BLIND
spot

KATANA COLLINS

This book is a work of fiction. Names, characters, places, and incidents are the product of the author's imagination or are used fictitiously. Any resemblance to actual events, locales, or persons, living or dead, is coincidental.

Copyright © 2016 by Katana Collins. All rights reserved, including the right to reproduce, distribute, or transmit in any form or by any means. For information regarding subsidiary rights, please contact the Publisher.

Entangled Publishing, LLC
2614 South Timberline Road
Suite 109
Fort Collins, CO 80525
Visit our website at www.entangledpublishing.com.

Embrace is an imprint of Entangled Publishing, LLC.

Edited by Candace Havens
Cover design by Cover Couture
Cover art from iStock

Manufactured in the United States of America

First Edition August 2016

embrace

Chapter One

Shelby

My entire life — all twenty-one years — can fit in sixteen boxes. Putting the car into park, I looked over my shoulder into the backseat at the meticulously stacked brown rectangles. The half of the car I packed was thoughtfully arranged from large to small, with the boxes marked "fragile" placed on the top. My best friend Reagan's side was jammed in like a failed Tetris game. Not that I really cared. What was really going to break? A five-dollar picture frame I got from Target? The most valuable thing I owned wasn't packed inside a box, but the car that contained everything — my mom's 1969 MG Midget.

Reagan bounced in the passenger seat beside me, clapping her hands. "Dude, you've got to chill out," I told her. "You're like a freaking jackrabbit on speed over there."

"And *you're* acting like a sloth. How are you not more excited about this?" She flashed me a big, toothy grin.

I *was* excited. Even if I didn't wear my emotions on my

sleeve like Reagan, that didn't mean I wasn't feeling them. Getting out of the car, I looked up at 148 Congress Ave — a beautiful, modern building that stood tallest of any residential complex in Charleston. Reagan wobbled out of the passenger seat, teetering in heels and a fuchsia miniskirt. I raised an eyebrow in her direction. "I thought you said you'd have no problem moving boxes in that," I said, grabbing a box out of my backseat and hoisting it onto my hip.

Her chin tilted centimeters higher. "I won't have a problem. I might just be a little slower than you two. Anyway, not all of us are comfortable wearing a dirty T-shirt littered with churro crumbs."

I looked down, and sure enough, the Nintendo logo was covered in crumbs and cinnamon sugar. Damn. I hated when she was right. "Um, excuse me, this is *vintage*," I said, brushing the crumbs off the 80s T-shirt I had managed to grab at Goodwill a few years ago. It was my favorite, and the cotton was so buttery soft. *Mm, butter.*

Harrison slammed his driver's side door before giving a whistle, looking up at my new building. The truck bed was filled with what few pieces of furniture I had acquired in the last few years. Thank God for friends with trucks, right? "Pretty nice looking," he said. "More than a step up from being a resident advisor over at the dorms, huh?"

"Yeah." And it only took me three years, four jobs, and endless persistence to get the place, since I wasn't exactly a prime candidate to most landlords. A parentless girl up to her neck in student loans? Yeah, doesn't really instill much confidence.

Reagan grabbed a couple of boxes as well. "Let's get this over with. I was promised pizza."

Moving sucks. Usually. But this time? I would finally be in my own apartment — a place where freshman wouldn't come knocking every time a roommate ate their yogurt. One where drunken eighteen-year-olds wouldn't lock themselves out and come crying to me at four in the morning. It was mine.

I'd been saving for years and had enough in my account for a year's worth of rent and then some. I managed to get the smallest, cheapest apartment in the building—size didn't matter to me. I know that all women say that, but I actually *meant* it. At least, when it came to apartments, I did. For all I cared, this place barely needed a kitchen. As long as it had the keypad lock and the twenty-four-hour doorman, I was set. Luxury was for suckers. But security? Safety? That was key.

Holy shit. I had a doorman. *Me.* For years, the closest thing I had to a doorman was the mouse that lived in my closet, and my "security system" was the bat I kept next to my door. While standing there, unmoving, frozen like an idiot, I made eye contact with the doorman through the floor to ceiling windows in the lobby. Though he was dressed professionally in business attire, his messy blond hair, blue eyes, and tanned complexion implied that he spent more days at the beach than sitting inside at a desk. His full lips turned up into a welcoming smile.

He rushed for the door, directly toward me. I *knew* he was just coming to open the door for me. I *knew* my friends were right there, and that it was broad daylight. And yet, even with logic and rationale on my side, that familiar panic of a strange man charging at me festered, clawing at the base of my ribs. *Come on, girl. Get it together. A hot guy opening a door for you is not a reason to flip the hell out.* He grabbed the handle, and as the door opened, a breeze caught my hair, flipping it up into the wind. Insecurity rose, and I quickly smoothed my bangs over the scar at my left temple.

As I gained my composure, he stood tall, gesturing for me to enter. Maybe he hadn't seen my damned-near anxiety attack. Maybe, just maybe, luck was on my side, for once.

"Thank you," I said. I stepped into the entryway as that

momentary panic reduced to a low simmer. He was just a normal guy, doing his job and helping the new girl get into the building.

Without thinking, I lifted my lashes, and our eyes connected. The bolt of adrenaline was more potent than pure caffeine.

His grin widened. "No problem," he answered in a raspy drawl that was all southern gentleman with a touch of bad boy. "Welcome to the building."

I opened my mouth to say thank you again, just as Reagan slammed into me from behind, sending the items in my box flying across the floor.

Yep, that was more like it. My life in a nutshell. I wasn't the girl who demurely stepped past a hot guy. I was the girl who face-planted in front of him. Heat rushed to my cheeks as I dropped to my knees, gathering the spilled items.

"Sorry," Reagan squealed, peeking out from behind several tall boxes loaded in her arms. "Harrison forced me to take more, and I didn't see you there."

I waved her apology away. "It's fine. Here." I grabbed my new set of keys, tossing them to her. "You and Harrison go on up—fourteenth flour, apartment 1420. I'll be up in a second."

Harrison followed her to the elevators. "You sure?"

I nodded, and as the doorman crouched beside me, Reagan grabbed Harrison's sleeve, tugging him onto the elevator. He handed me some textbooks that had gone flying, pausing to look at the cover to my Advanced French book. His gaze drifted from the book back to my eyes—and, holy shit, his were such an electric shade of blue that a current resonated down my entire body.

Jesus, you'd think I'd never seen a hot guy before. I took the book from him and tucked it back into the box. "Thanks."

Yes, Shelby, he is hot. He is also your doorman. A guy you have to see on a daily basis. Oh God. What if my toilet overflows? What if I clog my toilet, and he's the only one working and—

And then he grinned again. Any concern I had about seeing him every day evaporated. That smile created two dimples on either side of his mouth. Wow. Just…wow. Those dimples—I'd seen them before. You don't forget a smile like that easily. I caught my bottom lip, eyes narrowing as I studied his face. "You look familiar. Do you go to CSU?"

He leaned back on his haunches, his stare lingering for more than a second on my lips. When he finally met my eyes again, he offered me that sexy little half smirk thing once more. "Yeah, I do. I thought I recognized you, too. I don't really see you out much, though."

I shrugged, grabbing some random items—Chap Stick, deodorant, lotion—that had fallen and stuffing them back into the box. "I keep really busy. You must work a lot, too, though, right?"

He gave me an odd look, cocking his head. "What do you mean?"

My hand shook as I grabbed a box of Tic Tacs, the last item that spilled from my box. I was almost back to myself. *Almost back to normal Shelby—or as normal as Shelby gets.* "Moonlighting here as the doorman must take up a lot of time." I smiled. I liked that he was a student and held a job—just like me. And working in the service industry was thankless. As a waitress at Charleston's most notorious five-star historic restaurant, I should know. Though—thank *God*—I could finally cut back my hours there.

He pushed off his knees, leaning once more against the counter. "Oh, sure. I keep busy," he answered. "What about you? Find yourself *moonlighting* anywhere?" There was a twinkle in his eyes, and he loosened his tie.

I gave an exaggerated eye roll. "Who, me? I thought only heiresses and trustafarians were allowed to live here."

He raised a brow. "So, you're an heiress then?"

I pulled out the hem of my Nintendo shirt and did a twirl for him. "I'm offended that you can't tell."

For a moment there, I wasn't sure he got my humor. He regarded me cautiously, as though sizing me up. Then, taking in my worn jeans, retro tee, and (I'm sure) messy ponytail, his mouth twitched with that same smirk. Only this time, it didn't quite reach his eyes. "Of course, of course." He mocked a bow, tipping an invisible hat. And when he looked up through a web of thick lashes, my breath nearly gave way.

"You know I'm screwing with you, right?" I matched his grin and hoisted the box onto my other hip.

His smirk widened, slipping into a smile. And hot damn, that smile. It could easily be responsible for global warming. "Oh, you can *screw* with me whenever you want, darlin'."

I opened my mouth to answer, but the words got completely lost on the way out. Like, they disappeared into a different universe or something. The tingle moved to a full on electric bolt through my body, and to my absolute disbelief, the tips of my breasts responded as though I had walked into a freezer.

Normally, that kind of line would scream asshole, but from him it was hot.

He laughed at my lack of response and gestured to the box. "Can I help you with that? Shelby, right?"

His voice slid into me, under my skin, where I was pretty sure it could take up permanent residence. I nodded. God, I needed to get a grip. "Yeah, Shelby. And—I...no. But thank you. Someone needs to stay here by the desk, right?"

"Right, right," he said. "Someone's gotta open the door for all those heiresses." Amusement flashed in his eyes, and he laughed, dropping his head. "I have to tell you, I'm not—"

Harrison and Reagan popped out of the elevator, interrupting us. Harrison walked quickly by for the next load of boxes, while Reagan stopped in front of me, putting hands to her hips and tapping her toe. "You two are adorable and all, but I am not moving *all* your shit for you." Pressing her palms to my back, she gave me a gentle push to the elevators.

I shrugged, and the guy grinned back at me as another man, older and also in a suit, came up from the basement. He shook hands with the hot guy, who waved before pushing through the front door, relieved of his shift for the day.

Damn. I hadn't even gotten his name.

. . .

A few hours later, I put the last book onto my shelf with a contented sigh, straightening the framed picture of my mom and me beside it. Done. For the first time in three years, I was actually glad to have spent my adult life in the dorms. It made for a quick and easy move. Harrison gave me some of his furniture—a bookshelf, a futon, a trunk that I'd be using as a coffee table, and a couple other odds and ends.

The minimalist lifestyle suited me well. And the lack of furniture made the small apartment more roomy. Glass half full, right?

From above us came a pounding noise, not dissimilar to the sound of elephants stampeding. I stole a quick glance at the clock—a little past eleven. "What the hell are they doing up there?" I looked to the ceiling as though it held all the answers. Music, heavy on the bass, pumped through the vents and the walls vibrated with the pulsing rhythm.

Reagan followed my gaze. "It's the fifteenth floor up there, right? That's the penthouse."

"So?"

She shrugged. "So nothing," she said. "Just, I bet they throw some kick-ass parties."

I snorted, curling my lip at the thought. "Of course they

do. And they get away with noise pollution while they're at it."

Harrison snaked an arm around my shoulders and pulled me in for a hug. "C'mon. Don't let the penthouse folks ruin moving day. This place is amazing."

I rolled my eyes and gave him a gentle push. "Oh, please. You both live in Newbury Commons. Your apartments are triple the size of this place."

Reagan dropped herself onto the futon—my futon—and kicked her feet up on the trunk. "Sure, if you like buildings that are a hundred years old."

"You live in the historic district. *All* the buildings there are a hundred years old."

She shrugged and rolled her eyes, grabbing a slice of pizza. "Whatever. All I'm saying is that you live in a brand new building. With state of the art everything."

My stomach flipped. I did, didn't I? And it was officially mine. "It *is* pretty great, isn't it?"

Another slamming sound came from above, followed by a chorus of shouts.

Harrison grinned, ignoring the party, and looked to me with raised eyebrows. "It is. My dad says it's one of the safest buildings in Charleston."

"Then how come *you* didn't get this place?" Reagan asked, dabbing the grease off of her slice with a napkin.

Harrison grew quiet and looked down at his shoes. "Oh, you know…it's a little small for me." He looked up sheepishly, and a stray bit of dark hair fell into his eyes. He brushed it back with a shrug.

That same excitement I had been feeling all day dropped, and my stomach turned. "Is that how I got this apartment?" I asked quietly. Part of me didn't want to know the answer. "Did your dad pull strings to get me in here?"

"Naw." He shrugged, turning away, and dropped to the

floor, reaching for his own slice of pizza.

I dove forward, sliding the box away. "Harrison…" I warned, narrowing my eyes at him.

Finally, he sighed. "Fine…kind of. When this apartment opened up, it was too small for me, but I also knew you had an application in for the building. He made a call." My glare hardened as heat burned through my gut, and out of instinct, I brushed a finger over the scar at my temple. It sliced down my hairline to the base of my ear. My knuckle swept across the wisps of my long bangs, and I swallowed, my throat suddenly dry. "One call." Harrison threw his hands into the air. "That was it, I swear."

"I don't want his help. Ever." That man had made my life a living hell for years. I didn't care if he was genuinely trying to make amends. It was too little too late.

He continued to stare at the corner of the trunk. "All right. I'm sorry."

"Harrison, I mean it—"

"I *know*. I get it," he said, finally looking at me. "I'm sorry. But for the record, he did it for me as much as you. It means a lot to me that you're in a safe place, especially now that your mom…" He trailed off, swallowing. "Now that you're on your own. Don't make it into something bigger than that. You're happy here. Let yourself be happy."

I gave in, nodding. Harrison loved me—he was the closest thing to a brother I'd ever have, and he was just trying to make my life easier. I couldn't blame him for that.

I slid the pizza box back over to his end of the table.

"If it helps, I don't think his call even did anything. Your application was next up, anyway." He grabbed a slice and grunted as melted cheese slid off.

It did help. A little. But I wasn't about to say that out loud. "Should we study?" I grabbed the used French book I had just picked up for classes tomorrow and crossed my fingers that the person before me was some sort of genius who took awesome notes in the margins.

Ugh, French. The necessary evil I needed to pass in order to get my international business degree. I'd known Spanish for years. And Italian was relatively similar, but French was a bitch. Languages never came easy for me to begin with, so why I chose *international business* was a mystery, even to me. Well, except the fact that it was almost a guaranteed job placement. Business degrees were solid, and international business? That meant I wasn't limited to only domestic jobs; I had my pick of the world—in theory.

I cracked open the French book, reviewing what I had learned last year as another round of screams came from above, this one followed by the sound of a glass shattering. "Oh, for the love of God, come *on*," I shouted to no one.

"Just ignore them, Shelby."

"I *can't*." I popped to my feet, grabbed a broom from beside the stove, and slammed the tip into the ceiling. "I am not going to spend an entire year dealing with this." I grunted with each strike above.

"They're not gonna hear you," Harrison offered gently. "Let's just put on our own music and drown them out."

Twenty minutes passed, and a headache throbbed behind my eyes. "Is it just me, or is it getting louder?"

Harrison put a hand to his temple, rubbing in circles. "Okay, it's not just you." He nearly had to shout to be heard over the music.

"We should join them," Reagan squealed. "Classes haven't even started yet. What the hell good does studying do us?"

Harrison looked to me with a raised eyebrow. "She's got a point there."

"Because," I said, standing and snatching the broom once more, banging it on the ceiling. Not that it was working the least bit. "There was summer reading, and sometimes they give tests on the first day." I threw the broom down, rushing to the security phone on the wall.

Reagan rolled her eyes, muttering, "They never give tests on the first day. Who are you calling now?"

"The lobby," I muttered.

"Again? You've called twice already." She fell back into the couch and put her book on her face.

"She's right, Shelby. All they've done is turn the music up louder with each call."

I muttered a curse. "You're right." I hung up the wall receiver and grabbed my cell. "Yes, hi, I'd like to file a noise complaint. Can you have someone come to 148 Congress Ave?"

Harrison rolled his eyes. "Making enemies already."

"It's the penthouse. You'll hear them when you get here, I'm sure."

On the other end, the dispatcher was polite but curt. "It will likely be anywhere from thirty minutes to an hour before we'll have an officer there."

My stomach dropped to my feet. "An *hour*?" There was no way I was putting up with another hour of this noise.

"Sorry, ma'am. It's a busy night and 'noise complaint' isn't exactly a priority." I heard her shrug in the half-hearted apology.

"I understand." Was murder a priority? Because if this noise didn't stop soon, I was going to kill someone. I tossed my phone onto the table and grabbed my apartment key.

"Where are you going?" Reagan jumped up, following me, and Harrison was only a step behind her. "Shelbs, you don't even have *shoes* on."

"I'm going up there." I said, stomping down the hallway. I jammed my finger into the elevator button once. Twice. Then a few more times for good measure.

"How? Don't you need a special elevator key for the penthouse?" Harrison asked, following Reagan and I out the door.

The elevator dinged and stuffed inside were a handful of students I recognized as CSU people. "Apparently not." I smirked at Harrison over my shoulder and stepped on the elevator—they both followed me. I leaned into one of the girls who swayed unsteadily on her four-inch heels. She reeked of vodka already. "Do you know whose party this is?" I quickly picked a name—any name that seemed common. "Joe invited me, but I wanted to thank the host when I get in."

"Oh, Joey invited you? How is he? Is he coming tonight?" she slurred and fell into the guy behind her, breaking into a fit of giggles. I studied the guy—he also looked like a college student. His hand crept to the girl's waist, and he smelled her hair. My jaw tightened as I sent him a death glare.

"Hell*o*?" the girl said, breaking me out of my trance. She tipped her head back, resting it against the guy's chest casually. Fun. Carefree. There was a time I'd been those things, too. A short-lived time.

"What?" I asked, having completely lost my train of thought.

"Joey. Is he coming tonight?"

"Oh, right. Um…maybe…I don't know."

"You want me to introduce you to Tate? He's a doll." A tiny bit of eyeliner smeared down one side of her face. Before I could thank her, the elevator pinged open to the penthouse lobby.

I ignored the looks that passed between Harrison and Reagan, and instead marched into the marble foyer, momentarily awestruck. *A college kid lives here?* I held back a grunt, reminding myself that my two best friends came from wealth as well and were wonderful, loving, hard-working people. Money did not automatically equal corruption and laziness.

I scanned the sea of people, looking for anyone who gave an indication of living in the apartment—a greeting, a tour, something. I walked deeper into a huge kitchen that opened into a living room decorated with a black leather sectional and chrome accents, and dread filled my stomach. This was going to be like searching for an M&M in a bowl of Skittles.

I turned to Harrison and Reagan, ready to admit defeat, when from my left I heard that same slurred, tinny voice squeal, "Tate."

I spun to find the sexy doorman from earlier swaggering toward the drunk girl from the elevator. Did they send him up here to quiet everyone down? He leaned in, giving Vodka Girl a kiss on the cheek, and my chest squeezed as I watched, unable to tear my eyes away. His hair looked even more messy, as though he'd spent the whole day running his hands through it. The black dress pants from earlier now hung lower on his slim waist, and the button-down shirt was loose at the collar and untucked on one side. His tie was slung carelessly beneath the popped collar, and he looked like he stepped out of an Armani ad. *Wait—did she just call him—*

"Tate," she pouted, running her hands down his arm. "I missed you all summer."

He looked up, and I knew the moment he saw me by the way his grin spread across his face, still creating those two delicious dimples. My nerves prickled, and the air between us crackled to life like a roaring fire.

Not only was this guy *not* my doorman, but he was the boy next door...or in this case, the boy above. The *rich* boy above. And if I wasn't careful, I was gonna throw up all over his rich boy Kenneth Cole shoes.

Chapter Two

TATE

When I looked away from Chrissy, I found myself face-to-face with Shelby, AKA, the new girl, AKA, the girl I wanted to lift over my shoulder caveman style and throw down on my bed.

She still wore her retro Nintendo shirt that she'd worn moving in, and jeans that fit nicely around her slim curves. I followed the line down those jeans to strong legs and…no shoes? Huh. That was weird.

"Well, hey again." I made my way over to her, and she glanced up through a veil of thick lashes, all furrowed brow and stern frown. "Whoa," I said on a chuckle. "Rough day?"

"You *live* here?" She looked around my apartment as I shrugged off her disbelief. Jesus, people, get over the apartment already. Yeah, it's nice. But it's not *mine*. My parents might as well own the damn place along with every item inside. Buddy, my golden retriever came barreling down the hallway and landed both paws on Shelby's shoulders. He was nearly taller than her, stretched up on two feet like that.

"Buddy, down. *Off.*" I snapped, and he quickly leaped off of her, sitting between us and wagging his tail.

"And you have a dog." She shook her head as though she were trying to make sense of everything. Her blond ponytail swung with the movement, and I found myself wanting to run my fingers through it. To take the elastic out of her hair and let those long strands fall over her shoulders. "But, pets aren't allowed in the building," she continued.

I shrugged. *They are when your dad's the governor.* But I didn't say that. I doubt it would have bothered her, though. Almost every student who lived in this building was here because of an affluent parent. Or an "heiress," as she put it earlier. It was the only way you could get into the damn building, let alone afford it. And being that it was the most secure apartment complex available in Charleston, you found a lot of celebrity students and kids of politicians here.

"Shelby," I said, remembering the name her friend called her earlier. I finished my beer and dropped it into the recycle bin next to the kitchen counter as Brad handed me a shot glass spilling over with some sort of brown liquid. I sniffed it and my stomach turned. I sat it on the counter instead of shooting it down.

"You said you were the doorman," she snapped, and I couldn't help but grin at the edge in her voice.

There was a teeny part of me that felt guilty for the lie. I hadn't meant to leave without telling her the truth, but her friends ushered her away, and I had to get to the basketball luncheon. "No, *you* said I was the doorman. I just didn't correct you."

Her mouth fell open. It wasn't until that moment that I noticed the guy behind her—the one that helped her move in. I knew him—we'd had some class together the year before. Economics, maybe? I gave him a short nod. Damn, I hoped he wasn't her boyfriend. "Hey, man, what's up?" I looked to her girlfriend—the redhead in the miniskirt. "I'm Tate," I said to her.

"Tate," Shelby repeated, practically spitting my name back in my face.

"You say my name like you're cussing," I said.

She rolled her eyes. "Well, Tate *is* a four-letter word."

"It's really nice to meet one of Shelby's neighbors," the redhead cut in, shooting her a look.

"Yes," Shelby said. "My very *loud* neighbor in the penthouse."

I slipped my hands into my pockets, rocked back onto my heels. "Ah, you got the apartment down there." I nodded to the floor and shrugged as my pulse jumped. "I think you'll like being under me," I added quietly.

With a roll of her eyes, her cheek dropped to her shoulder. Not many girls pulled off cute while angry, but she had it down. "Oh, I don't think so." Even though she narrowed her eyes at me, the frown stayed right in place. "I like the top. And I like it *quiet*," she added pointedly.

I leaned in, landing my hand on her hip. "Then I've got news for you, darlin'. The guy on bottom ain't doin' it right."

Her frown deepened into a damned sexy pout. She was different than the other girls at Charleston Southern University. Naturally beautiful, not the kind that had to cake their faces with makeup to look halfway decent. Not that I didn't love some seriously sexy red lips now and then. But this sort of instant attraction was different, the kind of tension that made me want to kick everyone out of this damn apartment and have her all to myself for the whole night. Those pink lips parted as the tiniest breath escaped, and she swallowed, pulling back. "Can you just try to keep it down?"

I nodded, bringing my hand back to my hip. "I will. Sorry about the noise tonight. But since you're here, come on in. Have a drink." She couldn't leave yet. It was unnerving just how badly I wanted her to stay and hang out.

I stepped to the side, and Shelby's friend zoomed past us with a quick, "Okay." She attempted to link arms with Shelby and pull her inside as well, but I had to hand it to the girl, she held strong, feet firmly planted, jerking her friend back to the doorway.

"We can't," Shelby answered, looking directly at me. Those amber brown eyes had flecks of chocolate just around the pupil, and I took the chance to study her, to drink her in. "We need to study."

"Study?" I snorted. "For what? Classes haven't begun."

"That's what *I* said." The redhead smirked at me, then glanced back to Shelby with eyebrows raised. The guy stood silently behind, arms crossed. "Harrison, what do you think?"

He looked to Shelby and tilted his head in a silent question. Their eyes connected, and my spine stiffened. The guy—Harrison apparently—put a hand on Shelby's shoulder. I took a deep breath and turned back to the redhead. She was my best chance at getting Shelby to stick around a while.

"I didn't catch *your* name," I said to her.

She grinned and held a hand out. "Reagan."

"Reagan," I said, taking that hand. "We've got sangria…"

"Shelby's favorite," she responded, smiling and slowly turning back to her friend.

Shelby rolled her eyes, finally dropping her hands to her sides. "Okay, fine. One drink." Buddy seized the moment, nudging her hand with his nose, and with his big tongue, he lapped at her fingers. Her face split into a grin, and she scratched Buddy behind the ears. I automatically liked anyone who liked my dog.

"C'mon," I stepped back, letting Reagan and this Harrison guy go ahead, and as Shelby moved past my shoulder, I curved my arm around her stomach, resting the weight of my hand at the waistband of her jeans. She jumped at my touch and licked her plump, pink lips, stealing a look at me from over one shoulder.

Oh, boy. This girl was trouble. The only question was, did she intentionally cause it, or was she the type of girl it just followed? Something told me it was the latter.

Harrison looked back at us and gave me a quick, foreboding glance before Reagan dragged him to the punch bowl.

"So," I said, reluctantly pulling my hand away from her hip. "Sangria?" I grabbed a red plastic cup, moving to the pitcher I kept in the fridge.

"I can get it," she answered quickly, grabbing her own cup from the pile and heading toward the punch bowl. With a gentle touch, she brushed her side-swept bangs from her eyes, her hand lingering at her temple.

I scrunched my nose. "I dunno that I would drink out of the community bowl," I said, pulling out the pitcher of leftover sangria. "I have some right here that's more likely not to have backwash and God knows what else in it."

Her cheeks flushed, and she furrowed her brow, setting the plastic cup back down. "I'll take one of those bottles of water instead."

She stiffened as I passed a look over her face, her eyes flashing with challenge. Shrugging, I tossed her a bottle that was on the door. I didn't care if she drank, so long as she stayed.

She inspected it for a second before throwing it back to me. "This one's open already."

"Oh, sorry." I grabbed another, checking the cap for the seal before setting it down in front of her. "There you go." I grabbed myself a beer then leaned my elbows onto the counter, which brought me just below her eye level.

She took a sip and wiped the corners of her full lips with the back of her hand. "So…" She blinked before meeting my eyes with a steely determination. "Why'd you lie to me?"

I grinned, slugging a gulp of beer. "I had a feeling it'd be fun." I wiggled my eyebrows. "And I was right."

"It's fun lying to people and making them feel ridiculous?"

"Aw, it wasn't a full on lie. More like…a practical joke."

She snorted, turning her back to me and leaning her ass against the counter. I paused, allowing myself a moment to study that fine curve before I sidled up next to her. "I'm sorry," I said. And I meant it. I swayed to the right, bumping her with my shoulder. "Really. I was just messing around. And if it gets too loud up here, don't hesitate to give a call or a text—let me know to quiet down."

Behind her thick lashes, amber eyes glittered. A breath caught in my throat. "Really?" she asked, eyes narrowing. "Because I called the doorman three times, and you turned the music *up*, not down."

"I can't say I'm not glad, since it got you up here." A smile tugged at my lips. "But I promise, from now on as long as it's *you* doing the asking, I'll always turn it down. I'm not totally unreasonable."

She pursed her lips. "Thank you."

I tore a napkin in half and wrote my number on it. "You can always feel free to swing by in person instead of calling, too." I sent her a wink, and a laugh finally broke through the scowl—like a rainbow slipping through the clouds after a storm.

"Okay, Casanova."

I don't know why I did it, but I reached over and pinched a section of her hair, running my thumb and forefinger down the length. It was just as soft as I had imagined, and smelled like coconuts.

She raised her eyebrows, one side of her mouth curving. I met her smile and raised her a dimple.

My knuckle brushed her arm as I dropped the piece of

hair, and I noticed a track of goose bumps racing toward her elbow. For a moment, I considered leaning closer and brushing my lips against hers. She had on some sort of Chap Stick, and it smelled like watermelon. I inhaled that scent deeply, burning it into my memory. But even as I drew in closer, there was a waver in those cheeks; that smile she sported so effortlessly, so beautifully, trembled and dropped a fraction of an inch. I immediately pulled back.

I wet my lips, and distracted myself with yet another sip of beer. "What were you studying?"

"Studying?"

"You mentioned to your friends earlier…"

"Oh, right." She sighed and picked at the corner of her water bottle label. "French."

"*Ah, le Français? C'est la plus belle langue du monde.*"

Surprise flickered across her delicate features, and she gave me an odd look. "You speak French?"

"*Mais, oui.* I spent summers in Nice growing up."

Air pushed out of her lungs in a loud sigh. "Of course you did."

"You have a problem with travel?"

She gave me a sarcastic smirk and batted her eyes. "I just prefer Rome…that's all."

"So why study before classes have even started? French giving you a little trouble?"

"*No.*" She answered too quickly and knew it. "Maybe a little."

"I could help, you know." Why exactly was I offering to help? There were easily eight women at this party that would strip off their clothes for me without an ounce of effort. They'd do things to me you normally only see online. But tonight, none of them appealed. I wanted this one. The odd girl who wore no makeup and fucking awesome thrift store T-shirts.

"No, thanks," she finally answered. She jerked a nod to

Chrissy who was now on my coffee table, dancing with her skirt around her waist and thong-wearing-ass in the air. Her tongue was out as she gyrated to the beat. "Now, *she* would probably take you up on your offer for some *French*."

"I don't want her." I moved around to stand in front of her, and she raised her chin defiantly. "I want you."

She shook her head, laughing in a bemused way. "You don't even know me."

"So? Let me get to know you. This weekend. We can celebrate your move into the building."

"Thanks," she said and moved in a step closer. She wet her lips slowly, with intent. Her eyes lowered in a sexy, hooded way and she nibbled her bottom lip. "But no thanks," she finished and offered me a patronizing pat on the chest before brushing past my shoulder and heading to her friends. "Trust me, Archie. This Betty's not interested."

I rushed to follow her, chugging the rest of my beer. "If I recall, Betty was *quite* interested in Archie."

She turned, walking across the room backward. "Not this time." Her eyes flicked to Chrissy, still shaking her ass on my coffee table. "You'd do better with Veronica."

Jesus. I looked back and forth from Shelby to Chrissy. I could have Chrissy tonight...easily. Only, damn, I didn't want her. Didn't want any of them, just Shelby. I shook myself out of it. It was the challenge, that was all. It had to be. Falling into bed with girls was just too damn easy these days, especially while at a party. I watched her cross the room, landing next to Harrison. She leaned against his shoulder, and he draped an arm casually around her, as though it was second nature for him to touch her.

Annoyance and jealousy seethed through me. Yeah, fucking irrational, I know. I tossed my empty bottle into the recycle bin and grabbed the shot Brad had poured earlier. Squeezing my eyes shut, I swallowed the liquid, and it burned the whole way down to my stomach. I hissed a curse, pressing the back of my hand to my lips, and slid the shot glass to the end of the bar. "One more," I called to Brad, who leaned there next to the bottle of José, checking his phone. I turned to the fridge, grabbing two more beers. Why, exactly, had I been taking it easy tonight? Because I had class tomorrow morning? So what. It was a double fisting kind of night.

Chapter Three

Shelby

My mind reeled, running like a vengeful toddler on a sugar rush. Walking away from Tate took all of my effort. He was clearly just a flirt. But dang, did it feel good to flirt back. It had been months since my last date—I just didn't have much time for it. And to be honest, the guys weren't exactly knocking down my door to get to me.

What would I have done if he had called my bluff and kissed me, right here in front of everyone? I shivered and the tremble caused my nipples to harden. Shit. Clearly I *wanted* him to kiss me…whether or not I wanted to admit that to him or myself, it was the truth.

Harrison pulled me in tighter. "Everything all right in there?" He tapped the tip of his finger to my head and I nodded.

"How's the sangria?"

He handed me his cup with a smirk and I drank the fruity deliciousness. Seriously, who would drink beer—something that tasted like the devil's piss—when drinks as amazing as sangria existed? I had another sip then handed it back to Harrison. He pushed the cup back over to me. "No, you can have it. You seem to be enjoying it more, anyway."

Reagan leaned in, her eyes floating somewhere past my shoulder. "He wants you."

Harrison snapped his head up, his glare darkening. "Who?"

Reagan rolled her eyes. "Who do you think? Tate. Duh."

Harrison tensed beside me, and I tapped my elbow to his ribs, offering a comforting smile. "He wants anyone with tits. Especially if that someone says no." My neck burned with the desire to turn and look at him, but I was proud of myself that I didn't. I could feel his eyes on me, searing into the back of my head. "Trust me. He wants nothing more from me than another name he can brag about at poker night."

"Then he's a fucking moron." Harrison gave me a small smile, and I returned it, finishing the sangria.

"I dunno, Shelby," said Reagan. "He's seriously staring at you. I think you *want* him to be like the other guys. It's easier to run if he is." Her tone was light, but she looked right through me to my soul. Reagan might be the sort of girl who can pound drinks and get us into any club…but she was more than tight skirts and lip gloss. The girl was smart and intuitive. And she knew me too well.

"Reagan, c'mon…look at the guy. He's slamming tequila like there's no tomorrow." This time I did steal a glance at him. He clinked his shot glass with a group of friends and tipped his head back. "That must be his third shot in the last ten minutes. You're telling me *he's* someone 'different'?" I made air quotes around the word.

She arched a brow, looking down her perfectly ski-sloped nose. "He only started doing those shots after you turned him down."

"I think we can all agree that it doesn't hurt to be careful," Harrison countered quietly.

"Yeah, but it also doesn't hurt to let loose a little. You can't always let your past dictate your future. Just because some asshole—"

"And this is why I love you guys." I linked my arm with Reagan's, resting my head on her shoulder. "Thank you for watching out for me. But trust me—that guy? He is not the person to 'let loose' with."

"Why's that?" she asked.

"Because, he's only in it for the chase. For one night."

Reagan smiled and pinched my cheeks. "Then he's *exactly* the guy to let loose with."

The phone rang near the elevators, and Tate rushed over, hopping over the back of his couch to reach it. Buddy barked, chasing him through the house. "Buddy, go play dead," he shouted, and the dog ran to the living room, dropping onto his back.

"Hello," he said, picking up the receiver and leaning against the wall. "The wha—? On their way up?" He raked a hand through his hair and hung up the phone. "Shit. Hey," he called, turning to the apartment. "Police are on their way up. Anyone under twenty-one? Get the fuck out through the stairs in the back!"

A handful of kids ran down the hallway, and the girl dancing on the coffee table stumbled, landing in some guy's lap with a giggle. "Who the fuck called the police?"

"Who the hell knows?" Tate shrugged and swayed, tossing an empty beer into the bin beside him. My lungs tightened— was he drunk? Tipping the other bottle in his hand back, he finished it off with several glugs and aimed to throw it in the recycle bin. The bottle grazed the side, bouncing off and smashing onto the floor. Glass shattered, a few shards jumping out and landing near his toes. I looked down at my bare feet and gulped. Oh, yeah. He was drunk.

My face burned as I looked over at Reagan. She gave me an uneasy smile, and Harrison squeezed my elbow. "It's okay. They'll just tell him to keep it down and it'll be fine."

"Maybe we should go?" I whispered.

Reagan shook her head. "That'll look even more guilty. Tate already knows you were pissed about the noise."

"So what?" Annoyance lurched in my chest. "I was *right* about the noise."

"Yeah," Reagan offered quietly, "but do you really want to start a war with your new neighbor? Who also goes to our school?"

Harrison moved toward the stereo, turning the volume knob down.

"What're you doing?" Tate shouted. "Leave it on. It's a *party*." He pressed a button on his phone and the music blasted once more.

"When did he get so drunk?" I said to no one. "He seemed totally sober when we got here."

"You drove him to the bottle, girl." Reagan jabbed me in the ribs with an elbow. "Or he's trying to impress you with his antics."

I rolled my eyes, hugging my stomach. "Guys are morons."

Harrison walked over to Tate with his hands out. "Come on, man. My dad's a police commissioner. Just turn the music down. They're gonna come up here, give you a warning, and then they'll lea—"

"I know the drill. We're just going to have a little fun with them first." He exhaled and the noise sounded oddly similar to air escaping from a leaky tire. "Bet you a hundred bucks I can have the cops laughing with me in a matter of minutes, golden boy."

"Golden what?" Harrison repeated and looked back to us. I shrugged, and he turned back to Tate. "All right, man.

Whatever. Make your own bed."

The elevator dinged, and two cops stepped into the foyer. I held my breath, steeling myself for some serious shit to go down. My stomach somersaulted at those blue uniforms. *Most cops are good. Just good men trying to make the world a better place*, I told myself. Almost every cop I'd dealt with had been wonderful. Except one. Even the thought of him sent an icy chill surging through my body. A shiver ran the length of my spine, one that no amount of layers could have helped. Reagan put a hand to my back, giving me a reassuring smile.

"We're gonna need you to turn that down," the first officer said over the music.

"What was that?" Tate shouted. "I–I couldn't hear you over the music."

My breath hitched. Oh God, what was he doing? This was his idea of funny?

And apparently, his friends thought it was. There were a few snickers around the room, and he shot them a grin from over his shoulder. The quick movement caused him to lose his balance and he swayed on his feet, using the wall to keep himself standing.

"Turn it off," the second officer shouted.

"I still can't hear you. Here, let me turn the music off."

Harrison heaved an annoyed sigh, folding his arms as Tate clicked a button and the room fell silent.

One officer strolled through the kitchen, eyes narrowed, looking for signs of misconduct. He stopped a few feet shy of me. My breath stilled as his eyes wandered beyond me and into the room. "Got anyone underage in here?"

Tate gave a regretful frown and worried his bottom lip. "Just one. But he only had one sip and ended up passing out on the floor."

"Is he okay?" The second officer, a younger man, not so plump around the middle, grabbed a walkie-talkie from his belt. "Randy, think we'll need a bus?"

"We need to see the boy. Now. How old is he?"

Tate shrugged. "He's twelve."

"Twelve?" the officer gasped.

"I'm sure he's fine. He usually sleeps all day anyway. Follow me." Tate gestured, and the officers followed at his heels. He stopped as his toe tapped his dog. "Buddy, Buddy, you all right? Get up, boy. Show the good officers that you're okay." Buddy rolled off his back, hopping around the apartment.

Everyone at the party burst out in laughter—all except us. I leaned in to Harrison. "I told you we should have slipped out the back," I whispered.

Harrison nodded, swallowing. "I'm thinking you were right."

"Okay, funny guy. You're coming with us." I cringed as the older officer grabbed Tate by his elbow and gave him a quick pat down, inspecting for any weapons. "Let's see if you're still laughing after spending the night in the tank."

Tate snorted. "Aw, come on. It was just a joke. You know… because it was my dog. Seriously, have you ever seen a dog play dead for that long? It's a little impressive, right?"

"Jim, get the ID's of the rest of these kids. Make sure they're all legal." He moved Tate into the elevator as the younger officer made his way through the crowd.

"I owe you a hundred bucks, golden boy," Tate called as the elevator doors closed.

"Oh my God." Despite the effort to keep my voice steady, it still shook. And I was certain Reagan and Harrison heard it, too. "Th–they're arresting him?"

I looked up to Harrison just as the muscle in his jaw jumped. "Yeah. Because he's a fucking drunk idiot."

"Yeah, but *I* called the cops on him. I didn't think they'd take him in." I dropped my voice even lower. "Is he going to be okay?"

Reagan shifted a look from Harrison to me. "I'm sure he'll be fine."

The cop's handheld ID scanner beeped from the other side of the room, and he moved on to the next partygoer. Reagan opened her purse, and Harrison pulled his wallet from a back pocket.

"Shit." I exhaled, running my clammy palms over my empty pockets. "I left my purse down in the apartment."

Harrison rubbed circles over my back. "It'll be fine, trust me. I'll call my dad—"

"No."

Reagan swallowed beside me. "Come on, Shelby. I know you don't like the guy, but don't be unreasonable—"

"I said no. My ID is right downstairs. Surely, he'll let me grab it—"

"Maybe, maybe not," Reagan said. "It depends how pissed off Tate made them."

"At least if I text my dad, I can give him a head's up if they decide to do something stupid like drag you in—"

"I said no, Harrison." Cursing my shaky hands, I folded my arms, refusing to look at him.

Harrison sighed and rolled his eyes. "Stubborn like your mom."

My blood went cold. "What did you just say to me?"

"I—" Harrison's voice cracked, but I didn't let him finish.

"Don't talk about my mom."

He was quiet a moment as the officer inched his way through the crowd in our direction. "She was like a mom to me, too, you know."

"Guys, come on..." Reagan tried to cut in. Only nothing would stop me. Nothing stopped the anger and sorrow and sheer pain that radiated through my heart.

"Yeah. Except you still have a mother somewhere. You

still have the hope that she could come home one day. I have no one." My voice broke and I cleared my throat quickly to cover up the catch in my voice.

"I'd much rather have twenty-one good years with a mom like yours than eighteen years of wondering if my mother would ever think I was worth coming back for." He threw the words back at me, and I deserved it.

We were all silent for a moment, and the few people left here at the party hummed quietly with chatter. I squeezed my eyes shut and ignored that familiar burn of tears at the back of my sinuses. My mom always thought of Harrison like her own son, and if she'd heard me say that about his mother, I would have been scrubbing the bathroom with a toothbrush for a month. Just because I was sad, and nervous around the cops, didn't excuse me using him like a punching bag. Twenty-one years. That was all I got with her. But Harrison had even less time with his mom—time he barely remembered. I didn't have a future with my mom, but at least I had the memories. "You're right. That was a shitty thing to say. I'm sorry." And if anything, I only proved how right he was. I am stubborn. So was mom. But we'd always *had* to be. There was no surviving without that trait.

"I'm sorry, too," Harrison finally offered.

"I know," I whispered.

"I love you, Shelbs."

I swallowed. "I know that, too."

As the officer moved closer and closer to us, the feeling of dread in my stomach deepened. It was like being in a guillotine, forced to watch the blade come down on your neck.

Finally, he reached us. My fingers trembled, and I shoved them into my back pockets to hide my nervousness.

"IDs please." He was tired, but polite. Reagan and Harrison eyed me as they handed theirs over.

"I live in the building…" I started and my voice cracked,

a burning heat tightening in my chest. "A-and I left my license downstairs. It's literally one floor directly below this apartment."

His eyes narrowed and traveled the length of my body. They widened when he reached my bare feet, and an understanding smile tugged at his lips. "Well, that would explain the no shoes. You been drinking?"

I shook my head. "Barely anything."

He nodded, his face softening. "Once I finish up the rest here, we can go down to your apartment together for your ID."

Even though I was prepared for this answer, fear struck me fast and sudden like a bolt of lightning. My knees locked, the muscles in my thighs twitching.

"Can she go down and grab it real quick right now while you finish up?" Reagan asked.

Thank God for that girl, I thought, as tears stung the back of my eyes.

"I'm afraid I can't do that. Protocol says we're not allowed to let anyone out of our custody until after their identity has been verified."

"Well, then we should be able to come downstairs with you, right?" Harrison added. His voice was harder than Reagan's, more brittle and ready for a fight if needed.

The officer didn't hesitate, not even for a moment. "Of course, that's fine. Let me finish up these folks, and we can go down."

Harrison squeezed my shoulder lightly. "Breathe, Shelbs," he whispered, and I sucked in a breath. How long had I been holding it?

"Thank you," I whispered. His smile was a ghost of the Harrison I used to know, but he flashed me a quick grin anyway.

"Anytime. You know that."

Chapter Four

SHELBY

The next morning, I pulled into Turner Hall, lucking out with a spot right by the front door. Putting my mom's MG into park, I leaned back in the driver's seat, and it absorbed my weight, almost as comforting as a hug. Mom's face flashed into my mind, pressure clamping my throat. God, I missed her. She would have called me this morning...my first day of school. Just to check in. Just to make sure I had woken up in time, even though I'd only ever missed class once, my freshman year after pulling an all-nighter studying.

Despite the car being forty-seven years old, the leather of the steering wheel was still silk-smooth beneath my palms. She had bought this thing brand new in '69 with every penny she had. It was her baby—well, up until I entered the picture. But even then, this car was always a close second. Almost every memory we had together centered around this hunk of junk. Beautiful junk, yeah...but junk all the same. It broke down constantly, could never handle any temperature below forty-five and though having a convertible kicked ass, it was dangerous. *Extremely* dangerous.

If I closed my eyes and thought really hard, I could almost smell traces of her perfume on the seat. Sorrow seeped in, but before it consumed me, I grabbed my messenger bag from the passenger side. Locking up, I looked into the morning sky, streaked with blue and frothy white clouds. Humidity sat hot and heavy on my shoulders, and the clouds swelled with moisture.

I was fifteen minutes early for my first class of the semester—exactly how I liked it in life. There was plenty of time to choose my seat for the year, relax, and grab a coffee from the cart outside—

I stopped in my tracks as Harrison walked toward me with two paper cups in hand.

"For you." He dipped his head in a bow. "As a peace offering."

My mouth tipped into a smile, and I took a sip of the creamy, foamy cappuccino. It was perfect. "If anything, I should be the one bringing *you* the peace offering. Oh, wait..." I pulled a small box of mini glazed doughnuts out of my messenger bag. "I *did*." I opened the box, offering him one.

Harrison grinned, and with that one smile, I knew we were totally okay. "Doughnuts?" he asked. "Feels like some sort of crack about my criminal justice major."

"Look, if you're going to enter the justice system, you need to start incorporating these into your diet."

He took a bite as we walked across the parking lot. "We should both say stuff we don't mean more often."

"You mean I'm *not* stubborn?" I asked with mock incredulity.

"You are as stubborn as I am handsome."

I scrunched my nose. "So not at all, then?"

"Ha *ha*," he said, rolling his eyes. "Serious moment?" he asked with a change of tone. I nodded. "I'll try to keep you and my dad as separate as possible, if I can help it."

I opened the heavy front door, flashing my student ID at the guard sitting out front. "Thanks. I know it has to be hard for you—"

Harrison slid my messenger bag from my shoulder, relieving me of its weight. "Nothing compared to what you go through, I'm sure."

I managed to shrug his comment off casually. "Really, I'm fine. I just want to avoid him, if possible."

Harrison nodded. "I get it. I'll try."

We approached Room 106, and Harrison pulled the door open for me. After a brief pause, he cursed under his breath.

"What?" I turned to find a sunglass-wearing Tate walking directly toward us. His plump lips twitched—was that little half smirk meant for me? Did he even see me standing here? He veered off toward the coffee cart, and I exhaled the breath I'd been holding. "Oh." I turned back, pretending as though him not seeing me didn't hurt a tiny bit. As I slipped into the classroom, Harrison followed closely behind.

"I don't like that guy," Harrison said, shutting the door behind him.

"Like him or not, he's my neighbor."

Just as I had hoped, no one was here yet, not even the professor. Harrison and I settled into our seats by the windows on the other side of the room.

"Feel like grabbing some dinner tonight?" Harrison kicked his feet onto the seat in front of him, slouching into the chair.

"No. I've got to work, and then I don't know how much homework I'll have after that."

"At Magnolia's Manor?"

I shook my head, a face splitting grin stretching from ear to ear. "Nope. I won't be at Magnolia's much this semester—only if and when I need the extra cash." Thank God, the manager there loved me and was willing to let me pop in whenever.

"Hell, yeah, Stevens!" He offered me a high five, and I had to stretch to reach his hand. Damn these tall guys. "So tonight you're…"

"Still working at the tutoring center." I shrugged. "Only because I love it there. And they need me."

He nodded. "Well, let me know if you change your mind. Reagan and I can bring you something to eat if you think you'll run late."

A few more students shuffled in, and Harrison pulled himself up into a seated position. I busied myself with getting my notebook, textbook, and pens in order. The door slammed open, hitting the mahogany wall behind it, and I jumped. Tate stood in the doorway a moment and then slowly made his way into the room like he owned the place. Though sunglasses still rested on his nose (despite being indoors), I felt his stare as he wove through the desks.

A few girls giggled and jumped to their feet, throwing their arms around his neck. "Where you been all summer, Tater?" One atrociously high-pitched voice squealed, and I cast a sideways glance at the bleached blonde girl in teeny low-cut jean shorts and a skimpy tank top. A bit of ass cleavage showed at the waistband of her jeans, and I rolled my eyes. *How* is that a cute trend?

Tate pulled his glasses down, and his eyes wandered over the girl's shoulder, landing directly on me. I jerked my gaze away, becoming suddenly interested in my blank notebook. Guilt burned in me—it was my fault he'd been arrested last night. Well, *his* fault for being an ass to the cops, but still. I was somewhat responsible for them showing up in the first place.

I inwardly rolled my eyes. No. Harrison was right. That was not my fault, and I wouldn't take the blame. He had several chances to turn the music down, and he didn't. He had the choice to not try and "make them laugh," but he fucked with them anyway. Tate got arrested because he was an arrogant ass who thought his bank account elevated him above the law.

Tate stood next to me. His presence was demanding, and I wanted to look up at him, despite my better judgment. The flutters were like no other I'd experienced. I was far from a blushing virgin, but still, no man had been able to cause chill bumps to surface with just a look. Until now, apparently.

His fresh scent caught in my throat. It was simple, like soap with hints of cool spice, and something else, too. Something that was entirely unique to Tate. I hated myself a little bit for already being so affected by that smell. For even *knowing* it already.

I finally twisted in my seat, locking eyes with him. He held my stare, dropping into the chair next to me. Harrison's glare lowered, and he snorted. "Well, if it isn't the rebel without a cause," Harrison murmured, dipping his nose into his book.

"Hey, golden boy," Tate said with a jerk of his chin. Pulling out his wallet, he pinched a crisp one hundred-dollar bill between his fingers, holding it out to Harrison. "Here you go. You won fair and square."

"I didn't take the bet," Harrison said, scowl deepening.

"Sure you did," Tate responded, still holding the money out.

"Dude, seriously. I don't want your fucking money."

Tate sat there an extra moment, then shrugged, tucking the money back into his wallet. Then he matched my stare once more, eyes burning into mine.

I raised a brow. "So, Joker. How'd you get out?"

His lips curved at the corners and he took a sip of coffee. "Joker? Please, if I'm anyone, it's Bruce Wayne. I charmed my way out of that drunk tank."

"By 'charmed' do you mean 'called daddy'?" I gave him a sideways glance just in time to see his grin widen.

"Didn't need to. Turned out, the officer on duty was a fellow dog lover. Showed him a few pics of Buddy on my phone, and he let me out in less than an hour." He pulled his sunglasses down on his nose and sent me a wink.

I rolled my eyes and cracked open the French book. "If you're fluent in French, why are you in this class?"

He sank into his seat. "It's an easy A."

Of course. Guys like Tate went for the easy things in life. The easy A. The easy laugh. The easy girl.

Then why is he going for you?

I pushed the thought away. "What's your major?"

He shrugged. "I don't know yet. Liberal arts for now."

My forehead crinkled. "For now? What year are you?"

"I'm a senior."

I shook my head, bringing my attention back to the books in front of me. I needed better radar on people. When we first met, I thought this guy was a hard-working student with a job—and yet, the reality couldn't be further from the truth.

"That bothers you," his voice hitched a few notes higher, and his eyebrows arched.

"*You* bother me," I snapped. I immediately regretted looking when I was met with his smug grin.

"I like a challenge," he offered with a head tilt.

"Well, then, consider me your Everest."

"Is that an invitation to climb on top of you?" he asked, his eyebrows lifting, awaiting my response.

I shook my head because, seriously? That line was cheesy. It also made my skin tight and tingly. "If those lines have ever worked, then I feel really disappointed in my generation." I managed to keep my composure with the retort, even though my mouth felt dry.

I'm disappointed in myself. Why did that easy smile and stupid, smug line have me blushing? I'd never in my life needed a cold shower—until this very moment. The flush heated my cheeks and sent tingles of awareness spiraling down to the tips of my breasts. The very thought of him crawling on top of me caused my skin to reach to lava-like temperatures. I took a sip of coffee to calm my frazzled nerves. Holy hell, could he sense how he was getting to me? Thank God the professor chose that moment to come in and call the class to order.

The first thirty minutes or so was spent with him handing out the syllabus and speaking exclusively in French. I hated when teachers did that—they think it forces you to learn the language, but mostly it just results in me zoning out. I struggled to keep up, only catching every fourth word or so, and when I stole a glance at Tate, he was doodling in his notebook. He flicked a glance at me, smirking, then tore out the sheet, sliding it over to my desk.

It was a sketch of Archie, giving Betty flowers with a word bubble above that said "Fuck Veronica." I snorted and covered a hand to my mouth. The professor caught my eye with a stern look, and I flipped the sheet over quickly.

Once he went back to his French (i.e., gibberish), I snuck another glance at Tate, and a tremor skimmed across my chest. I couldn't tear my eyes away from that cobalt stare of his. It was as though he could hypnotize me into a trance, and with a snap of his fingers, I would reveal all my secrets, all my fantasies, which I was perhaps even too afraid to admit to myself, to *him*. I swallowed against my drying throat because, shit, that scared me.

Where is this vulnerability coming from? I'm not a girl who grows weak in the knees.

I wasn't the sort of person who melted when a cute boy looked at me, and the fact that he *could* weaken me with one simple glance was terrifying.

Something rustled in front of me, and I looked to the seat in front of me to find Harrison handing me a pointed stare and a stack of papers. I startled, taking a page and passing the rest down. A test? On the first day?

Son of a bitch—I was going to kill Reagan.

Chapter Five

TATE

"Tatum Gordon Michaelson, so help me, you will straighten yourself out. Do you hear me?"

Mom's voice shrilled higher with each passing second.

I debated saying nothing, just to hear her go supersonic. "*Tate*. Are you listening?" she screamed, and I jerked my head back from the deafening sound. Even Buddy perked, tilting his head at the odd noise.

"Yes. Jeez, Mom. I hear you. Every dog in the building can hear you."

There was an exasperated huff from the other line. "Don't you sass me. Besides, that mutt of yours is the only dog in the building, and you know it. We had to pay three times what a normal pet deposit would be." Mom had the quintessential southern belle drawl—a perfectly practiced one considering she was born and raised in Illinois and didn't come to South Carolina until college. "You should call your father and thank him for getting you out of this jam. Again. He almost let you sit in jail all night this time."

I sat down in front of my laptop, firing it up. I didn't doubt that for a second he wanted to leave me there. But there's no way he would—it would hurt his precious campaigning too much. "I will, Mom."

"Your community service is two hundred hours."

My stomach lurched. "Two hundred hours? That's—that's like a month of full-time work. It'll take me months to finish on top of classes."

She was silent for a moment. I imagined her sitting at our dining table, sucking in her cheeks. "You're right. It *is* a lot. And maybe next time you'll think twice before mouthing off to an officer. Maybe if it had been your first offense, they would have lessened it."

"Seriously? Come on…I get it. I learned my lesson. Couldn't we get that talked down a little more?"

"Yes." The word was clipped, and I knew the conversation was over simply from her tone. "We could. But your father and I chose not to."

Sighing, I opened up my email. "Fine, I get it. I'll do my penance."

"You start tonight."

"Tonight?" Jesus. Much notice? "Mom, I've got plans tonight—"

"Then cancel them," she boomed, then cleared her throat. It was such a rarity that she raised her voice, I had no doubt she'd strained her delicate vocal chords. "I'll text you the address. It's an inner city tutoring center."

I hung up on her before she pissed me off even more, and tossed the phone down beside me. They were really great at cherry-picking parenthood. And usually their best parenting happened when my dad was campaigning and there was a camera around to capture the moment.

Buddy trotted over, dropping his head in my lap. I patted

the couch next to me, but he didn't jump up right away. He just stood there, staring at me with chocolate brown eyes. "Oh, come on. Don't tell me you're taking their side. It was just a joke." Buddy sat down, tilting his head, but not breaking eye contact. "Okay, maybe it was a little stupid to use you for a laugh at the cop's expense. I'm sorry." I should probably be apologizing to the cops, not my damn dog, but it was a bit late for that now.

Buddy finally jumped up, circling before lying down beside me. His tail thumped against the leather, and I scratched the sweet spot above his tail. My mind wandered to Shelby—she was…odd, that's for sure. And while I certainly didn't love it when girls went out with me for my money, I liked it even less when they didn't go out with me at all.

Why was she on my mind? Since when did I let one girl—admittedly a fucking gorgeous one—get so far under my skin that I couldn't even focus in class? I squeezed my eyes shut, willing her face to leave my brain, and leaned my head back against the couch. The empty apartment surrounded me with silence, and her soft, husky voice rang in my ears. She wasn't whiny or shrill like other girls our age. She was sexy in an understated way.

I groaned, opening my eyes and willing my focus back to my email account. There were a couple of unread emails, one spam, another from my best friend, Brad.

Hey,

Is poker still on for Saturday? Feel free to ante up with your sweet Audi. I look forward to calling it mine.

PS – I know your bed's been empty lately. Maybe the hum of the computer screen will replace the nonexistent hummers. =P

At the bottom was a link, and I sunk into the couch even more. Yep, leave it to Brad to send his friends porn. I rolled my eyes. I watched it every now and then. I wasn't opposed to it, but didn't depend on it like some people I knew. Then again, maybe today it was just what the doctor ordered.

I clicked on the link and *holy hell*. I shook the fog from my brain, because for a moment, I swore it was Shelby on the screen. Upon a second glance, it clearly wasn't, and relief flooded me. Not that I didn't want to see the girl on her knees, full lips sealed around my cock, but no man wanted to date a porn star. Well, except maybe Brad, I thought with an eye roll. I watched closer as the woman on screen went down on the guy. She didn't even really look like Shelby other than the dark blond hair that caught on her eyelashes, and her big, golden-brown eyes. But even with a naked woman right in my line of vision, Shelby's was the face I thought of. Porn stars were supposed to be hotter than real world women, right? Wasn't that the whole point of a fucking fantasy? Since when did real girls infiltrate my daydreams?

I sighed. *Since Shelby, that's when.*

I closed my eyes, feeling excitement stir in my pants. Moans echoed from my laptop but in my mind, Shelby's face was all I pictured. Would she nibble her bottom lip, and writhe in pleasure as I tasted her? How would that husky voice sound first thing in the morning over coffee…or better yet, screaming my name in the middle of the night? I wanted to know her body—every curve, every hot spot, and every birthmark that existed on her smooth skin.

I wanted to know *her*. And this wasn't the normal desire to just throw a woman into my bed. I wanted to take my time, savor her. Study her. I snorted, closing my eyes. I should know better. That never ended well.

My thoughts went immediately to Katie, and all those warm fuzzies Shelby brought about shriveled into a dried out raisin. I pushed my ex out of my mind. Shelby wasn't Katie—I mean, I barely knew Shelby, but Katie would have never been caught dead in a thrift store T-shirt. She'd be in pearls…and demanding that I buy her the matching earrings.

That same twitch in my eyebrow that always surfaced with memories of my ex was back, and I rubbed a chilled hand over it to stop the convulsions.

I forced my eyes open to focus on the woman on the screen. The woman that was nothing like Shelby, and she clearly wasn't doing it for me. I slammed the laptop shut, dick still in hand, rock hard with thoughts of the girl downstairs.

My phone buzzed, and I gave up, zipping up my pants and reaching for my phone. Great, just great. I had thirty minutes to get to my community service. "Hey, Buddy, you wanna go tutor some kids for me?"

He whimpered, burrowing his nose deeper into a pillow, and I sighed. "Yeah, me neither."

...

I pulled into a pothole-riddled lot in front of a simple concrete building. Checking my phone once more, I made sure it was the correct address—and unfortunately for me, it was. Where the hell was I? Because I was pretty damn certain my life was at risk simply in the walk from my car to the front door. Most of the kids who came here probably walked from their homes, or even took the bus. It was hard to imagine, and I swallowed as I tugged the heavy door open. A plump woman smiled at me from behind a plexiglass window.

"Hi there," she said with a welcoming grin.

I nodded, hesitating before moving up to the counter. "Uh, hi. Tate Michaelson. I'm here for, uh"—I cleared my throat, lowering my voice a touch—"community service."

She nodded, flipping through some papers. "Yes, right. We

got your paperwork this morning. Come on back." She hit a button under the desk, and the second door buzzed loudly. I slipped through, following the woman to a large room. There were several crappy circular tables spaced through the middle, and a handful of students sat quietly working. They ranged from young—maybe nine or ten—up through high school age. Around the edge of the room were rectangular tables holding a few ancient looking desktop computers, which hummed loudly, whirring as though the technology was straining to stay alive.

"Your mom mentioned that you have a knack for languages, right?"

I nodded, turning my baseball hat around so that it was backward. "Yeah, I guess so."

"That's great. We have a lot of high schoolers who need help with their level one Spanish classes. What else do you excel at?"

I shrugged. "I don't know. I always liked science, I guess."

"Great." She made a mark in her notebook and handed me a stapled packet of papers. "This was faxed over from the courthouse this morning. You'll need our director or assistant director to sign off at the beginning and end of every shift you make. They'll record your hours, and at the end of each week, we will fax it in. Make sense?"

"Yep." I glanced around the room, already incredibly bored with the process. Shit, this was gonna be a long few months.

"Great—I'll grab one of the program managers to get you situated and find you a mentee for your time here. Have a seat." She gestured again to the table, and I sank into a plastic bucket chair. The dingy gray carpet was stained beneath my feet, and several holes had worn away in patches across the floor. There weren't a whole lot of volunteers there. About fifteen kids in all, and maybe half as many adults. What did that mean? Would I be stuck with more than one kid at a time? Jesus, I dropped my face into my hands and rubbed my fingers across my brows. "I think I would have preferred jail." I groaned into my hands.

"You're new," A small voice in front of me said and I slowly looked up to find a little girl—probably one of the younger ones—smiling back at me. She must have been around ten, maybe eleven. I don't know…I wasn't exactly good at pinpointing the age of kids.

"Uh…yeah," I said, shifting my eyes around and leaning my elbows onto my knees. "Just started today."

"I don't have a mentor yet," she blurted out.

I sucked my cheek. "Right. Well, I'm sure they'll be assigning you to someone soon."

She sat down next to me and pulled out a few books from a backpack that looked damn near as heavy as her. "I'm Sophia." She gave me a sideways glance, tucking her black hair behind one ear, and I nodded back.

"I'm Tate. What you got there?" I angled my chin toward one of the books in hand.

She groaned, her lip curling back around slightly crooked teeth. "Math. I hate math."

"Yeah, me too." I leaned back and tipped the chair onto two legs. "And don't believe what they say. You don't use half of it in the real world."

Her eyes widened, and she slammed the book down onto the table. "I knew it."

I shrugged. "It's the truth. Unfortunately, you still need to learn it and get good grades."

She clicked her tongue and gave me a doubtful look. "Why?"

"You want to go to college, right?"

She looked down at the books, keeping busy with flipping the pages. "I don't know. Maybe."

"Aw, come on. Of course you do. College is awesome. Trust me." I wiggled my eyebrows at her. "You *want* to go to college."

Her ears turned a pinkish color, and her chin dipped. "It's too expensive."

Something tightened in my throat. She probably couldn't afford it. And I knew nothing about this girl. I had no idea if she was smart or hard working, or if she was good at sports or anything else to get her into a school somewhere.

"That's what scholarships are for, right?" A familiar voice crooned behind me, and I knew that voice. Immediately.

Shelby.

Slowly, I twisted around in my chair and caught her glare, focused directly on the back of my head. I raised one eyebrow in response and allowed a lazy grin to spread across my face. Maybe this whole community service thing wouldn't be so bad after all.

Chapter Six

TATE

"That's absolutely what scholarships are for," I answered Sophia.

"You have to be, like, really smart for scholarships, though."

Shelby sank to a crouch in front of the little girl and put a hand to her knee. "*You* are smart. Because smart people know when they need a little help now and then. And you're a great singer. You could get a scholarship for that someday as well."

The girl shrugged, her cheeks reddening. Shelby gave a couple of reassuring pats to Sophia's leg before hoisting herself back onto her feet and bringing her eyes to me once more. "Tate, let's talk over here." She gave a little nod and turned toward a private room.

I followed her as she stood in the open doorway, waiting for me. Her mouth was settled into a firm line that pinched at the corners. So different from yesterday when we met in the lobby. She had been giddy, carefree, and fun. Maybe a little nervous at first, but that loosened pretty quickly after I helped her clean up her box. She was like a completely new person since she learned I lived in the building. I dropped into a mismatched chair and propped my feet on the table. Shelby took the seat across from me, looking over some paperwork.

I scanned the room, eyeing the seventies faux wood paneling and the crappy wallpaper that was peeling in the corners. Water stains covered the cheap dropped ceiling, and I shook my head. "Holy hell, this place could use a makeover."

Shelby snorted. "If we had the budget for that, we wouldn't be killing ourselves to get every bit of grant money possible," she mumbled, then set her paperwork down, meeting my eyes.

"So, what are you doing here, Betty? Find yourself in a little trouble, too?" I wiggled my eyebrows and popped a piece of gum into my mouth.

One side of her hair was clipped back and the other cascaded down her face in a curtain of soft waves. "I almost did, thanks to you. But, no. That's not why I'm here today." Her answer was curt.

"Thanks to me? What'd I do?"

She slapped her pen down and glared at me. "When you mouthed off last night, the other cop went around checking IDs—"

My stomach plummeted. The thought of Shelby being thrown in jail because of me nearly made me barf right there on the table. "You're underage? Shit, why didn't you run ou—"

"I'm not underage. I'm twenty-one. But my ID was downstairs in my apartment."

The tension released from my shoulders. "That's it? That's not a problem. Even if they had taken you in, you would have just shown your ID and—"

"That's not the point," she interrupted. "You're reckless.

And careless, with yourself and with others—"

"Whoa." I held out two hands. "Jesus, I'm sorry. I didn't see you come in, *Mom*." If looks could kill, I would have dropped dead right there at that conference table as Shelby's expression iced over into a frozen tundra. "So, if you're not here for community service, why are you here?"

Her glare hardened even more. "Some of us *work* here— and volunteer here because we like helping out. It's not always to get something out of it, you know."

"So which is it…do you volunteer here or do you work here?"

"I'm the assistant program director. Yeah, I get paid, but believe me when I say I'm not here for the money."

I kind of loved that she worked here when she didn't have to. And I loved that she was pissed and didn't let my smile thaw that anger. I nodded as her brown eyes glittered, challenging me to mock her for this job. I didn't. I couldn't. Damn, if it didn't make her even hotter. Clearly, if she was living on Congress Ave, she didn't need the money. So she was doing this…why? The answer was obvious—because she loved helping. "Wow," I finally managed through my cotton mouth. "Good for you. That's awesome."

Her eyes widened a fraction of an inch before she regained her composure. "Thanks." She paused. "It *is* awesome."

"So…I guess this means we'll be working together for the next couple of months." I gestured at my paperwork and dropped my feet from the table. "Does that make you my boss?" A smile turned up my lips. Shelby responded just as I'd hoped—with a tiny twitch of her own lips. Not a full on smile, but I'd take it.

"In a way, yeah." She dove into the paperwork, whistling. "Two hundred hours? Wow." She looked up, eyes wide, and I shrugged it off. She's so eager to help these kids, how would that look if I seemed bothered by it?

"I'm sure they're making an example out of me. What else would I do with that time, anyway?" There were at least a dozen things I could do with that time, half of which involved Shelby in my bed with her legs straddling my face.

She exhaled a puff of air. "Well, let's get you started, then. You seemed to get along well with Sophia. She doesn't have a mentor yet and could really use someone who will be stable in her life for a few months while she gets a handle on long division."

Nerves clenched in my chest. "She's a little…young. I thought I'd get one of the older kids. A guy, preferably."

Shelby's fierce eyes shot up like she saw right through me—saw that by hanging with a teenage boy, it'd be more like I was hanging out with friends in my living room than at a tutoring center. She cleared her throat. "Unfortunately for you, all the older guys have mentors already. You'll be with Sophia."

Ugh. "Great," I lied. "How often am I expected to come in?"

"As often as you can, but the kids do a lot better when there's a set schedule. Monday through Friday after school would be ideal. Sophia's mom doesn't get home from work typically until seven, so she's here every day."

I pulled out my phone, scrolling through the calendar. "Hmm, can't do Tuesdays. Basketball. Thursdays are tough, too… Thank God it's not the weekends, right?" I looked up to find that hardened glare back, and I grinned at it. I couldn't help it. "The schoolteacher glare is pretty damn cute on you."

"Cute?" Her eyes widened to epic proportions.

Oops. Did I say that one aloud? I leaned back in the chair and folded my hands across my abs. "All I meant was you pull off the 'boss' thing well. I like it." I winked and wiggled my eyebrows once.

With a sigh, she rolled her eyes, making a note. "Do you

think that a little wiggle of your eyebrows disguises the fact that you're being an asshole?" She paused, raising her gaze with her chin still angled down, and holy hell, if she didn't look like a sexy librarian in that moment.

"Nope." I shook my head and forced a light-hearted laugh. "I don't think that any more than you think rolling your eyes hides the fact that you're attracted to me."

Her brow furrowed as she licked her plump, pink lips. "*Anyway*, I can cover for you most Tuesdays if Sophia needs help. Other volunteers can also pick up the slack on Thursday if I'm not here. Otherwise, we'll expect you to be here. I looked at her homework list today already, and it's not much. You'll have an easy start, and the two of you can get acquainted."

"Today?" I let the chair drop to the floor, and it clacked against the linoleum. "Huh. I just figured today would be fast. Like an orientation of sorts."

"It is." Shelby dipped the edge of the pen into her mouth, chewing lightly on the tip. Holy. Shit. The tip of her pink tongue peeked out at the edge, and her lips curved around the plastic. My dick jumped in my pants, and I was feeling about ten degrees warmer than two seconds ago. "It's also your first day on the job, and you're expected to work. A word that I'm *sure* is foreign to you…but then again, you're good at languages, so I'm confident you'll decipher its meaning contextually."

My smile twitched higher. "Christ, who pissed in your lemonade today?"

"I told you earlier. You bother me."

"Well, Betty—"

"*Shelby*."

"Yeah, I know. I have a solution that could help both of us. You don't want me around here…*clearly*. I don't want to *be* here any more than I have to." I lowered my voice, glancing around the room, just in case. "Just sign off some extra hours, and I'll be out of your hair sooner rather than later."

She gasped, those brown eyes widening to orbs. "I can't do that."

"Sure you can." I tapped the papers with two fingers. "The assistant program director can sign off on hours, according to the woman out front. I'll still show up, make appearances so that your superiors don't get suspicious. I'll still do the work… it'll just be an extra hour here, thirty minutes there. And I'll be out of your hair a month earlier, easy."

From behind tense lips, she ran her tongue across her teeth. It was so easy to get under her skin it was hilarious. I knew girls like this from prep school. They were wound too tight. Came from money and privilege and justified their own luck in life by helping those less fortunate. It was nice and all. But clearly the girl needed to let loose a little.

Before she answered, a man walked into the room, giving me a quick nod and leaning down to Shelby. He was tall and wore ironed khakis and a button-down shirt. One hand sprawled out on the table and his other rested on her upper back. *What a tool.* She couldn't possibly be interested in a geek like that, could she? She tensed at his touch but quickly eased into it. My fists balled around the arms of the chair, and I bit my cheek. His nose was wickedly close to her ear as he whispered something, and his eyes drifted briefly to her rounded breasts beneath the fitted T-shirt she wore.

I felt the primal urge to grab her from his hold and crash my lips down onto hers. Tearing my gaze away from them together, I forced the barbaric feelings to take a backseat to common sense. As much as I'd like to think I could, there's no way I could go around grabbing random women and claiming them with my mouth. Especially not a woman like Shelby. Opening my eyes, I blinked slowly at her, meeting her challenging stare with my own, and felt the grin turning up the corners of my mouth.

Her skin flushed a rosy color from cheek to cheek and across the bridge of her nose. The faintest freckles appeared with her flush, and I held back a chuckle. She was mad. Again. Clearly there was something about me that sparked her flame, and I was looking forward to setting that fire ablaze.

Chapter Seven

SHELBY

"What the eff, right?" I crossed my legs, leaning forward in the booth toward my warm plate of pancakes. I was lucky that I hadn't run into Tate since Monday night. I spent most of Tuesday doing homework and brushing up on French for this morning's class before checking in on Sophia.

The waitress swung by, filling my coffee mug to the brim, and as steam billowed out, I inhaled that nutty scent. I stabbed the next bite on my plate, shoveling it into my mouth. "He actually thought I would just sign off on extra hours for him. Because, what, he had cute dimples? Because he was so thoughtful as to grace me with his flirting?" I snorted.

Reagan's eyebrows shot up. "Well…"

"Well *what*?"

She shrugged. "I'm not saying he's right for asking, but hell, girl, this is college. People call in favors from their friends—"

"We are *not* friends."

"Fine. From their peers, all the time. It doesn't mean he's a good guy for asking, but maybe he's not quite the asshole you make him out to be." Reagan cracked one hardboiled egg, peeling the shell and removing the yolk, placing it in her napkin. I eyed her carefully as she tore the egg white into bits, placing a piece in her mouth.

"You didn't eat much at dinner last night, either," I noted quietly, and her eyes shot up, flashing with…something. When was the last time I saw Reagan eat something hearty? We had pizza on moving day, but she insisted that we order gluten free and only ate one slice, which she peeled the cheese off of.

"I did *so*. My salad was huge."

"Yeah, it was a giant bowl of lettuce, no protein and barely any dressing." I swallowed. "You're not…again…are you?"

"No." She gritted her teeth, and I wet my lips, nodding.

"Because if you are—"

"I'm *not*." After a deep sigh, she popped another piece of egg white into her mouth. "I just have an audition coming up, and I want to look good. It's senior year. I don't have a lot more chances to get a leading role."

I nodded, knowing that desire. That drive to be in the spotlight. My throat tightened as I remembered the ballet slippers my mom had framed in a shadow box for me. My first pair ever. Like anytime I thought of my mother, I was met with a complex symphony of grief and fury. Sorrow was common, but it was the rage that surfaced even more. An all-consuming anger at everyone—at her doctors for not doing more to save her, at the insurance companies for not covering the drug trial…and at my mom.

For leaving me.

How fucking stupid was that?

Who gets mad at their own dead mother? She did nothing but love me. She gave everything in her life for me. And I was still irrationally pissed, as though it was her fault for getting cancer. As if she could have fought any harder than she already had.

But mostly, I was angry with myself for not appreciating her while I had her. For not visiting more often.

Those combative feelings of sorrow, rage, and guilt were such a driving force that I had to push my fingernails into my palm to tamp it down—replace that emotional pain with something physical.

I cleared my throat, wiping my hands on my jeans, palms still stinging and indented with marks from my nails. "Just be careful, okay?"

She brushed me off with a wave of her hand. "Okay, *Mom*."

Which one of us is the mother here? My mom's playfully chastising voice rang in my memory, echoing Reagan. Those words stabbed into me and no amount of fingernails in my palms could make that pain subside.

"Shit. I'm so sorry. I didn't mean it like that—" Reagan apologized.

"It's fine," I said and her eyes lifted to mine. "I mean it." I added more gently. "It's fine."

All she did was nod. And that was all I needed. For now.

I poured another glob of syrup over my pancakes and forked a chunk into my mouth. "So," I said between chewing, searching for something—anything to change the subject. "What's the audition for?"

She took a deep breath. "*Singin' in the Rain.*"

"Oh," I squealed, offering her a smile. "You'd be a fantastic Kathy Selden."

"I know, right? Let's just hope Jim sees it that way, too."

"After the audition, we'll go celebrate with ice cream, okay?"

Reagan rolled her eyes, but her smile slipped through. "Okay, okay. A *small* ice cream." With a quick glance at her phone, she popped up, dropping some cash onto the table. "We better go."

I did the same, pulling out my tips from a couple weeks ago and dropping a ten onto the table. Reagan handed it back to me. "I got this one," she said, and I gave her a look.

"You had a boiled egg. I had pancakes. You're not paying for me."

She waved the bill in front of my face. "Yeah, but you got pizza Sunday."

"Because you helped me move."

Reagan sighed, dropping her arm. "Shelby, come on. Just take the help. I asked you to breakfast—otherwise you never would have come out on your own."

"Yeah, but I did. And that was my choice. And it was my choice to order the full breakfast, not just one pancake." I grinned at her and dove for my ten, snatching it out of her loose grip. She relented, gathering her dance bag onto her shoulder and leading the way to the door.

We crossed the brick-lined street, and I froze.. Up ahead, Tate stood with a couple of friends, the vodka girl among them, leaning against Tate's shoulder. Reagan tugged me onto the sidewalk as a horn beeped from somewhere over my shoulder. "What is it?" she asked, turning to face Tate and the girl. "Oh. Maybe they're just friends?"

I swallowed. What a shitty morning this was turning out to be. "Yeah, maybe." But I didn't feel very comforted by that.

"Seriously, look at them more closely. She's leaning on him. He doesn't have his arm around her. He's barely touching her."

That was true. He didn't seem all that into her. "I wish I could do that," I whispered, the words slipping out before I had the good sense to stop them.

"Do what?" Reagan asked. "Wear a miniskirt? I've got a million you could borrow."

She was trying to lighten the mood. But I didn't feel very light. I felt heavy, weighed down by self-doubt and loss and all the potential failure lurking in my future. "It's not the skirt. It's... Well, she clearly knows what she wants. And she's going for it with unapologetic abandon even though Tate's not really reciprocating. She looks so free." I blinked back the tears dancing at the edges of my lashes and turned to examine Reagan. "Like you. I've always admired how brave and free you are."

Reagan's face softened, melting into something melancholy. "Free," she repeated. "We're all bound by something, Shelbs."

"Yeah, I guess. We've all got demons."

She cleared her throat, and as quickly as the sadness had come on her, it was gone. "Real bravery is being in a show in front of hundreds of people." She winked. "How about you audition for *Singin' in the Rain* with me? Get Shelby Stevens back on the stage."

I snorted. "Yeah, right. You'd have more luck getting me in one of those miniskirts of yours and to a club."

"Done. No backsies. I'll have you in a short, tight skirt before the year's over. Just you wait." She grinned, but her smile didn't quite carry the same spark as it did earlier.

Just then, Harrison ran over from the parking lot. "What's so funny?"

"We're just talking about how sexy Reagan is." I grinned.

His pupils dilated, his gaze sweeping over Reagan's body before his eyebrows lowered. And not for the first time, I wondered if his feelings for her ran deeper than best friend level. "And how sexy Shelby is," Reagan interjected.

As his attention shifted to me, his lip curled, and it almost looked like he was disgusted by the thought. "Oh...okay."

Reagan rolled her eyes. "I know you two have that familial bond or whatever, but you should *still* be able to admit that she's sexy."

"She's like my sister," Harrison answered, giving Reagan a look. "I can't comment on her sex appeal. It's weird. And gross."

"Hey," I said, slapping his shoulder. "Gross is a bit extreme. Can we at least both admit that Reagan is sexy as hell?"

He licked his lips, briefly clearing his throat before studying the sidewalk as if that would hide the way his eyes lit when he looked at her. "Yeah, sure."

With a sigh, she dropped her hand to her thigh. "I give up." Spinning, she threw a wave over her shoulder, running off for the theatre building.

Harrison and I moved toward French. "I know we're all best friends, but sometimes I just can't keep up with you two."

As we passed Tate, Harrison brushed my elbow with his in a comforting gesture.

"You don't like him," I said, and though I meant it to be a question, it came out more as a statement.

"And you do?" Harrison asked quietly, studying me through a side-eyed glance. I forced myself to look away from Tate as Harrison held the door to the language arts building for me. I slipped inside, hoisting my heavy bag higher onto my shoulder.

"Yeah." I sighed, waiting until we were out of earshot to answer Harrison. We slipped into our same seats as Monday, and I pulled out the French book.

"Yeah?" His voice cracked with the accusatory question.

I shook my head to clear my thoughts, like a dog shaking off water. "No. I mean, no. He's exactly the sort of wealthy snob I've sworn off since—"

"Okay, I get it," Harrison cut me off, facing forward in his seat.

"Besides…" I cleared my throat as, from the corner of my eye, I saw him enter. "I can guarantee he wants nothing to do with me after the other night," I said to Harrison. I squirmed, steeling myself for the silent treatment—or worse, ready to get completely berated by him and his friends for refusing to sign off on extra hours. Instead, he slipped into the seat next to me, his lips curving seductively, and flipped his sunglasses to the top of his head.

"Morning," he said with a grin.

"Um...hi?"

His mouth twitched higher. "Was that a question?"

I exhaled through the side of my mouth and my bangs flipped up off of my eyelashes. "I just wasn't expecting you to...to sit here. After Monday."

He shrugged. "Why not? I don't blame you. I mean, it's something I would do for a friend, but I get not everyone's as awesome as me." His grin split into a full-on smile, and yep... there were those frickin' dimples again. Was it possible to loathe something you wanted to lick so much?

I opened my mouth to correct the "friend" comment and quickly snapped it shut. Reagan was right. Peers should be friendly to each other in college. And we had a whole semester together in this class where I should probably make an effort to be nice.

So, I said nothing, which only made his grin widen more.

"*Bonjour*, class." Professor Ceele entered the room, stack of papers in hand and called out names one by one. My muscles clenched—our tests. Between calling names and passing out the tests, the professor said something about the drop period lasting for only another two weeks.

I raised my hand, hearing my name called, and he paused before dropping the paper face down on my desk. I stole a glance around the room and just barely lifted the corner of the page. An air bubble formed in my lungs, and for a second there, I thought I might throw up. My test was bleeding. Red marks covered it like slashes, and at the top of the page in giant red numbers was a "53."

I stuffed the test into my bag, my belly rumbling like an earthquake. When I finally gained the courage to look up, I caught Tate's eyes on me, and my skin flared red. Jesus, did he see the grade? His lips twitched at the corners momentarily before he turned his attention back to Professor Ceele.

His test sat face up on his desk for the world to see—a giant "100, Great job!" in red ink at the top. Now I really *was* gonna throw up. Life was so not fair.

. . .

After class, I packed up my bag, and Harrison's hand fell to my back. "Is it that bad?"

I swallowed, shaking my head "no" even though I was screaming "yes" on the inside. "I don't want to talk about it."

He nodded. "I could help, probably."

I rolled my eyes, hoisting my bag onto a shoulder. "What'd you get on your test?"

Harrison's face flushed, and he shrugged. "Only an 83. But still…even mediocre help is better than nothing."

At the other end of the classroom, Tate stood with one of the girls from class. His shades were already pulled down onto his nose despite the fact we weren't even close to being in the parking lot yet. It shouldn't annoy me, but it did. *He* did.

"Shelby? Hel-*lo*?"

"Don't you have poly sci?" I glanced at my phone. "Like, right now?"

He craned his neck to look at the time and cursed. "Shit. Okay, I'll catch up with you later." He ran for his car, and I sighed, taking my lumbering time to get out the door.

"Ms. Stevens," Professor Ceele called from the front of the classroom. I cringed and crept toward his desk.

"*Oui?*"

He waved away my French, but a small smile softened the dismissal. "I just wanted to say, you have time to catch up. And if you can't, don't hesitate to drop the class. You'll be just fine without mastering French IV."

I swallowed, needing a giant glass of hydrating water. I definitely could not drop the class—not as a senior. If I didn't take it this semester, I'd just be back in the same place come January. "Actually, I'm an international business major." I blew a soft breath out of lightly parted lips. "So, I won't be 'just fine' not mastering French IV."

He winced in sympathy. "Well, then, I would suggest some caffeine and a study partner. I know a few tutors I can recommend, but they don't come cheap." He offered me a small smile, and it deepened the wrinkles around his light eyes. "It'll be a tough semester for you, but if you plan on working in international business, then French is a necessity, isn't it?"

I nodded, tilting my chin and giving the best faux confidence I could muster. Which, admittedly, was probably not all that convincing. "Yes, sir. I can catch up. I always do."

His smile was warm as it widened and spread over his whole face. He pushed to his feet as well, and gestured for the door. "I hope so."

I slipped out to find Tate leaning against the wall right outside in the hallway. I nearly ran into him and quickly dodged his elbow, which stuck out into the doorway. "Jeez," I said, mostly to myself.

He kicked off the wall, and I sped up to avoid a conversation with him. Or *tried* to. But he was faster, and soon his steps fell into rhythm beside me. "What was that about?"

"None of your business."

"Whoa." He put both hands up, surrender style, and jumped ahead of me to open the door. "I was just asking. Damn."

I sighed, walking faster into the parking lot, closing my eyes briefly against the warmth of the sun hitting my skin. Students milled about after class, hanging out on the benches and near the coffee carts. "I know. Sorry," I added in a mumble. Why did he have to be so nice? And yet, he was an asshole. Was there such a thing as a nice asshole? Digging my keys out of the front pouch of my bag, an idea crept into my brain. Tate had offered me his help at the party. He spoke French fluently. What if he tutored me until I caught up to the rest of the class? He still stood next to me as though waiting—waiting for me to ask for the help we both knew I needed.

I gulped, and he plucked the car keys from my hand, looking at the set. "No shit," he gushed, looking around the lot and taking off toward my mom's cherry red MG Midget. I still couldn't call it mine…for as long as I owned the car, it would be my mom's. "This ride is yours?" He circled my car, eyes wide. "I was wondering whose Cherry Pie this was."

My smile deepened, and though tired, it was genuine. "Yep. She's beautiful, but breaks down every time the wind changes direction."

"Aw, come on. It must be worth it. Damn, it's in great condition, too. Restored?"

I shook my head. "No…my mom just took really good care of her before giving her to me."

He smiled and put his hands in his pockets. "You talk like it's a person."

"It might as well be. She was always part of the family." My only family now, I thought as my eyes traveled her sleek lines. Unless I counted Harrison. But he wasn't blood. And as much as I loved the guy, he'd never take the place of my mom. That lump in my throat threatened to take up residence permanently, and I swallowed it down before it grew roots.

He put the key in the door and hopped into the passenger side. "Take me for a ride." His eyes glistened with intent. *Oh, hell. I'll take you for a ride, all right.*

I crossed my arms over my chest. "Don't you have class?"

He didn't even look at his watch, but leaned over, sliding the key into the ignition. "Not until twelve." Then, with a twitch of his head, gestured for me to enter. "You?"

I hopped in the car, pointedly waiting for him to get out. "Twelve thirty."

"Great, you can give me a ride home." His grin split wider.

There was no reason to not give him a ride home. How long would the drive take? Five minutes? I could manage being in the car with him that long. I rolled my eyes, cranking the car to life. "You're really something, you know that? How'd you get here?"

He buckled up, leaning the passenger seat back. "A friend gave me a ride."

"Oh." *A friend.* Perhaps the same friend who was hanging all over him before class? I pushed the jealousy to the side. How fucked up was I? I didn't even want this guy, and here I was bothered that he got a ride with a "friend."

"So, how do you like Ceele?"

I swallowed, veering right out of the parking lot. "I think he's…very understanding."

Out of the corner of my eye, Tate's fingers brushed across his lips like he was deep in thought, studying me. "How'd you do on the test?"

I shrugged, trying to remain as cool and casual as he was. "Okay," I managed to croak. Then I added, pretending I hadn't snuck a peek at his test, "You?"

"Okay," he repeated, and I had to stop the snort before it exploded out my nose.

"'Okay,' my ass. You and I both know you got a perfect score."

His lips relaxed and he barely registered emotion as I called him out on the lie. "So, if we're being honest now…

how'd you *really* do?"

I sighed, rolling to a stop at the red light. "Not well." My cheeks flamed and mortification seeped into my chest. "I knew I wasn't gonna do well, but I didn't think I'd do quite as bad as I did." I cleared my throat, taking off as the light turned back to green. "Actually, I've been thinking…"

"Dangerous, Betty," he said. "You do that too much."

"As I was saying…I've been thinking. I'm willing to sign off more hours for you at the center." His brows arched, but he said nothing, so I continued. "If you help me pass French this semester. I just…I don't know, it doesn't come naturally. I freak out when it's test time. I can usually speak it all right, but when other people speak in French, it's like gibberish. I can't understand a damn word of it, and I've been at this for years now."

"So…" He steepled his fingers below his clean-shaven chin. "You're saying that if I tutor you, you'll cut down my hours at the center?" He pressed his lips together, wetting them before they stretched into a grin.

"Well…" I gulped, and granted, I'd only been mulling this over for a couple of minutes, but I didn't make it this far in life by playing by the rules. Sometimes, you had to get scrappy. "I–I'm pretty sure it's illegal. But I'm hoping if we get caught, we can both plead ignorance. I'm only going to sign off on the exact amount of extra time you spend tutoring me. So, technically…*technically*"—I put a finger in the air to drive the point home—"you're still doing the actual work. It's just not for an accredited organization. And the more often we can do the work there at the center, the better."

He said nothing more, simply lounged back in my passenger seat, examining me as I drove. He ran a hand over the camel-colored interior leather. "She's a beauty."

The stress that tightened my shoulders cranked up a notch. Would this guy ever give me a straight answer? "Yes, she is."

"It suits you. This car."

"Thanks. But you clearly don't know her insides very well. They designed her entirely for looks. She stalls constantly and ends up at the shop almost weekly."

"So, she looks really capable, but in actuality she needs a little help now and then? Nothing wrong with that," he said quietly.

I tried to swallow beyond the knot in my throat, but it felt oddly suffocating. "Yeah, well, some of us aren't as easily fixed." The scar at my temple flared with pain, and I knew it was just in my head. I was no fucking Harry Potter, for God's sake.

"You mean cars? Some cars just aren't fixable."

"Yeah, that's what I said." I fish-hooked into our building's lot, turning the car off. Thank God we made it all the way home. I didn't have enough of a balance left on my credit card to afford a tow truck this week.

"So?" I unbuckled, curling my leg under me as I turned to face him. "What do you say?"

"Shelby…"

I groaned. I knew that tone. That was a "thanks but no thanks." I put a hand in the air, waving him away. "It's fine. Really. I'll just see if Harrison can—"

"Your place or mine?"

I froze, halfway out of the car. "What?"

His dimples appeared along with a soft smile. "Your place…or mine?" he said, slower this time.

Relief flooded through me, and I sighed, closing my eyes. "Yours. It's bigger." Why was he being so nice to me? Not just tutoring me—he was getting hours off his community service in exchange for *that*. But everything else—in the lobby when we met, at his party, sitting next to me in class, worrying about my test score. I was about as congenial as a starved gator.

"How about tomorrow after class?"

He pushed out of my car, shutting the door gently behind him and running his hand over the hood. His nimble fingers brushed the lines where the convertible top met the windshield, and I stared in awe at those able hands. "Maybe someday I'll be lucky enough to take her out for a spin myself."

There's no shame in admitting when you need help.

It wasn't only my mother's voice reciting those words. It was mine. I had just said nearly that exact same thing to Sophia the other night. But it wasn't my failing grade on the first test that bothered me. It wasn't even the fact that I needed help from a tutor. It was that I needed help from someone like *him*.

Chapter Eight

Tate

There was a firm knock at my door. I grabbed the beret from my coffee table and jumped to my feet, sliding toward the door that separated my kitchen from the foyer entrance. Buddy ran at my heels, barking and hopping behind me. I had gone all out for this one, though I didn't know why. I loved France—it was the only time that we traveled as a family without worrying about Dad's work interfering. Mom had no country club to visit, no luncheons to attend or plan. It was the only time in our family history that we could just be together, visiting landmarks or going to the beach. My mom worked on her tan, and we actually *talked*. I had no friends to go running off with, and Dad had no meetings. It had been utter perfection.

    I had laid out a spread of baguettes, Brie, and macaroons, along with Orangina to wash it down with. I skidded to a stop in front of the door as nerves bounced around in my stomach. It felt empty—despite the fact that I had already dug into the stash of macaroons. I swung the door open, "Bonjour, Mademoi—"

Brad, wearing a smirking face, leaned against my doorway with his arms crossed. "My fucking hero." His grin spread wider, and I rolled my eyes, sliding the hat off.

"What are you doing here?" I turned away, heading into my kitchen, and grabbed a bottle of water.

"Sorry, man." He casually dipped his hands into his pockets, looking around the apartment. "I didn't know you'd be having *company*."

"It's nothing." I waved off his innuendos. "Just a study thing."

"More of this community service shit?"

I swallowed as Shelby's face popped into mind. "Something like that."

Brad leaned back against the counter, resting his weight back on his elbows. "Man, your parents are a piece of work. When're they gonna ease up?"

I shrugged, glancing at the clock. Roughly five minutes until Shelby came up. I needed to ditch Brad ASAP. She was already skittish around me—throw my dumbass friends into the mix, and she'd be out of here in seconds flat. I mean, Brad was a good guy and all, if you were one of his bros. But as a woman on his radar? Yeah, not so much. "So, is this a courtesy call, or do you need something?"

"Just popping in to let you know b-ball is cancelled for tonight."

I nodded. "Okay…that warranted a visit?"

He shrugged, his lopsided grin growing higher on one side. "Thought we'd go grab a beer instead." He looked around as one eyebrow shot up. "But even I can take a hint. Let's just hope this girl is in it for the bulge in your pants, not the bulge of your wallet, right?" He slapped me on the chest and those words cut deeper than I'm sure he intended. I opened the door to the foyer, tapping the elevator call button. Normally, the penthouse needed a key to open into the apartment, but I liked an open door sort of policy, and I had a tendency to leave my floor unlocked while I was home. I examined Brad, in his wrinkled shirt and the jeans I recognized from yesterday. Maybe it was time to change that life practice.

"Oh, before I go...check out this girl I went out with last night. She looks like Raven Marx, right?" I rolled my eyes at that. Brad talked about the porn star as if they knew each other. It was weird. But despite his compulsion, he was for the most part a good guy. He pulled out his phone, searching through some buttons before handing it over to me. A selfie of a waif thin girl with tits bigger and rounder than beach balls came up on some social media site.

"Yep, pretty, er, hot." *Yeah, not hot at all.*

"Shit, man... Hot, but looser than a fucking—"

"Okay." I laughed, guiding his shoulder toward the elevators. "I don't need all the details, man." This was really not the conversation I wanted to be having right now. Not with Shelby only a few steps away.

Brad held up his hands, laughing. "Since when?" His smiled dropped momentarily as he looked around, finally taking in just how far I'd gone for this day. "Ohhh," he said quietly. "You really like this one."

I snorted, busying myself with scratching Buddy behind the ear. "Don't be an idiot. I just met her."

He nodded, sucking the inside of his cheek. "Okay, okay. That's good, man. It's good to finally see you walking with the living again."

I rolled my eyes. "Please. I've been partying with you all fucking summer."

"Yeah." He backed toward the door. "Physically you've been present, but when it comes to chicks? You haven't seemed to really care since Katie—"

"I don't want to talk about her." Acid burned in my stomach. I hate that all my friends knew how dumb I'd been. They'd witnessed it from the beginning, how, despite their warnings, I moved forward, completely blind to her. "Besides. I've been with girls. A lot of them." I wasn't trying to brag—just reminding him that I hadn't joined the priesthood.

"No, you've fucked a lot of girls. You haven't 'been' with them."

My expression fell quickly at that, and I sighed, scuffing my shoe across the floor. "Since when did you become a fucking poet, man?"

"So I worry about my friend. So what?" Brad shook his head, stuffing his hands into his pockets. "Anyway, when do I get to meet this new mystery girl?" His grin split wider.

I snorted at that, tossing him a macaroon. One hand slipped from his pocket, just in time to catch it, and he stuffed it into his mouth all at once. "You? Oh, hell no," I said, laughing. "If I have my way, she'll stay as far away from your ass as I can keep her."

The elevator slid open just then, and Brad's grin stretched as he shot me a wink. "I can see why," he said quietly.

I groaned. Standing there in a fitted button-down shirt and jeans was Shelby. She was dressed simply. No, not simple... classic. And beautiful. She wore her hair down. The dark blond strands fell straight beyond her shoulders, and the ends of her wispy bangs swept, as always, to the left and caught on the tips of her long eyelashes.

She blinked, looking between Brad and me, her eyes landing on mine. My heart thundered inside my chest, and I was certain Brad sensed it. He snickered from beside me, and stepped onto the elevator. "You must be Tate's community service?" He leaned into the elevator doors, holding them open. "I'm Brad." One hand darted out, lifting Shelby's into a lingering shake before she even offered it.

"Shelby," she answered cautiously.

Brad pulled back, flashing her a wide smile. "It's really nice to meet you," he added more quietly, and there was a genuine tone in his voice that made me remember why I kept that asshole around. "Have fun you two." He winked at me as the elevator slid shut.

She spun to me, cheeks red. "What exactly did you tell him we'd be doing?"

I sighed, holding the door open for her. "Nothing. I just said I had plans."

There was a noise that rumbled at the back of her throat like some sort of gargling. "Sure." She lifted a worn-looking messenger bag from one shoulder, setting it on my counter.

"It's true."

She picked up the beret, which I had left sitting on the counter, and held it up, her mouth tipping into a haughty smirk. The kind of smirk that I wanted to kiss away.

"And what's this?"

"I had a little plan." I leaned in, gently taking the beret from her grasp and placing it on my head. "To introduce you to the French lifestyle."

"Is that guy code for you wanting to try a ménage?"

I choked on my own spit, and her grin widened into a heart-melting smile. She tilted her head. "Kidding, kidding." She spun and wandered into the living room where I had set out my food spread. "Well, well, well…you really *did* go all out."

"Did you doubt me, Betty?"

She smiled and sank into the corner of my couch, pulling her feet under her, and I followed, lowering myself beside her, propping an ankle across my knee.

She pulled her French book out, setting it on my coffee table. "You don't want to know the answer to that," she mumbled, then lifted a macaroon and wrapped her lips around the cookie, slowly taking a bite. I groaned, watching those lips pucker and nibble the cookie away. That must have been intentional, right? No girl naturally looks that fucking sexy without even trying.

Her eyes fluttered closed, and her deep moan crawled inside of me, setting my body on edge. She chewed slowly, savoring each bite, and as she swallowed, she let a satisfied sigh escape.

Goddamn. That was the sexiest thing I'd ever witnessed.

She blinked, a soft smile tilting her lips. "Those are amazing," she rasped. "Where did you get them?"

I examined her closely—did she really have no fucking clue what she just did to me? Or was she a tease? All innocent and sweet and *oh, the macaroon. What?*

I shook the fog from my brain. "Um—Jolie Bakery. Th– they came from Jolie. Down by the waterfront."

At the corner of her mouth, a crumb stuck to her Chap Stick. Again—this had to be a setup, right? My eyes were locked on her full bottom lip.

"You have a crumb." I pointed. Her lashes lowered, and she darted her tongue to the wrong corner of her mouth, missing the cookie. All the blood rushed to my pants so quickly, I swear I got light headed.

Was this all in my mind? She didn't seem aware of what she was doing as she brushed her index finger over the wrong side of her mouth. I slid a little closer, waiting to gauge her reaction, and her breath caught, almost like she was swallowing a gasp. A good gasp? One that was laced with need, I hoped. My pulse thundered, and my arousal was so thick it clawed at the base of my pelvis. But something more profound skimmed higher in my chest. Something new that flipped and somersaulted and wasn't altogether unpleasant.

I leaned in some more, still hesitating. She seemed the skittish type, and I didn't want to rush her. "You still missed it," I said. Lifting my finger to her lips, I brushed at the crumb stuck there. I knew it was too soon, too fast. But God, I needed to taste those watermelon-scented lips, to feel them against mine.

I'd been slowly moving closer for the better part of thirty seconds, and as I tilted my chin down, her sharp breath and firm nipples were all the confirmation I needed. "Don't worry," I whispered. "I'll get it." I brushed my lips to hers, running my tongue along the seam of her mouth. That damn watermelon Chap Stick she wore was purely intoxicating. Her gasp spiraled to the very tips of my body, and she whimpered into me. A hand fell on my chest, and her soft touch feathered across my shoulders and up to the back of my neck. I groaned, deepening the kiss, and her lips parted. She flicked a tentative tongue against mine, exploring. That silken stroke surged through me right down to my toes. My cock pressed against the zipper of my jeans, and I grunted as I wrapped my arm around her hips. My thumbs landed at the sliver of skin between her shirt and jeans. She was like satin beneath my touch, soft skin pulled tightly over firm muscles that only seemed to tighten with every stroke of my thumb. Tugging her closer, I shackled her body against mine, holding my weight above her.

She grunted, that hand tightening around my shirt, and she shoved me back. I blinked, dazed by the sudden change. Her hand rested on her lips, and she shook her head. "No," she said quietly, jolting to her feet. She snatched her book from the coffee table and grabbed her bag with the other hand, rushing for the elevator. "Why did you do that?"

"Are you kidding me?" I drove a hand into my hair and stood, following her. I'd thought she was a little on edge, but this was extreme. Had it been all in my head? I thought back to the quiet sigh that had vibrated against my tongue, and the way she scooped clawed at the back of my neck. It definitely wasn't all in my head. She'd been kissing me back. I was certain of it. "I thought you wanted—I mean, didn't you—"

"No. I need to study, Tate. I'm going to fail this class, and I can't. I can't...be distracted. I'll lose my scholarship." Her bottom lip wobbled, and her eyes brimmed with glossy tears.

Oh, fuck. Please don't cry. She turned, her hand moving toward the elevator button, but I stepped in her way.

"Look, I'm sorry. Shelby, stay. I can help you with your French."

She inhaled a ragged breath. "No. You've made it clear what you're *actually* interested in, and it's not my language skills."

"Shelby." I chuckled, and her eyes darted to mine. The tears were gone, replaced with fiery anger.

"Are you laughing at me?"

"No, it's just..." I leaned back against the elevator doors. Damn, there was no way to say this without sounding like a complete and utter ass. "I just thought you wanted it, too. I'm sorry that I read the signals wrong. Come on...come back inside. We'll go back to studying. *Just* studying." What I wanted to say was you kissed me back and seemed to be enjoying it for a hot second. But based on her reaction seconds earlier, that probably wouldn't fly.

"You won't kiss me again?" She narrowed her eyes and looked at me sideways, the muscles at her shoulders bunched tight.

I shook my head. "No. I won't kiss you again. Unless you kiss me first, in which case, all bets are off."

Relaxing her shoulders, she rolled her eyes. "That won't be happening." She moved, backing into my kitchen once more. "But I'm only doing this because I have no other options, and despite your clear character flaws, you are some sort of French speaking wunderkind."

I had to smirk at that one. "Wunderkind, huh?" I liked

that. She sat on my couch once more, this time all the way in the corner, and I sat an arm's length away.

"You know…I promised not to kiss you. And I keep my promises. But I bet you'll be kissing me before Ceele's next quiz." I grinned, and her mouth dipped into a frown.

"Why? Why would you even *want* me kissing you?" she blurted out. Was she seriously asking why? She couldn't possibly think that I didn't want to kiss her. But she wasn't like the normal girls who lived in this building. She came from wealth, but she didn't constantly dress like she had someone to impress. Outside of that kick-ass car, she didn't seem to spend a lot of money in general. And I didn't have to worry about her being only after my trust fund—something my parents loved to caution me over.

"Oh, really?" Her sarcastic voice snapped me back to the present, and I realized I hadn't yet answered. "Well, that's just fascinating. I'm so desirable that you can't even come up with reasons, huh?"

I laughed and grabbed a macaroon for myself. "Well, why *wouldn't* I want to kiss you? You're beautiful, smart, sweet—

Her face twisted. "Sweet? You think I'm sweet?"

I snickered. "Well, okay, not always to *me*. But I also kind of like that you give me shit back."

She opened the French book. "Prince Charming at work, I see."

"Hey, Shelby," I said, my grin widening. "*Est-ce que tu veux sortir avec moi ce soir? J'aimerais bien ça.*"

Her mouth opened, and the blank look on her face took a few moments to pass. Finally, a soft smile splayed her mouth. She rolled her eyes, and her neck mimicked the movement. "No, I would not like to go out with you tonight. No matter how happy it would make you."

• • •

An hour and a half, eight macaroons, and a whole baguette later, we had tightened her verb conjugations considerably. According to Shelby, she was able to speak well enough to get by, but it was the reading comprehension and especially the listening sections of the test that killed her. I spoke in French almost the whole time, slowly at first, and then sped up as she got the hang of it.

I noticed Shelby checking her phone. "*Quelle heure?*" I asked.

"*Trois-heures quinze,*" she said, barely looking up.

"Actually, if you're going to answer with three fifteen, you need to add *de l'apres midi* at the end. Or say it in military time."

"Shit," she muttered, shaking her head. "I knew that, too."

I shrugged, grabbing the last bit of baguette and tossing it to Buddy. He caught it with a massive chomp of his jaws. "It's okay. It's an easy thing to forget. You did really well today." I grabbed the empty plate, dumping it in my sink. "What happened on that test? You seem to grasp the material at a C or B level."

She tilted her head, giving me an exasperated glance. "I don't know. I think when test time rolls around, I just start panicking. I can understand things okay, but when I'm under pressure I freeze, and it all becomes gobbledygook."

My smirk twitched. "Gobbledygook, huh? I think that's the scientific term for it."

She puffed out a breath, packing her books away. "It's as scientific as I get, that's for sure."

"Hey," I said, pushing off the counter and falling to the couch beside her once more. "I have an idea."

Her eyes widened, and one eyebrow arched. "Oh?"

"Let's go grab some dinner and find a French movie sans subtitles. You know, in the spirit of continuing the lesson."

That eyebrow climbed even higher, pushing up past her

bangs. "That sounds like a date."

"But it's not. It's studying…Tate style."

Despite the hardness in her voice, a smile broke through as she pushed to her feet. "As fun as 'Tate style' sounds, I need to go. Sophia's waiting for me."

"Sophia? I thought you didn't go in on Thursdays?"

"Normally, I don't." She shrugged. "But the only way I could justify in my mind signing off on your hours was if I put the extra time in at the center myself. I'd feel bad if a kid was getting stiffed for my own selfish reasons."

Whoa. I didn't quite know what to say to that. I opened my mouth to speak, but the response blistered in my throat, hot and burning, and making it impossible to talk. And so, I said nothing. I didn't even say good-bye to her as she slipped out my door with a little wave and hopped onto the elevator. No amount of preparation could have readied me for the emotion that skittered across my heart. My body wasn't responding to her gorgeous eyes or her pouty lips or even her hot little curves. No. My body was responding to *her*.

I looked down at my arms, where goose bumps raced across my flesh, and Buddy made his way to me, sitting at my feet. "Something tells me she's gonna be worth the wait, Buddy."

Chapter Nine

Shelby

My heart pounded, and as soon as the elevator doors closed, I collapsed. The mirrors of the elevator absorbed my weight easily, and were cool against my heated skin.

Okay, I needed to weigh my options here. Studying with Tate—a guy who knew his French like *lived* his French—was good for my grades. But studying French with Tate—a guy who was already sexy as hell and made even sexier by the foreign language gliding off his skillful tongue? Yeah, not so great. Not for my mind, heart, and certainly not good for my grades to have such a distraction around constantly.

But the weirdest part of speaking French with Tate was that *I* felt sexy while doing it. And "sexy" was a word I seldom used. Cute? Sure. Smart? Well, usually, when it didn't involve French. Sassy? Damn, almost always. But sexy? Not even a little. Around Tate, though, my body responded differently, physically pulsing for him. God, that was scary. Yes, I'd had sex before. It was always fine—sometimes good. But never mind-blowing. Never good enough to push me over the edge into the brink of orgasm. I couldn't blame the sex or the guys I had been with because I wasn't even able to bring *myself* to that level.

I'd tried. Damn, had I tried. Porn didn't really do it for me, and I could never bring myself to purchase any sort of sex toy.

I let the thoughts of Tate, and that quick glimpse of abs I stole from under his T-shirt, drift away into the universe as I unlocked and went into my apartment, tossing my bag onto the futon.

One by one, I shredded each layer of clothing until I was stripped down, and then I turned the shower on. Steam filled the bathroom almost immediately. That's how I liked my showers—so hot they practically gave you third degree burns. Water pelted my skin as I ran a bar of soap all over myself. I closed my eyes as my hand drifted down my stomach and fluttered between my legs. Visions of Tate's lips on me— down there—flooded my mind, and I moaned as the unusual tightness took hold of my body once more. Would he look up at me from his knees, those pale azure eyes connecting with mine? Would I be able to see his dimple as he smirked from between my thighs?

My pant, followed by a low, throaty moan echoed in the shower, and I fell back against the wall, speeding up the movement of my fingers. It felt good—it felt right, what I was doing. Sparks danced across my nerve endings as the feelings intensified, rippling low in my belly, and heat uncoiled there as I inserted a finger deep inside myself. The muscles tightened in response around my knuckle.

The memory of Tate overcame me as I thought of him hovering over my body, his muscular arms bearing the majority of his weight, flanking either side of me. I imagined myself pushing my hips into the air, grinding myself into the obvious erection that had brushed my thigh earlier this afternoon.

But just as quickly as his image had flashed into my mind, the repressed memory I fought so hard to tamp down filled my thoughts. An overwhelming stench of sweat and coffee breath. A massive amount of male weight pinning my face between his legs despite my muffled pleas for him to stop. His deep grunt followed by a clumsy thrust into my mouth. I winced at the hazy flashback, my breaths becoming shorter, more panicked. They strangled in my throat and constricted on my chest.

Placing both hands on the tiled wall, I turned, pressing my body against it—a trick the therapist taught me. The steaming water hit my back and though I was safe, home in my own shower with no threats present, blood rushed and throbbed in my brain. I deepened my breathing, taking air low into my diaphragm like Reagan had showed me, and slowly it returned to normal.

Through the shower glass, I saw my cell phone sitting on the edge of the sink, and a hollow sadness echoed in my chest. Normally, this would be when I would call my mom—I wouldn't need to tell her what set me off or what brought on the memories. She would just listen and talk me down to a calmer state. Now who was I to call? Harrison? Reagan? It wasn't the same—it would never be the same. My rock was gone.

Tears pricked my eyes, and I quickly shoved my face under the running water as a few escaped down my cheeks. I didn't want to know which drops were from the shower and which were from my eyes. I just wanted them gone, washed down the drain.

When I finally calmed down, I buried my face in my hands. I didn't always flashback during a sexual experience. But my PTSD was an ever-present ghost.

I turned the shower off and wrapped a towel around me.

Sliding my hand over the fogged mirror, I saw the scar at my temple reflected back at me—always the first thing. I quickly looked away, brushing my wet bangs down over my forehead.

Once my scar was covered, I forced myself to look at my reflection, just as my therapist said to do.

"The fear is real," I chanted against the tightness in my throat.

"But the threat is not. The fear is real, but the threat—" My cell rang beside me, cutting through the quietness of my apartment. *Mom,* I thought. A blast of potent grief burned in my stomach, and I immediately pinched my eyes shut against the swell of tears. The reflex to believe a call was from her, or that a knock at the door was Mom surprising me with a milkshake after a final exam—would that ever go away? I wanted to throw my fist into something. Those same deep breaths I'd nearly fucking perfected lodged in my chest, swelling and blocking the airway. The phone rang again, needling into the weakest points of my soul.

I collapsed onto the floor, pulling the towel tighter around my body. There was no use answering the phone, because whoever was on the other line didn't matter. It wasn't her.

It would never be her again.

Chapter Ten

Shelby

Friday's French class flew by — and while I still only understood a handful of Professor Ceele's discussion, the class was less daunting with Tate as my tutor. I may not get an A, but I could pass with a good enough grade that someone would hire me after graduation.

A few hours later, I sat next to my student at the tutoring center, showing her the proper way to outline a paper. But no matter how hard I tried, my eyes magnetically drifted to Tate every few minutes. And each time I did so, he was already looking my way. By the third time it happened, his lips lifted into that dimpled smirk.

I smothered a chuckle and pointed to Sophia, mouthing, "Pay attention." His grin widened, and his fingers tapped the back of Sophia's chair as he finally dipped his head, directing his focus back to his student.

If I wasn't mistaken, he actually seemed to be enjoying his time with Sophia. She had him laughing as she mimicked his mannerisms, everything from the way he tipped his chair back on two legs to how he would tap his pen when thinking.

If someone had asked me a week ago if I thought Tate Michaelson would be good in a room full of kids, I would have rolled my eyes at them. But this Tate? The one helping Sophia and not aiming to impress a class full of friends and girls? He was attentive and nurturing and playful. And the sight of it sent tingles racing down my spine.

"Shelby?"

"Huh?" I snapped my attention back to Kendall, my student.

"Is this right?"

"Oh. Here, let me have a look."

A snicker came from a table away, where Tate sat, eyes on me, all hard muscle and sexy dimples. I touched a hand to the corner of my mouth to make sure I wasn't drooling like a Labrador.

Damn him.

"Distracted?" Tate asked.

"Nope." I pressed my lips together, shook my head, and brought my focus back to my student's notes. "Not even a little," I lied.

I made some notes on Kendall's outline, and got her set up at a computer to begin writing. There was a ton of paperwork that Ryan had left for me, so I slipped into the back room to finish up. Grabbing the stack of donation forms, I opened the spreadsheet to put in the amounts for bookkeeping purposes.

The sense of a presence behind me grew thick, and I stiffened, my body clenching. I held my breath, waiting for Tate's voice.

These stupid nerves of mine made no sense. He was just a guy. I didn't need to freaking collapse into a bumbling pool of stress every time he walked by. I turned to say hi, and standing there behind me wasn't Tate. It was Ryan—my boss. I looked around and realized Tate wasn't even in the room—he was still out in the common area with Sophia. It had all been in my head. My stupid, over-reacting, awkward head. I felt a twinge of disappointment needling the base of my rib cage at seeing Ryan, not Tate. He gave me a warm smile then quickly looked back to the screen, reviewing my paperwork from over my shoulder. "Hey," Ryan said. My cheeks flushed red—oh, Jesus, I hoped he didn't think I was hitting on him. He was young—a couple of years older than me—and had graduated from CSU a few years before. But still, damn, that would be embarrassing. "I hate doing the bookkeeping—it's the main reason I keep you around," Ryan said with a wink.

He put a hand to my back, squeezing my shoulder before setting his own stack of papers on the table beside me. He slid into the seat, and I buried my nose in the laptop and the stack of paperwork. Why, oh why, did I have to be such a spaz?

I cleared my throat. "It's the *only* reason you keep me around." I smiled, though it was tight, more forced than usual, and he narrowed his eyes, seeming to notice immediately.

"I'm sorry." He leaned forward, gathering his papers. "Did you want to work in here alone? I can go into the other study room." He hitched a thumb over his shoulder and pushed to his feet. "I just hate working in my little cubicle. It's so stuffy."

I slid a hand across the table and placed it over his stack of work. "No, it's fine. I'm sorry…I thought you were someone else at first."

He nodded, eyes narrowing just barely. "The new kid, right?"

I swallowed. Was I that obvious? "No…I–I thought Kendall's computer had frozen again."

Ryan's face relaxed, and he leaned back in his chair, that easy smile returning. "Oh, good. Geez, those dinosaurs. I can't believe they're still running."

I froze once more, fingers hovering over the keyboard.

"Good?"

He shrugged, grabbing a pencil that was tucked behind his ear. "Well, yeah." He made a note in the margins of his top sheet but looked up at me as a bit of brown hair fell over his forehead. "Good."

I sank into my chair, the heat rushing to my cheeks. Sure, Ryan and I were friends. And he was always really nice to me. But he couldn't *seriously* like me. I mean, he was older than me—an adult in the work place, and I was still just a student. That would be weird, right?

"The new kid's not so terrible, you know," I said. "We have classes together."

Ryan snorted. "Maybe not. But according to the clerk who sent his paperwork, his parents are just awful. Paid off a judge to get the community service without facing a trial." He met my eyes, one brow arching. "His dad's a senator or governor or something."

I gulped. I knew his parents had to be loaded, of course. He had the friggin' penthouse apartment. But I'd had my share of political parents, and it was plenty for one lifetime.

Ryan's face crumpled with concern. "You okay? You're looking really pale."

"I–I'm fine. Just been a long day, you know?"

He nodded, pushing to his feet and grabbing a paper cup from the water cooler. "How's the waitressing going?" He filled a cup to the brim and set it next to me.

I took a sip as he pulled his chair closer. "Eh, not so bad now that I cut my hours. I'll be popping in for a shift this weekend, but otherwise, I'm hoping to stay away." I managed to sound pretty normal. "I don't want to be a professional waitress for the rest of my life," I said, my mind drifting to my mother.

"You'll be totally done with it soon." He grinned and pulled his ankle up to his knee. "Then you'll never have to pour another cup of coffee again. You'll be off to London or Paris, making an amazing living."

I groaned. "Anywhere but Paris."

He glanced at the window beside the door where Tate was waiting. "Looks like your boyfriend needs something," he said, eyes darkening. "And he doesn't look all that happy, either."

Standing, I headed to open the door for him. "Ryan, could you give us a moment?"

Tate stepped inside, his eyes darting back and forth between Ryan and me.

Ryan gathered the papers, tapping them together on the table before slipping out. "Sure thing. I'll be in the other study room if you have a question about those donations."

I shut the door behind him and took my seat. "What's up?"

Tate stared at Ryan as he left the room. "Is he the reason you stopped our kiss?"

Shock registered deep in my hollow stomach. "What?"

Tate didn't seem exactly angry as he lowered himself into the seat Ryan had just occupied. But there was something darker to him than before. "Is he your boyfriend?"

"*No.* Not that it's any of your business. He's my boss and…a friend." Why did I feel the need to validate that we weren't just colleagues? Maybe because of the way I would catch Ryan looking at me, or tugging on my hair. If I'd noticed it, then clearly Tate had, too.

"So, he's just a friend?"

I nodded.

Tate exhaled and leaned back, a soft smile splaying his lips. "You might want to tell *him* that, then."

I rolled my eyes, suddenly exasperated with Tate once more. The guy had my emotions running the gamut—I was going to have whiplash before the semester was over.

"Anyway, are you done with Sophia for the day?"

He nodded, sliding his time sheet over to me. "She's finishing up her homework—almost done with math. I think she's got it down, but she might trip up on one or two questions."

I scanned his sheet. "So, let's see...you got here at four." I glanced at the wall clock. "It's now five and change. And you spent forty-five minutes with me yesterday, so I'll give you two hours for today." I made some scribbles, and Tate moved to take the sheet from me, but I pulled it back. "Let me file it. I don't want a superior looking at it and seeing that you left earlier than I jotted down."

Tate nodded and pushed to his feet. "You wanna come? Maybe grab some fries somewhere?"

I sighed. "Fries would be awesome, but I have paperwork to finish up here, and someone's got to wait with Sophia until her mom comes, and answer any homework questions she may have." I shrugged.

Tate drifted back down to the seat, and I went back to working on my spreadsheet. I felt him, though, his eyes studying my every movement. When I finally flicked a glance his way, sure enough, he was still sitting there, leaning his elbows on his knees. But where there would normally be a playful smile, he was thoughtful, with relaxed lips and eyes that tilted down slightly. "So you're picking up my hours from Sophia again?"

I paused, holding his eye contact before nodding. "Someone has to."

"But you get paid for that time, right?"

I shook my head. "I clock out when I'm covering those hours." It was wrong not to. It would essentially be allowing the tutoring center to pay for *my* French lessons.

He nibbled the corner of his mouth before sliding his hours sheet back and looking at it once more. "Tell you what.

I'll stay—do my full time with Sophia…"

My eyebrows shot up nearly to my hairline. "Really?"

He nodded, and his smile curved. "*If* you'll let me take you out to dinner after your shift here."

My blood slowed within my veins. The whooshing pulse in my head was louder than a waterfall, matching its rhythmic beat thrumming in my throat. On one hand, it would be nice not to have the extra work of helping Sophia…and it would be good for her to have Tate as a more stable fixture in her life. And I *did* want to go out with him. Surprisingly, I really enjoyed Tate's company. So, why was I not letting myself indulge a little?

Because he's everything I've sworn off. And when it doesn't work out, I'll have to see him every day. Idiot.

"What about Buddy?"

His smile widened. "I have a dog walker I can call on nights I can't make it home."

"Of course you do," I said under my breath, then I gulped the last bit of water Ryan had given me before answering aloud. "Fine. For Sophia's sake, I will grin and bear a dinner with you—"

Tate laughed, hopping to his feet.

"*But*." He froze and spun to face me once more with an eyebrow raised in question.

"But?"

"But—it's not a date. And I get to choose the restaurant."

He chewed that over for all of a second before nodding. "You got a deal, Betty."

...

Every sip of water I took landed hard in the pit of my stomach, like dropping a quarter onto a trampoline. My insides were bouncing with anxious energy. And as I watched Sophia skip away hand in hand with her mother, something sweet knotted in my chest. Watching them should have made me sad, but if anything, it offered a small slice of what I'd been missing the last few months. A moment of peace and love between mother and daughter.

"You ready?" Tate's deep voice vibrated behind me. And just like that, the trampoline was back.

I nodded and held up a finger. "Give me one minute to file these." I backed up toward Ryan's cubicle, which was created out of boxes and chairs and shelves, and slipped open the top folder of the metal cabinet. Tucking the time sheet for Tate into the first file, I let the drawer click shut. I stood there another second, the cool cabinet chilling my skin.

On a deep breath, I pushed off the surface to find Ryan standing in the doorway, watching. "You okay?" he whispered.

My throat closed, and I nodded. "Yeah," I said. "Just going to grab some dinner."

His smile lifted at the corners. "Be sure to order a mint chocolate chip milkshake, just for me."

"You know it," I answered and brushed passed him.

I jerked my head as I approached Tate. "Let's go." He pushed the door, propping it open for me with a foot as I swept by his shoulder.

Keys jingled in his hand. "Should I drive?"

I shook my head, taking the lead and falling into a faster step. "Nope. It's just across the street."

Tate's face was tinted red in the glow of the diner's lit sign. His eyebrows lowered for a moment before he grinned. "Sounds great." Test number one was passed.

"Seriously? I mean, the place doesn't offer caviar or anything, but it's got a damn good burger and amazing milkshakes—"

"Caviar?" His eyes narrowed. "Who the fuck said anything about caviar?"

I shrugged. "I just didn't know how casual you were willing to go. Now I know."

He curved my hand into his, and his palm was dry and warm despite the balmy September heat. With a gentle tug and a quick look both ways, he pulled me across the street. "Trust me. I'll take a burger and fries over caviar any day."

I reached the entrance first and pulled open the retro door, falling into a window booth near the front. "You're not going to be disappointed. This place has the best fries in town."

He glanced around. "As in, so bad they're good?"

"As in the best of the best. They're hand-cut and freshly fried to order. Not pre-made under some lamp in a moldy container in the back."

"All right, then. Let's put this to the test, shall we?"

Cathy came bouncing over to our table, a wide grin stretching across her face. Brittle auburn hair frizzed out of a high ponytail, victim of too many years of boxed color jobs. She pushed her reading glasses higher up on her nose, and the chain draped from the back of her ears behind her neck. In the decade or so that I'd known Cathy, she'd barely changed.

"Well, if it isn't my favorite do-gooder," she offered with a grin. "How are you, kid? Stand your ass up and give me a hug."

"I was getting there." I laughed and pushed to my feet, wrapping my arms around her. Her hands landed on my shoulders, gently holding me at arms-length when our hug finished.

"Let me have a look at you." I stood straight and caught Tate watching with a curious glance and an amused smirk. Cathy circled me as I stood rigid, mimicking a private in the army. She stopped in front of me and slapped the top of my arm with her ordering pad. "You're too damn skinny, missy." She never let the gap in between her two front teeth inhibit the smile at all. "But other than that, you're perfect as you've ever been."

"Right back at ya, Miss Cathy." I slipped into the booth across from Tate. "This is my friend from school, Tate. He's volunteering with me across the street. Tate, this is Cathy."

"Well, good for you," she said, tapping that same ordering pad on the table. "Start you with some fries?"

I grinned. "You know it. And—"

"Mint chip shake," Cathy cut in. "I know, sweet girl. Just like your momma." She gently smoothed my hair back and ran her hand down my ponytail before looking to Tate. "What about for you?"

"I'll do a vanilla milkshake."

"You got it."

Cathy ran off to the kitchen, and I arched a brow at him. "Vanilla?"

He nodded, matching my smile. "Classic."

I rolled my eyes. "Chocolate is classic. Vanilla's boring."

"Oh, Betty. The right person and the right place can make the most boring thing seemingly exciting."

I gulped. "Is that so?"

My eyes wandered around the diner I knew so well. Blindfolded, I could still find the bathrooms.

"You come here a lot?" Tate asked.

"My whole life, practically." I meant it to come out in a normal voice, but I barely managed anything above whisper.

The eight by ten picture behind the bar caught my attention. The cheap plastic frame had a tiny crack at the corner, and some glue had seeped out where someone had attempted a repair. My mom in her waitress uniform stood leaning on the counter while I sat at the bar, books open, looking up from my homework and grinning at the camera. Cathy had snapped the picture one day back when I was in high school. "I've been going to the tutoring center for years,"

I answered, feeling numb to the conversation, like Tate was miles away.

He nodded thoughtfully, following my eyes to the wall across the room where the picture hung. Of course, he probably couldn't see it from this far away. A photograph of a waitress serving at a crappy diner was probably not even on his radar. But it meant the world to me. I had the same photograph framed in my house.

Emotion swelled in my stomach like a balloon filling with water. I was grateful when Cathy dropped two milkshakes and the steaming plate of fries down between us. She sent me a quick wink and smiled. "Enjoy. Anything else tonight?"

"Chicken strips, please," I said.

"And a burger for me."

Cathy nodded and ran off once more to the kitchen. Tate grabbed a fry and hissed, dropping it back onto the plate with a yelp. He shook his fingers, pushing them into his mouth.

"Rookie mistake," I said, laughing. "I warned you they were fresh."

"I didn't think that translated to scalding." He laughed, too, dipping the burned finger into the ice water.

I took a sip of my mint chip milkshake, and a chunk of chocolate lodged in the straw, just like it always did.

"Wow, that's a really good fry," he said, chewing. He carefully took another, dipping it into his milkshake before taking a bite. His eyes closed, and they rolled to the back of his head as he gave a grunt of approval.

"Oh, no." I grinned. "You're one of *those* guys."

He scrunched his brows, tilting his head in question.

"You know," I said. "The fries in the milkshake kind of guy. It's a perfectly good waste of a French fry."

He laughed and grabbed another. "If you don't like it, then you clearly haven't tried it." He dipped it in the milkshake and passed it to me. "Go on, try it. It only works with a simple milkshake. Don't try it with the mint."

I rolled my eyes, taking the fry from him, and our fingers brushed. I bit the fry, chewing cautiously and swallowed. "Okay," I started, "it's not as bad as I thought. But, it's still also not good."

"Oh, come on." He slapped the table.

I shrugged. "Sorry, but it's true. It doesn't deserve the praise people give it."

"I'll convert you, eventually. It's better when you have bad fries…it masks the shittiness."

"Well, see? There you go. These fries aren't meant to be dipped."

"It's habit now, Betty." He paused, sipping the milkshake and looking up at me from over the straw. "So, what else?"

"What else?" I repeated.

"You said you've been coming here for years. When did you start working at the tutoring center?"

My heart thundered in my ears. Taking him here was stupid if I didn't want to explain myself, reveal who I really was. But I had to know if he'd be okay with this place—if he wasn't okay with my favorite diner, then there was no us.

No wait—there is no us. Why am I even entertaining this thought?

"I came here all the time with my mom. For as long as I can remember. The milkshakes are seriously the best I've ever had—I don't know how they do it. And I started volunteering at the tutoring center in high school."

His brows dipped as he mulled that over. "Your mom? Are you from around here?"

I nodded. "I've pretty much been in Charleston my whole life. You?"

He examined me cautiously, as though reading my conversational shift once more. "My parents went to college in Charleston as well, but I grew up in Greenville. Do you still come here with your mom a lot?"

"No," I said. His eyes were still on me, waiting patiently for my answer. What was I going to do? Never bring her up to anyone new ever again? *Baby steps.* "No," I repeated more quietly. "Look, my mom…she passed away a couple months ago. And I'd just rather not talk about it." I bit my lip before the tide of tears rose again. "If that's okay."

"I'm sorry. Of course," he murmured.

I turned my attention out the window, heat flooding my cheeks. I hated being looked at like that. With pity. With sadness. "Please, could you just sto—"

"Did you see Ceele's toupee flop over when he bent to get his pen today?"

I darted a glance back to Tate. He was grinning, but there was a dampness to his eyes. I swallowed, sniffing back emotion. "No…I was too busy trying to look up every fourth word he said. When did that happen?"

Tate laughed, leaning forward, and his fingers grazed mine as we both went for the same fry. He trailed his index finger across my knuckles before reaching instead for a different fry. And in that moment, as heat and energy and intensity buzzed between us, making the air thicker and my lungs tighter, I wanted Tate. I wanted him more than almost anything. And damn was that frightening.

...

Hours passed, and we had long since finished our meals. It wasn't until my phone buzzed with a text from Reagan that I realized how late it was.

"You have no idea how amazing it is getting up before the sun and hitting the beach with a surfboard. Even if you don't catch a single wave, it's beautiful just to sit in the water and watch the sunrise." The milkshake gave up its last remaining sip up with a slurp, and Tate grinned, biting the plastic edge of the straw.

"You make it sound so Zen. Like yoga or something."

"Exactly. And when you do catch a wave? It's like ten seconds of pure adrenaline."

It was late. And I should get home. But all I wanted to do was stay there with him and keep talking. I slid out of the booth, pulling out a twenty from my wallet. Tate's hand shot out, folding my money back into my hands.

"I already took care of it."

I paused, startled. "What? When?"

He slid to the edge of the booth, standing as well. "When I went to the bathroom."

Emotion bristled through my body, making all my hairs stand on edge. "This wasn't a date," I snapped. I told him that from the beginning, and it wasn't my fault if he didn't listen closely enough. "Here." I sifted around my wallet until I found a ten and held it out for Tate. "Take it."

He held up both hands, leaning away from me. "Shelby, it's fine. You'll get the next time." Except there wouldn't be a next time. Couldn't be. He glided past me, opening the door and waving to Cathy with his free hand. "Nice meeting you."

I gave Cathy a small wave, and as I passed by Tate, I grabbed his sleeve, pulling his ear close to my lips. "Did you tip her?"

"Of course." He rolled his eyes.

"Well?"

He licked the swell of his moist bottom lip and locked me into a staring showdown. "Of course," he said again. There was a darker timbre to his voice this time.

I released my hold on his shirt, pulling away from the sheer magnetism, and forced a smile for Cathy.

"You kids come back soon!" she called out, wiping down our table.

"We will, Miss Cathy," Tate said.

The parking lot was dark except for one flickering street lamp that was decorated with graffiti and stale pieces of gum. We crossed the pathetic excuse for a strip of grass and back over to the empty lot at the tutoring center.

"Shelby." Tate darted for my elbow, pulling me back against his broad chest. It heaved with thick breaths. "Stay behind me," he growled, and using that hand, he scooped me behind his right shoulder. "Something doesn't feel right."

I rolled my eyes and pushed forward in front of him again. "Tate, just because the neighborhood isn't white picket fences and trees and mansions doesn't mean you're going to—"

There was a click as a shadow stepped out from between the buildings. Moonlight sliced across the gleaming barrel of a small gun. I gulped, and my stomach convulsed, twisting upside down.

"Give me your purse and your wallet," a gruff voice said. "Do it now, or I'll fucking shoot."

Chapter Eleven

TATE

I should have trusted my instincts. As soon as we crossed to the parking lot, something felt off. It was too quiet. With my thumb, I opened the switchblade to the Swiss army knife that was attached to my keychain, just as the kid stepped out and pulled the gun on us. I put my hands up and Shelby did the same, her shoulders stiff.

He was young—probably not even out of high school. And he wore black from head to toe, including a hat. He said something about our wallets and jewelry, or some other bullshit he probably got off of TV.

On the left side of his neck, just above his collar, was a mole, and I searched his face for any other distinguishing marks. Hazel eyes. Small scar above his right eyebrow. "Easy," I said, sliding a look to Shelby. Her raised hands trembled, and I wanted nothing more than to pull her into my arms.

"Jewelry, too. Hurry the fuck up," he said, gesturing to my watch.

"Tate—" Shelby's voice was soft, and about as shaky as the boy's hand holding the gun.

My heart pounded, slamming into my ribs, but I took a deep breath, keeping my voice as even as possible. "It's okay, Shelby." Despite the gentle tone of my voice, my body braced for a fight. Adrenaline pumped through my veins. I wanted nothing more than to rip this little fucker's head off.

I took in every detail, from the tip of his hat down to the gun in his hand. Narrowing my eyes, I studied every inch of it, a wry grin twitching at my lips. I'd been hunting with my dad enough to know that real guns don't have plastic edging around the seams. But BB guns do. It might not kill us, but it would still hurt like a fucking bitch.

"I–I don't have any jewelry." She flipped her hands around.

"Look, man. You don't want to hurt us. I have cash in my wallet. Take that and go."

"Shut up!" the boy screamed, his voice cracking. He turned the gun on me. "Your watch. *Now*."

"You can have the watch." I moved slowly. My knife still clenched in my hand, but to the kid it just looked like I was holding a set of keys. With my free hand, I slipped the watch off my wrist and held it out. "Here, take it."

The boy licked his lips, eyes darting back and forth between Shelby and me. He was scared, and the whites of his eyes glistened under the street lamp. He didn't stray far from the alley, the brick wall nearly scraping his back.

Instead of taking the watch, he gestured to Shelby. "Give it to her. Have her bring it to me."

I gnashed my teeth. *Oh, hell no.* I didn't like where this was going. A quick glance at Shelby showed she was barely keeping it together. I wasn't sure she could handle walking, let alone handing over items.

"I'm grabbing my wallet," I said, the open blade of my

small knife squeezed into the flesh on my palm. A trickle of blood oozed through my fingers, but it was either that, or the kid would see that I had a weapon.

I fumbled to open my billfold, grabbing the cash in there, and held it up along with the watch. "Take the cash. Take the watch. And get the fuck out of here."

His unsteady hand teetered, but remained pointed at me. "Don't tell me what to do. *I* have the gun."

One side of my mouth tilted higher, and I let a nasty laugh escape. "We both know that's a fucking toy." Curling back, I hurled the money and watch into the alley.

And bingo. He shifted on his feet, head turning to where I threw the items. I lunged for the gun, snapping his wrist back, and the handle slipped clean from his palm and into mine. Getting my footing, I pointed the gun at him. "There we go," I said. "And lucky for us, you were dumb enough not to wear gloves. Do you know what that means?"

The boy's eyes glistened with imminent tears, and I wanted to laugh. Laugh the entire time I was sending him to a jail cell. This asshole? *He* should be in jail. *He* should be doing community service.

"Go. Get your shit. You can have the money. I'll be sending this toy, with your prints on it, to my dad, where it'll sit along with a file of this incident. If your prints show up anywhere else in the system, they'll log you in for this crime. If you keep your nose clean, you can take the money and get yourself a fucking job. Sound like a deal?"

The boy nodded, shifting on his feet.

"And if you ever bother her" — I gestured to Shelby — "or anyone in either of these parking lots again, trust me when I tell you my father will fucking eat you for dinner."

He took off running down the alley, not bothering to stop for my watch and cash. I called out after him, "And spread the word to your friends, asshole."

When the footsteps faded, I jogged into the alley and lifted my watch, sliding it back onto my wrist, and shoved the cash into my back pocket. "Piece of shit..." I muttered, walking back over to Shelby. When I looked back up, she was still standing there, staring down the alley with wide eyes and her arms still raised.

"Shelby?" I asked quietly, rushing over to her. "Are you hurt?" I swept a look over her from head to toe and saw nothing. No bruises, no torn clothing, no blood. A glazed look passed over her eyes, and a single tear fell down her cheek. The corners of her mouth trembled as though she was holding back a sob or a frown. Capturing her bottom lip between her teeth, she shook her head. She didn't need me to talk. She didn't need any "you're okays," or "I told you so's." Instead, I curled a hand around her neck and pulled her into me, guiding her over to my car. She fell into step with me. I opened the door and helped her into the passenger seat.

I brushed a knuckle down her cheek, and she shook my hand away, waving off her shock. "I–I'm fine. Just...just..."

I nodded and smoothed her hair with my good hand. "I know," I whispered, shutting her gently inside the car before taking my seat behind the wheel. I reached behind me to where I kept a box of tissues and put pressure to my bleeding palm. The cut didn't look so bad...maybe needed a stitch or two at most. I locked the doors to my Audi before I pulled out my phone.

"What are you doing?" Her voice was small, as though she were speaking to me through a tin can.

"I'm just calling the police—"

Before I finished my sentence, her hand shot out, covering the screen. "No."

"Don't worry, did you see that kid? He's not going to be bothering you any time soon. And we have to get this down to the station." I gestured to the gun.

"No." Her voice quivered this time, and she shook her head, another tear spilling. She quickly swiped it away, looking up as more moisture pooled in her eyes. "Please. No police."

I swallowed the dryness in my mouth, and with my other hand, brushed Shelby's bangs away from her eyes. She jerked from my touch, wincing, and pushed away from me. I put my hands up, pulling them into my body. The robbery seemed to have traumatized her far more than I originally thought. "Okay," I said quietly. "But I need to call my dad. Because if I don't tell him about this and at least get *him* the gun, he'll kick my ass."

She nodded, one single, sharp movement, before turning again and directing her vacant stare out the window.

• • •

It only took my dad's guy—one of the men from his security team—eight minutes to show up at the parking lot and retrieve my statement and the gun. He bagged it and was quickly on his way—as were we. Shelby rode the entire way in silence, and with each passing minute, I grew more concerned about her. I knew a little bit about shock, but not much.

I pulled into our building's lot and turned the car off. She pulled the door handle, slid out, and shut the door, hoisting her purse higher onto her shoulder and hugging it to her body. Her normally rosy cheeks and olive skin paled, and a sheen of sweat covered her forehead and her neck.

I followed her into the building and slid my key into the penthouse slot on the elevator. "Come upstairs with me for a while." I put a hand on her back, and she trembled, flinching away from my touch. When she didn't answer, I gently turned her to face me. "Shelby?"

She wiped a hand over her eyes. "I'm fine. I just need to sleep it off."

I shook my head and touched the back of my hand to her cheek. "I can't leave you alone right now. If you don't want to come upstairs with me, why don't I come to your place with you?"

"You don't have to do tha—"

"Yes, I do." I swallowed my anger and fear over what happened tonight. I took a major chance on that kid. Yeah, it was a BB gun, but under a challenge, he still could have hurt one of us. And if that one of us had been Shelby, I never would have forgiven myself. Seeing a gun drawn on this girl… I mentally shook my head—there was no more pretending that she wasn't special to me.

I circled my thumb across the back of her hand. God, I liked her. So much that she stayed on my mind constantly. But why? What was this power she had over my thoughts? Why did my chest swell and my pants bulge each time I pictured her face, her hair, lips, eyes…damn, those eyes. If today accomplished one thing, it was to cement the fact that Shelby was not Katie. There wasn't a deceitful bone in her body, and even if my radar had been totally off with my first love, there was no way I was wrong about this girl in front of me. This girl who volunteered places she didn't need to, and who wore nothing of value that even a dumb kid with a BB gun would take. She was the real thing.

All these theories that I was only interested for the chase and the challenge were utter bullshit. I mean, damn, we only met a couple of weeks ago. But there was something strong and real between us, something that I couldn't and wouldn't push away like I had with every woman since Katie—with tequila shots or one night stands or just plain stupidity. I didn't want to numb the feelings this time.

With a shiver, her hands fell onto my waist, my shirt wrinkling in her fists. She shook her head, sniffling. There was a sort of half laugh, half sob thing that exploded from her chest. "I'm just being stupid. Really."

"Then come be stupid upstairs with me."

She laughed, and I glimpsed the real Shelby for the first time since we stood with arms raised in the parking lot. The elevator dinged, and the doors slid open on her floor. She lifted her tearful eyes, wet like two stones after a rainstorm. The elevator doors slid closed in lieu of her answer.

My stomach clenched, and I wrapped one arm entirely around her waist, pulling her in closer. I didn't quite trust myself to speak right now. Part of me wanted to yell at her. What if I hadn't been there tonight? Another part ticked over the facts. She'd spent years going to that place. Why now? Why had one of those kids targeted her tonight? A thought struck me hard, like a bolt of lightning. It was *my* car—I'm the one that put us in danger. The locals probably knew Shelby's car, if she parked so frequently in that lot. But a red Audi R8? It stood out like a neon "come rob me" sign in that neighborhood. That douchebag probably saw it and waited for whoever owned the car to come out.

Shelby's shaky hand slid up my shirt, caressing the dips and curves of my abs and chest. A sharp breath caught in my throat and lodged there as a current took over in my veins. She was touching me. Shelby Stevens was touching me. She lifted her chin and looked up at me, her eyelashes spiked with the last of her tears. Her warm breath held remnants of mint and chocolate from her milkshake, and she licked her lips, holding my stare.

I gritted my teeth and closed my eyes as her other hand gently curled around the back of my neck, and I shuddered at the bold touch. Twirling her fingers through the back of my hair, she gave the strands a gentle tug. And then, she lifted onto her toes and pressed her lips to mine.

Chapter Twelve

Shelby

I grasped Tate, holding him firmly in my arms. I wanted to be with him, and it took a gun shoved in my face for me to realize that I was done hiding from my feelings, no matter how scary they were. What would Reagan do right now in my shoes?

And so, I took a page out of her book, and I kissed Tate. I kissed him for a lot of reasons. Because he saved me. Because I wanted to know how those lips would feel nibbling on mine. Because I was shaken and I needed a physical reminder that I was here and alive with blood pumping through my veins. But most of all—because I wanted to. I wanted to kiss Tate. And hold him. And feel his firm body pressed against mine.

I dragged my fingernails down his neck as his hands tangled in my hair. Then, fingers cupping my jaw, he pushed my lips off of him. As he gently ended the kiss, an unexpected whimper escaped my lips.

He pressed his mouth into a thin line and heaved a shaky breath. "Jesus, Shelby. I don't want to, but we have to stop a second—"

The elevator opened into his lobby, and I took his hand, giving him a gentle tug toward his doorway. He reluctantly followed, and I had to laugh at the crazy, sudden role reversal.

He shook his head, a hand rubbing behind his neck. "Shelby, wait—stop."

But I didn't wait. And I couldn't stop. Because if I paused long enough to think things over, or really consider what just happened tonight, I would be bogged down with doubt and concerns, and I didn't want that. Not right now. I pushed Tate into the wall behind him and nibbled from his jaw down to his neck. The taste of his salty skin tingled on my tongue, and the tiny bit of stubble from his morning shave scraped my cheek.

"Shelby," he whispered, and his hand landed gently on my hip. He spun us around so that my back was now against the wall, and with an arm over my head, he caged me in. With the other hand, he tilted my chin, angling my eyes to his. "I need to know you're okay. Are you hurt? This—this could be trauma or, or…I don't know. But you're kind of scaring me here."

His eyes shifted back and forth between each of mine, reading me—or trying to. Unfortunately for Tate, I was a book written in invisible ink.

I traced my thumb over his bottom lip, and his eyes fluttered closed, tongue darting out to lick where my touch lingered. "I'm fine, Tate. I'm better than fine. I feel…alive." My voice cracked, and a bitter laugh escaped as I admitted that fact. "I'm fine," I said again. Was I fine? I wasn't actually sure, but I knew I wanted him.

A muscle in his jaw ticked. "We shouldn't do this now. We should wait."

Scraping my fingers down the sides of his waist, I tugged his hips into mine. His erection pressed against my belly, and my eyes drifted closed, my head falling back against the wall.

My throat stretched with the movement, and I heard his sigh from above me. "Fuck, Shelby," he groaned, his voice more strained than I had ever heard it.

"Don't make me wait," I whispered. "I don't often allow myself this—" I looked to him, nibbling my bottom lip. "Please."

"You're not in shock?" he asked once more.

I paused—I didn't want to lie to him. I wasn't exactly *not* in shock. So, instead, I answered, "I know what I'm doing. And I want you."

He closed his fingers around my hips, sliding the other hand down and clasping his arm around my waist. In one fluid motion, he had me in the air, and I wrapped my legs around his waist, locking my ankles at his back. That erection now pushed between my legs, and a breathy whimper snuck through my pressed lips. He groaned as well, officially conceding, and with the one free hand, he wrapped his fingers into my ponytail, tugging my mouth to his. What I thought was going to be a ravenous kiss landed surprisingly soft on my lips, first moving with a tender coaxing, directing my mouth over his like he was the conductor and our kiss a complicated melody.

As always, remnants of rational, logical arguments itched at the base of my thoughts, threatening to swallow my current blissful clarity.

Will I regret this in the morning? What if I really am in shock? All it took was a quick thrust of Tate's hips to replace that with imagery of his slick muscles and the weight of him on top of me. I groaned, arching into his erection as that kiss turned into something more ravenous. I was so tired of being the girl who weighed all her options first. For once, just once, I wanted to throw all that caution to the wind.

I wrapped my entire arm around his neck, opening my mouth wider and running my tongue along his. The truth was, I wasn't fine, but not because some kid stuck a BB gun in our faces. Being around Tate had me unhinged and feeling like anyone but the Shelby I'd been my whole life. If he broke off this kiss, if he walked away from me, from us, it might wreck me. I was a thin sheet of glass stuck inches from a swinging pendulum, and one step in the wrong direction would shatter me.

We were moving, and before I knew what was happening, I was on my back in Tate's bed. The down comforter was soft, silky, compared to Tate's muscles, hard, heavy, and firm, pressing me into it. There was a faint smell of spice and laundry detergent.

Fumbling with the buttons on his shirt, I had it undone and torn off his shoulders in no time, tossing it to the floor, and Tate pulled my T-shirt over my head. The brief moments our mouths were apart were far too long, and our lips came crashing down on each other's again. I traced my nails down his spine, playing his vertebrae like piano keys, and his moan vibrated a seductive melody down to my toes.

He pulled back, resting his weight on his elbow, and traced my breast through my bra, taking extra time at my nipple before brushing his knuckles down the length of my stomach. They trailed over the top of my jeans, popping the button and tugging the fly down. But instead of continuing south of the border, his fingers went back to my waistband, until he landed on my other breast. With a flick of his hand, the sheer lace of my bra was undone and in a pile with the other remnants of discarded clothing, and I arched into his mouth as he lowered it to my nipple.

I pushed off my heels, lifting my torso, allowing Tate to undress me entirely. I didn't cower as he sat back on his haunches, his stare skimming across me like a stone skipping water. What was he thinking? Why was he staring for so long? His gaze left a shiver in its wake, and I forced myself not to cover up as he studied me with far more concentration than he ever showed his textbooks. I propped myself onto my elbows in a show of mock confidence and raised an eyebrow. "Approval ratings?"

His throat roped as he swallowed, working through the dryness. "Through the roof." He grinned, removing his cargo shorts, and grabbed a square foil from his nightstand.

I nearly choked, laying there watching him move around, so comfortably naked. Pleasant warmth spiraled through my body, and my skin puckered as though a chill in the air had set off a chain reaction of goose bumps. But there was no chill. There was no breeze. It was just Tate and me and those cobalt eyes that didn't leave mine for even a second. His sinewy muscles rippled with each graceful movement, and his cock pierced forward. I barely had time to register how glorious he was before he was on top of me once more, lowering his mouth to my breast. I cried out in a voice that was so unlike any sound I'd ever heard from myself before, I wouldn't have recognized a recording of it. What the hell was *that*? His skilled tongue slipped over my nipple, and he varied the motion by scraping his teeth gently against the sensitive skin, ripping open the condom as he did so.

My muscles were so tense that they actually hurt. Every one of my nerve endings was alive and humming with every touch of his hands. I needed him, needed this. My body begged for release, and for once, I was going to listen to it. Give in to that pleasure. Sex wasn't scary, but the intensity at which I cared for him was terrifying. I'd been with other guys, but the chemistry had never been so fierce and consuming as it was when I was with Tate. He didn't try to rush things; he didn't enter me yet, simply nestled his erection between my thighs and rocked against my clit.

I gasped at the shuddering pleasure, and he swallowed my moan, kissing me until I was left silent and aching with each pressure-filled thrust against me. Shoving my hands into his hair as he tried to pull away, I held him there against my mouth, needing that kiss to continue. Needing to feel more of his lips all over me. My eyes fluttered open, and I slowly ran my hands down the back of his neck, gliding my touch over the slick mounds of muscle and pebbled flesh before I raked my fingernails into his skin. With a body-trembling hiss, he shivered against the forceful motions of my hand.

I did that. I caused that reaction. Maybe all this time my inability to climax had nothing to do with my past. Maybe it had just been the wrong timing, the wrong guy, or not enough spark. Because *nothing* had ever felt like this before. Right here, in this moment, I actually thought I could come. My core tightened, and with every breath, I inhaled his light cologne.

Nibbling a trail down my stomach, he paused at a mole just beside my belly button, pressing a kiss there before moving down between my legs. I gasped, diving my hands into the sheets just as he ran his tongue over my clit, sucking it into his mouth entirely in a tortuously slow movement.

Oh, fuck. A jagged breath trembled in my stomach, and I threw a hand to the headboard, gripping it with white knuckles, as though it were a steering wheel and I had any control over where Tate was about to take me. I dug my heels into the bed and twisted the sheets between my fingers.

His index finger trailed a line up the inside of my thigh, circling my wetness, and with that simple touch, my body jerked in a reaction before it went completely limp. A pressure built inside of me like a balloon that was stretched with far too much air, ready to pop. And it—it was just too much. It was too much—everything. Feelings and emotion and tingles and, and—

No. I was so close. So, so close. A shaky laugh escaped me, and I quickly swallowed it down, pressing my palm to my eyes. "Sorry," I whimpered. But even as I made the apology, another nervous giggle spurted from my lips, and he looked up from between my legs, confusion tightening his brows. I took his face in my hands and pulled his lips to mine. A curious look passed over his features before I touched my tongue to his and answered any question he might have had about my enjoyment level. I tried to quiet my own racing mind with that kiss, too. It was just a small setback. Nothing that would ruin the night. This wasn't irreparable. I could salvage this; I *wanted* to. I just needed to get out of my own damn way and enjoy the release. I'd been so close before, closer than I'd ever gotten, even just by myself.

I sat up, and he took me into his lap so I straddled his erection. Circling my hips over his, he groaned, throwing his head back and offering his neck to me. I ran my tongue from the hollow point at the apex of his sternum, up to his jaw, nibbling at the bit of stubble piercing through. Pinching my chin, he matched my stare, and for all of a second, we did nothing but look at each other. Hold each other. His eyes were savagely hot, and the way he searched my face and brushed his thumb over my swollen, wet bottom lip was achingly tender, like I was something to be cherished.

Gently, he freed my hair from my ponytail, brushing his fingers through the strands. His eyes explored my face, and he traced the muscles up and down my back. "You are so beautiful," he murmured, more to himself than to me.

My breath expanded in my lungs, my muscles clenching with his declaration. For the first time with anyone, I honestly believed him when he said it. It wasn't a way of getting in my pants, or some phrase he was repeating from a movie. But even more important? The way Tate looked at me, I *felt* beautiful.

"Say it in French," I whispered.

His grin widened. "You know how to say that in French."

I nodded, taking his earlobe into my mouth. I whispered in French, "But I want to hear you say it."

His cock twitched against me, and he groaned the sentence. "*Vous êtes très belle.*"

"So formal," I said and kissed him again, nibbling on that full bottom lip I loved to watch speak to me in French. "*Merci*," I murmured against his mouth.

He groaned, falling back onto his bed with me on top. Me…in charge. It was scary, this new spark of electricity I experienced with him. But it was also empowering and thrilling in a way that I wasn't quite sure how to handle. I felt like I was on the verge of striking a match near a gas leak. It might be fine. But it might also explode into a fiery mess.

His dick stood erect, and I swallowed hard, taking in his body. I was staring, but I didn't care. He was something to stare at. Despite the nervousness that bounced in my belly, I found myself actually wanting to taste him. I could do this. And not just because it felt like I should, or it was my turn to reciprocate, but the thought of taking him into my mouth made me ache between my legs in the best possible way.

I kissed my way down his ridiculously defined stomach. I mean, seriously…the only other time a six-pack has ever touched my lips was that one awful night Reagan convinced me to try PBR. And Tate's six-pack was way tastier than any beer I'd ever had. I ran my tongue along the dips and curves, reaching the springy hair at the base.

With a sharp breath, I took him into my mouth, circling my tongue around his smooth tip. It felt…incredible. And sexy. He hissed through clenched teeth and dragged a thumb across my bottom lip as I withdrew him from my mouth. I squeezed my thighs together, tightening my muscles against the ache that throbbed there.

"Holy shit, Shelby." His head fell back on the pillow, and he threw an arm across his eyes with the moan. A smile curved on my lips just before I took him once again into my mouth, this time dragging my teeth gently down his shaft. "Oh my God." His hands dove into my hair. Before I realized what was happening, his right hand brushed back the left side of my bangs, pulling my hair away from my face. He tugged the strands away from where they clung to my lips.

It didn't hurt, but a flash of another man, another time, pulsed in my brain and my scar sizzled with the tug. I yelped, gagging on his erection, and when I pulled back, smoothing my bangs into place over my scar, there was a smear of blood on my fingers.

My body convulsed out of nowhere, and I was suddenly shaking so hard that I must have looked like I was having a seizure. The blood. Streaming down my face. My screams echoed in the recesses of my mind. A man's sweat dripping onto me like water torture. Grunting, pushing into me as I gagged on him over and over.

The dizziness was too much. Hands. My hands…my feet—I needed something to push on. To remember the here and now. But Tate couldn't see me like this. I stumbled to the side of the bed, shoving my legs into my jeans and scrambling into my shirt.

"Shelby, what the fuck…what's going on? Are you okay?" He was right in front of me, but his voice sounded miles away. And that's where he needed to stay. Miles away. I was too fucked up to behave normally. Why the hell could I have mediocre sex with other guys, but the second I enjoyed myself with Tate and gave in to what my body wanted, my brain freaked out? It wasn't fucking fair.

I looked again at my hand, and the blood was still there. I had no idea anymore what the hell was real and what wasn't. Nothing hurt…did it? Was I in pain and I didn't realize it yet? As I ran for the elevator, I brought a hand to my scar, feeling it…there were no cuts, no open wounds, no pain. So, what was bleeding?

Tate's hand clamped on my elbow, and I yelped as he

jerked me back into his chest. "Shelby, stop, it's okay. Look at me…" I clenched my eyes shut, not wanting to be here, having this conversation. I wanted to be home, in bed, under the covers.

My knees were still shaking as I pressed the elevator call button. "Please, Tate, just let me go."

I looked down at his hand around my arm—the blood. It was his. His hand. Relief and shame rushed out of me like a broken dam, and I nearly broke into a fit of tears right there. "Oh my God," I whispered, swiping at my running nose. The tears were already falling, and there was no stopping them.

"I'm so sorry…I thought—" He started and then stopped. "I thought my hand was fine, but our movement must have opened it again." He held up his palm, which clenched a red-soaked tissue. "See? Fine. I'm fine. It's fine—"

Fine. That word. I hated it. I must have said it a million different times to a million different people after "the incident," as my stepfather always called that night. He refused to acknowledge it as anything else. The elevator door pinged open, and a sob trembled in my chest as I shook my head.

"But *I'm* anything but fine," I whispered, getting in and hitting the button for fourteen. The elevator doors shut slowly, and as they closed, I saw a flicker of understanding pass across Tate's face.

Chapter Thirteen

Shelby

By the time I got downstairs to my apartment, I was already shaking less. My stuff. My books. My pictures. My mom's smile caught my eye, and my lip trembled as I lifted the picture frame, running a finger down her face. She was thin but curvy back when this image was taken. So different from the shell of the woman cancer had left behind. Here, she was beautiful, with this constant light that shone from the inside out. It was like a beacon that would call people to her. She made friends with just about anyone—unlike me.

Closed off.

Scared of everything and everyone.

She was my opposite in every way.

I gulped a ragged breath, swallowed it, and placed the frame back on the shelf. She and Reagan were more alike than I cared to admit; I think that was what pulled me into the friendship in the first place. Though far from maternal, she reminded me of Dee Stevens.

There was a quiet knock at my door. "Shelby," Tate whispered. "Let's—I don't know, let's talk."

My jaw clenched, and though it was irrational, I pressed against the wall, barely moving, barely breathing, as though this would help conceal me behind a closed, locked door. There was no way I was opening that door and seeing him. It was too humiliating.

There was a sigh from the other side. "Well...can you at least give me *something*? Just let me know you're here and safe?" He paused, and there was a tap against the door. "Please?" he added more quietly.

"I'm here," I choked out. "I'm safe," I added a little louder, just in case he didn't hear me the first time. "Please go. I just want to be alone."

After a pause, he finally said, "Okay." But there were no footsteps. "Shelby?"

I swallowed. "Yeah?"

He inhaled a sharp breath. "Thanks for letting me know you're okay."

He didn't wait for a response this time, and I heard him walking to the elevator. When the doors closed, I exhaled in relief and rushed for the bathroom, brushing back my hair. A little bit of blood was drying at my temple where Tate had pushed my bangs. I clenched at the sight, kicked off my shoes, and pressed my feet into the cool marble of the bathroom floor. The here and now. *I am in my bathroom. I am here. I am present.*

The fear is real, but the threat is not.

Tate was not forcing himself into my mouth. He was a good guy, and a little bit of hair tugging was not a reason to flip the fuck out on someone. Hell, he wasn't even tugging on it. He was brushing it back from my face *considerately*. But I'd never be normal. Never have a normal sex life like other women. I smelled him, still—not Tate, but *him*. That awful, shitty drug store cologne mixed with body odor. He wasn't even a bad looking guy—there was no reason he had to force himself on women, other than the sick pleasure he got from it.

I gulped.

That man had ruined me, and he would never have to pay for what he did.

And that wasn't something Tate should have to deal with.

When I opened my eyes again, the blood was still there but so was my consciousness. I ran some cold water, splashing it on my face and in my hair. Red circled the drain, swirling like a whirlpool. Snatching a towel from the rack, I wet it and scrubbed my face. I scrubbed my skin and hair until it was raw and red like my swollen eyes. And even when there wasn't a spot of blood left anywhere on my face, hair, or hands, I wet the washcloth again and scrubbed some more.

Because that's just how fucked up I was.

Chapter Fourteen

Tate

I spent my entire night tossing and turning in bed. To my right were traces of Shelby's scent—coconut and vanilla along with that little bit of watermelon Chap Stick she always wore. And to my left was a small splatter of my blood. The very blood that had sent Shelby running in pure panic. What the hell happened there? Did I do something? I replayed the events in my head for the millionth time, still yielding no great epiphanies. Guilt gnawed inside of me, even though I don't know what I did. I sighed, grabbing my phone, checking to see if she'd responded to any of my texts yet. Spoiler alert: she didn't. Rolling to my right side, I inhaled her scent deeply—I was doomed to insomnia.

The next morning, she was still all I could think about, and as soon as the first shred of daylight sliced through my window, I popped out of bed, threw on some clothes, clipped a leash on Buddy, and ran down to Jolie Bakery. At seven, I stood outside her door, croissant in hand. I pressed my ear to the door and faintly heard a bit of shuffling on the other side and then a distinct sound of a faucet. I exhaled...she was awake. She was okay—or at least, okay enough to be up and walking around. Taking a deep breath, I raised a fist and tapped my knuckles to the door. All the faint shuffling sounds halted, and the water cut off from the other side. Silence.

Buddy barked once, and I shushed him, dropping my forehead to the door.

She was just—afraid. Of what, I wasn't quite sure, because even though it had been a scary night, that wasn't what seemed to be bothering her.

With a sigh, I set the plastic box with the croissant and the éclair on the ground. "Shelby," I said through the door, running my fingers along the lock, tracing its circular pattern. "I'm leaving you some breakfast. You should eat something."

I waited there another second before tapping a finger to the door and pushing off back toward the elevators.

...

By three o'clock, I had sent her three texts and only gotten one curt response back. *I'm fine.* Fine? She made it quite clear the night before—shit, had even specifically stated—that she was anything *but* fine. Did she really think I'd let that pass?

I walked Buddy about six times, hoping to catch a glimpse of her somewhere. Anywhere. With no luck. The television droned the Saturday afternoon news in the background, and I half-heartedly watched, sipping my iced coffee. Buddy lay beside me, belly up, and I scratched his long, reddish fur.

My dad's face flashed on the TV, and I groaned aloud. Awful B-roll footage of him and my mom playing Putt-Putt rolled, along with an image of them glad-handing. Finally, there I was. I cringed at the video of the three of us carrying boxes from my car into the dorms. That freaking video had been filmed years ago—my freshman year. Heat rushed through me, and I winced as my grip on the remote tweaked my cut hand. His infamous tag line scrolled across the screen above a family photo of all of us. *Make it Better with Michaelson!* A knot tightened in my chest, along with that same rush of irrational anger I always got when I saw those damned commercials.

My phone pinged with a text, drawing me out of my rage fest, and I nearly jumped off the couch to grab it, shuffling the laptop beside me on the couch. Brad's profile pic flashed me the middle finger, and beside his avatar was his text: *b-ball?*

I sighed, dragging a hand down my face. Why the hell not? Clearly, I had no other prospects until tonight's weekly poker night—and even that was only if there were no good parties happening. I shut the TV off and texted a quick response before I hopped up to put my gear on.

I froze when I got to the lobby. The back of a blond ponytail swung near the mailboxes; her head was down, flipping through a couple of envelopes. "Shelby?" My voice was raw, hoarse with disbelief. Maybe that old adage was true. What was it? When you stop looking, that's when something pops up?

Her shoulders stiffened just before she spun to look at me over one shoulder. "Tate," she whispered, and her eyes widened.

Basketball was suddenly the furthest thing from my mind, and I rushed over to her. She fell back against the mailboxes, her eyes wide, fearful. *She's afraid?* Of what? Me?

I pulled back and instead leaned against the front desk, a few feet away from her. "I've been worried about you," I offered quietly, and a sudden rush of embarrassment burned in my cheeks. The last time I admitted that to a girl, she took the chance to scoop up the governor's son's heart and run with it.

Her eyes morphed into something steadfast and seemingly strong, though a feeling in my gut told me otherwise. "Well, you can see for yourself. I'm fine."

"There's that word again," I chuckled, a bitter crack snapping the back of my throat.

Her face softened, and she lowered the mail to her side. "This time, it's true. Look at me." She held her hands out. "See? Fine."

"And last night?" I lowered my voice. "Were you fine then?"

She swallowed hard and shook her head, casting her eyes to the floor. "No. I wasn't fine last night. And we should talk—but not now. And not here."

I closed the distance between us, placing a hand on her hip. "So, what happened?" I moved my thumb in slow circles, and her eyes squeezed shut.

"I just really don't like it when guys pull my hair," she whispered.

It was a lie. Or at the very best, a partial truth. I hadn't pulled her hair. Brushed it out of the way, yeah. Smoothed my fingers into it. But at least I had her talking. I'd take what I could get at this point. It wasn't a Katie kind of lie. She wasn't lying to get her way, or get what she wanted. It was self-preservation.

"Okay…I'm sorry. I didn't know."

She looked down to the side as though the patterns in the marble were something fascinating.

"Hey," I repeated, crouching lower to meet her gaze. Those golden-brown eyes connected with mine, and I wanted to thank God for the moment he gave us just then. Because, for all of a second, we got lost in each other. I didn't bother finishing my sentence just yet—I simply stood there, loving the silent peace of being with Shelby.

If I didn't say something soon, I'd probably come across

really creepy. "Can I make it up to you? Tonight?" I smiled, but didn't quite feel it in my heart yet. "We can go get your car, too."

She shook her head. "I have plans tonight until late. Like midnight."

"Tomorrow, then?"

She sighed. "Tate—"

"We have a French test coming up soon. Don't you need to study?"

She paused at that, nibbling her bottom lip, and it took every ounce of self-control not to run my thumb along that sinful pout of hers. "Yeah, I do. And we need to talk. I'll come over tomorrow afternoon," she finally whispered.

I grinned, this time feeling the pulse jump in my throat. "Yeah?" I raised my eyebrows, nodding in encouragement.

A small twitch of her lips flipped at the corners as she agreed. "Yeah," she sighed. "But Tate…*just* to study."

I backed up a couple of steps, giving her space, a smile lighting my face. "Sexier words have never been uttered."

She laughed at that, calling after me. "I mean it." Shutting the door to her mailbox, she locked it with a shake of her head. A truck pulled up in front of the building, and she pushed out the front door to where Harrison had parked. "I gotta go… my ride's here."

All that elation deflated quicker than you could say F-150 as I saw her hop in beside Harrison and give him that smile I worked so desperately hard to get. I waved as they sped off together, and in Harrison's side mirror, his eyes connected with mine in a stare down that was pretty damn intense for such a short window. At least I got her to agree to come over. I got the second chance—and that's what mattered most right now.

Remnants of her coconut and vanilla shampoo lingered in the air even minutes after she'd left, and I closed my eyes, inhaling that scent deep, as if that could somehow make her mine. As if clinging to that scent could somehow make her one with me. It had been years since I'd felt this happy with a woman. Shelby had some demons she was dealing with, that was for sure. But I could handle a little darkness. Because I had a feeling that deeper below that darkness was something blindingly beautiful and bright, ready to shine through.

Chapter Fifteen

Shelby

Work last night had been exhausting. I was glad that I'd picked up the shift at Magnolia's, but it had been packed. The bad news was I woke up with blisters. The good news was that I had a couple hundred bucks extra cash in my pocket thanks to a great night of tips. That two hundred extra bucks made it so I didn't have to pick up any additional shifts for at least a couple of weeks. I could focus on, and dedicate that time to, getting my French grade up.

The intercom phone rang, and I hopped over, lifting the receiver to my ear.

"Ms. Stevens, there's a Harrison here for you."

"Thanks, Lou. Send him up. My friend, Reagan should be here in a bit, too. Feel free to just let her in when she gets here."

I grabbed the plate I had dirtied yesterday, thanks to Tate's croissant and éclair, and tucked it into the dishwasher. The sight of the crumbs brought an emptiness to my chest.

It wasn't fair to him—I had stop whatever this thing was between us. And if that meant finding another tutor, I'd do it. Though, part of me hoped that wouldn't be necessary, because he was actually a great teacher.

Right, you want to keep spending time with him because he's a good teacher.

After I basically had a psychotic break right in front of him, I wasn't sure why he was being so nice. But it didn't matter. I was too fucked up for any kind of relationship. And until I was ready to be completely candid with someone, I shouldn't be stringing him along. There was a knot in my throat, and yet, I knew it was the right choice.

There was a quiet knock at the door, and I rushed to open it. On the other side stood Harrison, grocery bag in hand and smile on his face. "Hey, Shelbs." He leaned in, dropping a quick kiss to my cheek before rushing past me and setting the bag down on the counter. "I got us eggs and pancake mix and this pack of ready-made shredded potatoes. They're supposed to be foolproof."

"Sounds good to me."

There was another knock at the door as I poured us each a glass of water, my hands full. Harrison, laughed, gesturing for me to not worry about it. "I got it. It's probably Reagan."

I looked at the clock. "Mark it in the history books. She's punctual for the first time in her life."

Harrison's laugh cracked as the door opened, and his shoulders tightened.

"Harrison," Tate's voice came from the other side, and it was brittle.

"Hey, Tate." Harrison leaned on the door, blocking any entry Tate may have had.

I popped up from the couch and rushed over. I was still in my flannel pajama bottoms, a T-shirt, and my ratty robe I'd had since freshman year of high school—I didn't see the need to dress for an in-house brunch. Until now. "Tate?" I leaned around Harrison, and sure enough, there he was. He glared at me, one hand fisted around Buddy's leash, the other clenched around a box from Jolie. Then a smile tugged at his lips as he took in my jammies and ratty robe.

"I'm sorry," he said slowly, shifting his attention back to Harrison. "I guess I didn't realize you had company."

Harrison stood stiffly beside me, and I nudged him with an elbow. "Harrison," I snapped. "Why don't you go start the omelets?"

His eyes stayed fixed on Tate, but he finally nodded, stepping back. "Sure thing."

"He just got here." I hitched a thumb over my shoulder to Harrison. I knew how it looked—bad.

"Oh?" Tate seemed to examine me, eyes wandering from my wrinkled robe and slept-in T-shirt down to my bare feet and pj bottoms. "Well, I guess you don't need these." He wiggled another to-go box of something from Jolie.

A giddy sort of excitement twitched inside of me as he untied the ribbon and opened the box.

"Madeleines," I whispered. "That's nice of you, but not necessary."

He shrugged. "I wanted to make sure you were eating."

I swallowed. "And Madeleines were the most nutritional option?" I should have said that wasn't his concern, but I just couldn't bring myself to say the words.

That grin stretched wider, creasing his dimples. "You can only eat so many croissants."

I shook my head. "No way...they never get old."

"Noted." He stepped back, giving Buddy's leash a gentle tug. "I'll see you later, right? Study date?"

I chewed my bottom lip. God, this was going to suck. I'd never had to have this conversation, maybe because I'd never had such a strong connection with anyone before Tate.

I nodded. "I'll see you later," I managed.

He pushed the elevator button, and as the doors opened, Reagan hopped out and Tate got on. She carried a bottle of champagne and rushed toward my open door. "Guess what?" she squealed.

It took me a second, but I grabbed her wrist, squeezing. "You got the part? In *Singin' in the Rain*? Kathy—"

"Seldon!" she finished with me, and we both jumped up and down, screaming like a couple of sorority girls during rush. I ushered her inside, popped the champagne, and poured mimosas all around. I clinked glasses with my friends and grinned. "This is a good day."

Harrison sipped the mimosa and grunted, scrunching his face. "I think I need some guy friends," he groaned. "Just yesterday, you were crying to me on the way to get your car about how awful your night with Tate was—"

"I'm sorry, what? Your night with *who*?" Reagan screeched.

"Not like that," I cut in. Well, it was kind of like that, but Harrison certainly didn't need to hear those details. I'd fill Reagan in later. I sighed and repeated the story of how we were held at gunpoint, and how Tate was hurt and I didn't know it. I repeated the account of my meltdown pretty factually, leaving out the part where we were naked in his bed with his dick in my mouth.

"Oh my God." Reagan narrowed her eyes, assessing me, and I shook off her stare. "And he's still calling you? He must really like you."

I groaned, falling back onto my futon. "I have to end it." I didn't know if I was trying to convince them or myself.

"Yeah, but do *you* like him?" Harrison asked, whipping the eggs in a bowl.

I did. And that was the problem. So, instead of answering, I did what I do best—I deflected. "Not as much as Reagan likes her Gene Kelly lookalike, am I right?" I grinned, sending a wink to my girl. She had been swooning all through callbacks over the guy she was certain would get the role opposite her.

She fell into a seat beside me, rolling her eyes. "He got Cosmo. Can you believe it?" She crossed her arms, tipping the glass back and finishing the mimosa in a swig.

Harrison eyed me as he drank his champagne. Reagan went on and on about her audition and their first reading, but all the while Harrison watched me.

My face burned as I tried to ignore his scrutiny. I know that we hadn't all gotten off to a perfect start—him, me, and Tate. But was that any reason to award me with the glare from hell? I shivered, despite Charleston's morning warmth, and pushed off the couch. I needed to escape that icy stare. Those eyes that knew me better than I knew myself sometimes. "How are those omelets coming? Want me to start the pancakes?"

I turned my back on Harrison, pouring the pancake mix into a bowl, but I knew his attention was still on me, picking apart every tiny bit of movement. My hands shook as I smoothed my bangs over my scar, and I froze midmotion. Dammit. Harrison, my brother from another mother, knew every tic I had. He knew the second my shaky hand moved for my hair how nervous I was. I stirred the milk into the pancake mix, and I cursed my nerves as the hairs on the back of my neck stood on end.

Dropping the wooden spoon onto the counter, I spun to face Harrison. I don't know where this sudden surge of anger sprouted from. All I knew was that it had taken root and was spreading into a towering tree. "What?" I said. "What is it? You're clearly thinking *some*thing."

Harrison's smirk was infuriating, and he simply shrugged, flipping the omelet. "I didn't say anything."

I huffed a sigh and Reagan poured a second mimosa for all of us, cautiously setting the flutes between us. "You didn't have to," I grumbled, whipping at the batter once more.

"All I did was ask if you liked him," Harrison said again.

"But you don't, right?" I asked.

Reagan leaned in, carefully taking the pancake batter from me before I slopped half of it onto the floor. "You're ending it, though, Shelby," she offered carefully.

"No, I don't like him," Harrison said, interrupting Reagan. The utter calmness in his voice provoked me. It annoyed the hell out of me how composed Harrison managed to remain, even in the face of frustration. "But what does that matter?"

It mattered. He knew it mattered. Reagan and Harrison were my only family left in this world. Harrison was almost as close to my mom as I was. He was my brother, even if we weren't related by blood. And if he didn't like Tate—didn't like the only guy who'd ever made my body heat and my heart ache—maybe my mom wouldn't have liked him, either.

If that was the case, there was no hope for Tate. No one came between me and my family…alive or dead.

Chapter Sixteen

SHELBY

The elevator groaned to life, heading up to the penthouse. I wasn't sure if it was because of my nerves or the sudden movement in the elevator, but my stomach dropped to my toes.

Maybe I should call this whole thing off? The red stop button in the elevator tempted me, echoing for me to press it. One quick push and I could be off this elevator and back downstairs in my cotton pajamas. As I moved to lift my hand, my sleeve was lined with lead. Heavy. And by the time I had my finger shakily hovering over the button, the doors opened, revealing Tate standing there with a big grin and an even bigger box of Mellow Mushroom pizza. That smile of his was like an instant sedative, calming my frayed nerves.

Was this normal? This level of power Tate had over me? Most guys barely got me to their driveway, let alone inside their bedroom. But maybe it was time to let go. To free myself from the past and to try again, letting my body follow in kind.

As much as I wanted to, I was pretty sure that wasn't how this shit worked. Otherwise, why would people spend years of time and millions of dollars on intensive therapy?

"Hi," he said, breaking through my thoughts and right into my gut, where a nest of butterflies had taken up permanent residence.

"Hi," I managed to squeak.

"I wasn't sure you were coming." He held the door open, letting me enter first before he followed and dropped the pizza onto the counter. Buddy rushed toward me, hopping around as though he were still a puppy.

I was thankful for the distraction, and bent to pet the dog. Man, I always loved dogs. Always wanted one, too, only my stepdad was allergic, and once they divorced, my mom and I couldn't afford the extra mouth to feed.

"So," I said, standing after a final pat to Buddy's rump. "What's the lesson plan for tonight?"

Tate held up a finger, rushed to the TV, and pulled out *Amelie*. "We watch this without subtitles. *But*, to improve your listening skills, I'll pause it at random times and you'll have to respond to whatever dialogue line we end on."

Oh, boy. "So, it's like improv meets French class."

Tate shrugged. "The final exam is a thirty-minute conversation with the professor over coffee. If we can't improve your comprehension, you'll never pass this class."

Whoa. Harsh. But also true. I exhaled, scratching Buddy under the chin. "Tate…" I started quietly, but cleared my throat and added more loudly, "We need to talk."

The plates clattered as he dropped them to the counter. His grip on the edge tightened and he looked up at me slowly. "I'm not sure I like the way that sounds."

I ignored that statement. "Look…it's just…I have a lot going on right now. And obviously, as you saw Friday night, I have some stuff I need to work through. It's just not a good time to get emotionally involved with someone." I gulped and raised my gaze to find those cerulean eyes searing through me. "Even if that someone is sweet and smart and brings me baked goods daily." My lips lifted into a sad smile. "And this might just be easier if I find someone else to tutor me—"

"That's ridiculous," Tate spat, pushing off the counter and stalking toward me. I backed into the wall, bumping my head on a picture frame.

"Excuse me?"

"It's ridiculous. We have a test next week—you're not going to find another tutor to help you in that amount of time." He swallowed slowly, his jaw ticking behind clenched teeth. "Look…I'll be good, okay? That rule we established initially? I won't kiss you unless you kiss me first? We can do that again. But don't risk your grades because you're afraid to be around me," he scoffed.

I had forgotten about that rule from earlier. Unfortunately, I wasn't exactly to be trusted, either, when it came to Tate's lips and mine. If anything, I suspected my self-control was more lacking than his. But I did need help—this upcoming test was 20 percent of our grade for the semester. And if I didn't keep my GPA up, my scholarship would be gone, and I'd have to return to the dorms, go back to working at Magnolia's six nights a week, and become an RA again. This apartment was way too expensive without financial aid.

How honest could I be with Tate? Air caught in my lungs as I dragged in a breath. "I'm not nearly as worried about you behaving as I am about myself," I said quietly, dipping my eyes to the marble floor.

The sharp inhalation he took expanded his chest. Fuck. I definitely shouldn't have said that.

"Okay…" He sounded both thoughtful and cautious. "How about if we take things slow. Like, really slow, Snail stuck in tar, slow."

I squinted at him, and my eyelashes created a crackled web to see through. "What do you mean?"

"I like you, and I want to spend time with you." A smile twitched at his lips, and his dimple flickered momentarily. "I'd rather have hands off time with you than no time at all. I promise I won't kiss you. Until you kiss me. And even when that happens, I won't let you escalate things—not yet, at least. Not beyond kissing."

A warm surge tingled down my arms. He would do that? For me? Kissing I could handle…I knew that. But unfortunately, it was the other stuff I really wanted. "And what if I told you I wanted more than kissing?" I whispered.

He hissed a curse. "You're killing me here, Shelby. Which is it? What do you want?"

I swallowed. What did I want? It changed like the freaking weather. "I want *you*. But that's something that I'm really not used to. And it's scary."

He nodded, moving toward me, taking my hand. "It's scary for me, too. My bedroom's not really used to having repeat visitors." He grinned, but it quickly fell into something more serious as he cleared his throat.

I sighed. "So…what do we do?"

Lifting my hand to his lips, he pressed a kiss to each knuckle. "Why don't we just sort of roll with it. Let's see how we feel—do what it is we want to do, but if you get uncomfortable, you have to talk to me, Shelby. You say stop, and I will. No questions asked, okay? It doesn't need to be a big thing. We can just…go back to playing Scrabble or whatever."

I laughed at that. "Scrabble? When did we turn ninety?"

He laughed as well, dropping an indignant jaw at my response. "Scrabble is awesome—my nanny and I used to play all the time. And actually it'd be a great French lesson."

I grinned, relief washing over me. "So, what happened

to the French themed food? You slackin' off on me, Tate?" I nudged him, moving into the living room.

"Not even a little." He lifted the box of Mellow Mushroom pizza with a flourishing hand gesture. "French bread pizza. *Pour vous*, mademoiselle."

I wandered over to the TV, avoiding the eye contact that made my stomach flop around in my belly like a caught fish. "Do you always go to such lengths for your tutees?"

He shifted, grabbing a slice of pizza as the movie credits rolled and moving to the couch, taking the opposite end from me like he was intentionally putting a chasm of distance between us. "Considering the only two people I've tutored in the world are you and Sophia, I'd say no. You are definitely special."

I couldn't hide my smile, as Tate stared at me, so I took a bite of pizza instead, nodding. Only, his eyes didn't stray from my face. "What?" I asked, wiping a hand over my mouth? Did I have sauce on my jaw? Cheese? Parmesan stuck to my Chap Stick?

He shook his head, finishing the rest of his slice with a gigantic bite. "Nothing," he said, popping off of the couch. "Want any espresso?"

"Coffee and pizza? How very—"

"European?" He put fisted hands to his hips in a mock superhero way and gave me a lopsided grin.

"I was going to say weird."

"If you mean weirdly delicious, then you are right on. So…yes to espresso?"

I sighed, shrugging. "Why not?" I turned my attention back to the movie; I knew the plot pretty well, but even still, it was a struggle to understand each line. They spoke so damn quickly.

There was some clanking around behind me in the kitchen, when suddenly the screen froze. I jerked around to find Tate with the remote pointed at the TV. He raised an eyebrow, tamping down some espresso grounds into a metal thing. "Go," he said quietly.

"But—"

"But is an English word."

Fuck. What was the last line that was said? Something about...*qu'il aime et pop les bulles d'emballage en plastique?* Soooo, he likes plastic? No, that's not right. He likes... popping plastic? Bubbles! He likes popping plastic bubbles. "*Qui n'aime pas surgissants bubble?*"

"'Who doesn't like popping bubble wrap?'" Tate repeated my response, and his lips slipped into a soft smile. "Not bad." He slid back onto the couch beside me, a little closer this time, but still far enough away that if I stretched my arm, I'd barely touch him. Even *that* made my pulse race. "But also not great. That took too long to get a response—and I think it was a result of you not paying close enough attention." He handed me the steaming espresso. "Are you distracted, Shelby?"

"How can I not be?" I took a sip and nearly choked on the bitterness and strength of the brew. "Holy shit," I coughed. "That's like motor oil."

Tate shrugged. "International business major? You better learn to drink espresso like the Europeans. *Sans lait.*"

Damn him. I hated that he was right. "I'm going to be up for hours," I grumbled.

He licked his lips, looking away, and I thought I saw his cheeks flush the tiniest bit. Then again, maybe it was the motor oil he was sipping. "I bet we can find ways to fill the time." With that, he leaned back and hit play. "And if you pass tonight's lesson, we can watch *Midnight in Paris* after."

• • •

I made it through all of *Amelie* and about half of *Midnight in*

Paris before my eyelids fell. I must have drifted off sometime in the middle of the movie because when I opened my eyes, Owen Wilson was still hanging with Hemingway, and I was on my side, my legs strewn across Tate's lap. His white T-shirt wrinkled around the waistband of his basketball shorts, and I barely moved for fear of waking him. His chest rose and fell with evenly paced breaths, and after another minute, I shifted, stretching my neck to steal a better glance at him. His face was relaxed, neck turned toward the television, and his eyelashes fanned over the tops of his cheeks. Full lips barely rested together in a serene pout.

When I dared to glance down, I saw his hand draped gently across my calf. My heart stuttered at the gentle splay of his fingers against my bare flesh. What the hell should I do now? Do I wake him up? Slip out and down to my apartment without saying good-bye? No...definitely not the latter. He would kill me. I glanced at the clock—it was only just past eleven. Not late by college standards. Guess the motor oil didn't help keep us awake.

I pressed my lips together as his thumb moved in slow strokes over the back of my calf. Chills raced from the point of contact, up my body and torso, leaving tight nipples as evidence.

A breath dragged through my barely parted lips, and I wiggled my foot in his lap in an effort to wake him. I wished I were the fun, carefree girl who rolled with the punches and followed her instincts. That I could flip over and straddle his lap and claim his lips and body as mine. But that just wasn't me.

His head was still angled to the side, eyes closed. But his hands moved, stroking my feet, giving me a massage.

"Having a good dream?" I whispered, sitting up.

He held on tighter to my ankle as though he didn't want me pulling away from his touch. "The best," he answered.

Finally, his eyes fluttered open, wandering over my face and finally settling onto my mouth. His smile widened as he leaned into me, sweeping his thumb against the side of my lips. Oh God, was I drooling? The panic must have been written all over my face because he laughed and shook his head. "I think Buddy was cuddling with you in your sleep. You had some of his fur on your face. Sorry about that." He flicked a few strands of golden hair onto the floor, his touch drifting briefly to my cheek. I sighed into his hand, relaxed despite my highly aware state.

"Tate," I whispered.

Those skilled fingers dragged from my cheek down my throat, finally landing at the back of my neck. "Hmm?"

"I thought we were taking it slowly."

"That's right." He chuckled, stretching his arms overhead. The absence of his touch was cold and unwanted, and I wasn't really sure what to make of those feelings. "So don't you get any ideas."

I sighed, propping my chin in my palm. "What did you dream about?"

"A man never reveals his dreams." His dimple appeared again. After another second, it dropped. "Anyway, we should probably get you home, huh?"

Reluctantly, I stood up. Buddy did the same, jumping to his feet from where he had been sleeping at the foot of the couch.

Tate stretched, attempting to secretly adjust his erection before standing. I grabbed my things, flinging my messenger bag over my shoulder. "I hear cold showers do the trick."

He chuckled, picking up the espresso cups and putting them in the sink. "Is that so? I haven't had to take one of those since high school."

God, this was awkward. Leaving without a kiss, after you've already kissed before. And when you both clearly want to. Why couldn't I just get over my shit and date like a normal college girl? "Well, I'll see you tomorrow in class." I moved to the door, spinning to face him. "Why don't we go together—?"

"Do you want a ride—?" he asked at the same time.

His smile was large, even though he seemed contemplative. Or maybe he was just tired. "I'll come by at eight forty-five. Croissants okay for breakfast?"

I nodded. "They never get old."

He curled his fingers beneath my chin. For a moment, I thought he was going to kiss me as he leaned in. I thought he was going to draw my chin close and press his lips to mine. And if I were being honest with myself, the thought of him doing that made me feel giddy. But instead, he reached beyond my shoulder, pushing the elevator button.

"Good night, Shelby," he said, pulling back. That hand at my chin lingered an extra moment before he brushed his thumb across my lips, taking some Chap Stick with it. He pressed that same thumb to his mouth, closing his eyes with the contact. It was damn sexy, and I licked my lips where his touch had just been.

Shit. *I* was the one who needed the cold shower.

Chapter Seventeen

Tate

The next morning, I picked Shelby up outside her door. She stepped out with her backpack slung carelessly over one shoulder, a couple of books in hand, and startled when she saw me.

"Tate. Jesus, you scared me."

I shrugged. "I said I'd come by at eight forty-five."

"I know, I just didn't expect you to be *right here* when I opened my door." A cute little smile tugged at the corner of her mouth as she craned her neck into the box of baked goods. "So, croissants as promised?"

"And éclairs," I said, presenting her with the box of baked goods and handing her a to-go cup of coffee. "You ready to knock it out of the park with Ceele?" I asked as we got onto the elevators.

She sighed, bringing the steaming coffee to her lips. "I guess we'll see soon enough. This test Friday might be the death of me."

"It better not be. I need you intact."

She lifted her eyebrow. "Oh? For what?"

"I have something special planned for this weekend." Leaning in, I took a deep breath next to her hair. God, I just couldn't resist it. She smelled so amazing. I took the coffee, stealing my own sip while threading her fingers through mine. Almost immediately, her muscles contracted, cementing, and I could practically see her walls going up, see her fortifying against me. Shit, maybe even holding her hand was moving too fast. I almost pulled away. I almost let go. But I thought better of it. "This okay?" I asked instead.

Her eyes fluttered wider, pupils dilating in the dim lighting of the elevator. "Yeah," she said. "It is." Then she added, louder, "Especially if you bring me coffee every morning." Then, her hand relaxed into mine, holding on as if it could somehow also stabilize her. I hoped it did. I wanted to be that for her. She swallowed a gulp of coffee hard, wincing with the sip. "Whoa, sugar," she said.

"It's too sweet?"

Her face still twisted like she had sucked on a lemon. "Not if you bring me an insulin shot with it."

"Noted." I grinned, handing her my cup, which I'd only put one packet into. And just like that, she was back to being the Shelby I knew best. Goofy, sarcastic, sexy Shelby.

A few minutes later, we were parked and headed into the language building. I slung my arm around her shoulders, pulling her tight into my side with a nod hello to Brad and Chrissy. I nearly stumbled over my own damn feet at the sight of Katie across the yard. Every muscle in my body clenched as she tossed her curly dark hair over her shoulder and grinned that toothy smile at Logan, one of my basketball buddies.

"Oh, look," Shelby said in a falsely sweet voice that I recognized easily from numerous ex-girlfriends. Jealousy rang in the tone. "It's Veronica."

"What?" I snapped. How the hell did she know about Katie?

Confusion flickered across her face before she nodded to Chrissy. I sighed inwardly, brushing my nose to her temple. Oh, thank God. I'd have to tell her about Katie eventually—but not now. Not yet.

"Aw, come on. Betty shouldn't ever be jealous of anyone." I held the classroom door open for her, and she tilted her head as she slipped past me.

She took her seat behind Harrison. "I'm not."

A snort came from Harrison, but he didn't turn around. Shelby rubbed a palm across his back. "Good morning." She leaned forward, resting a chin to his shoulder.

"Apparently." He arched an eyebrow. "Guess you had a change of plans yesterday," he said to Shelby, his eyes sliding briefly to me.

"Yeah. Sort of." She pulled back, and that smile that I so rarely saw disappeared. "You're okay, right?" she asked Harrison, dropping her voice.

"Of course. Why wouldn't I be?"

Shelby snuck a glance my way, eyebrows tight, concerned, then looked back at Harrison. "You just seem…grumpy. Or something."

There was a definite shift in their interaction from just a week ago. Now, he just seemed like he was in a shit mood, which didn't really give him the right to treat her like dirt. I narrowed my eyes, studying them. Was there something more going on? It didn't always seem like it. They were close, sure, but I'd had friends who were girls before. Didn't mean I'd slept with them. But he and Shelby were tight. Closer than I was with Chrissy or any of my other female friends. Maybe he felt threatened by her spending time with someone else?

Whatever the answer was, this was a friend of Shelby's. If I was serious about her, I was pretty sure I had to find a way to make nice with Harrison. She didn't seem the type to dump one of her best friends for a guy she liked…and if she were that type, I probably wouldn't like her much. "Here, man." I passed him the box with the two extra éclairs Shelby and I didn't get to on the drive over. "We grabbed a couple extra for you this morning. Maybe it'll help cheer you up." In spite of Harrison's death glare, I forced a smile.

"Thanks," he said, taking an éclair from the box. His eyes steeled on mine as an arrogant smirk formed on his lips and made sure I understood clearly that "Thanks" actually meant "Fuck you and stay away from Shelby."

"Anytime," I answered coolly. *No fucking way, asshole.* "We go there a lot, so any time you want something, shoot us a text."

Harrison's nostrils flared at that, and I leaned back in my chair, breaking the last éclair in two pieces and handing the larger half to Shelby. Her cheeks flushed red, her eyes widened, and as she opened her mouth to speak, Professor Ceele walked in, calling the class to order.

・・・

It didn't take long for Shelby to pull me aside after class. "What the fuck was that?" she snapped, shoving my shoulders in a way that wasn't overly forceful, but certainly meant business.

"What was what?"

"You know what I'm talking about. Your little pissing match with Harrison," she whispered, eyes flaring to life.

My lips curved, but with my smile, her frown sank deeper. "Come on, I really tried with him. It's not my fault he was in a shitty mood. I offered him the last éclairs for God's sake."

"Don't lift your leg and mark me as your territory." She pushed passed me, stalking toward the parking lot, and when we reached my car, she spun, nearly bumping into my chest.

"Harrison and Reagan are more than just my best friends. They're family. If you can't get along with them, then there is no 'us.' Got it?"

I nodded, and a warmth spread through my chest. I loved that she cared so deeply for her friends. Even if it blinded her to Harrison maybe feeling something more than familial toward her.

Chapter Eighteen

Tate

Two days later, I showed up to Shelby's apartment, proud of the fact that I'd managed to keep my weekend plans for us a secret. We were only a few days away from Saturday night and there was no way she was getting me to blow the surprise.

When she opened the door, it looked like a bakery had exploded. Smoke filled the small room, she was wearing this adorable little apron thing, and she was covered in flour. A laugh bubbled up out of me. Covering my mouth with the back of my hand, I tried to stifle it—really unsuccessfully.

She threw a hand to her hip, tilting her head. "Well, that's the last time I ever try to do something nice for you."

I lifted a section of her bangs that were caked in white flour and something gooey. Was that…ew, was it egg?

She jerked away, smoothing her palm down her bangs, capturing a bit of the gunky mixture that gathered there. Crap, I forgot about not touching her hair. What had happened to her to cause such an extreme reaction? A biting pain twisted in my stomach at the thought that someone may have hurt her. I tried not to react, but tension pinched my expression through my forced smile. "You have egg or something in your hair." This time, I slowly brought my hand to her, scooping the goo out of her bangs. "There, got it."

Pushing her bottom lip out in an exaggerated pout, she looked up at me. Her brown eyes seemed even bigger somehow. "I was trying to make you croissants."

"You baked for me? Oh, you *so like* me."

She slapped my shoulder, and I caught her hand, pulling her flush against my body. God, I wanted to kiss her. That made it difficult to step away. Instead, I swept my thumb across her cheekbone, wiping off some flour there and holding my white-stained finger in front of her eyes. "I see the baking is going really well."

She laughed at that, her head dropping into her hands. "Oh my God, look at me. I'm a freaking mess."

"Maybe they'll be delicious."

"Maybe they'll taste like charcoal."

I swallowed, my throat feeling like something had lodged there. "Maybe I won't care."

"Maybe you have a death wish."

"More like a Shelby wish." Her playful smile slid away as I glimpsed the seriousness in the depths of her eyes. In a tortuously slow motion, her gaze dropped to my lips as she sucked in a sharp breath.

What had been a bearable warmth heating my pelvis flared into scorching heat. Her hand drifted down my chest, brushing over my pecs until she reached my abs, where she stopped. I grabbed her wrist, gently, so freaking gently so as not to scare her, and flipping it over, I drew it up to my lips, brushing a soft kiss against her pulse.

The knot in my throat unraveled, expanding. "We only have an hour until we need to leave for the tutoring center,"

I said, pulling my travel Scrabble set out of my backpack. I'd forgotten I had it until Shelby had mentioned the game when she called me a ninety-year-old the other night. It was something my grandmother bought for me years ago, and it had basically been collecting dust in my closet.

She stepped aside as I moved to her futon, dropping the game onto her coffee table.

"Harrison used to play Scrabble with me to help with my dyslexia. Of course, *nothing* really helped with it."

Dyslexia? I didn't know she was dyslexic. That would explain why she had so much trouble with test taking. If Harrison had helped her with that, then they must go way back. I mean, I knew that...sort of. But it didn't really register until she mentioned that. Little by little, I was stripping away at her barriers and learning more and more about her life. "You're dyslexic," I repeated. "Is that why French is so hard?"

She shrugged, brushing it off. "Maybe. Tests have always been really stressful. But my dyslexia is very minor compared to a lot of people's."

"You're like an onion, Shelby Stevens. The more layers that peel back, the more I learn."

Okay, if I thought she went rigid before, she was a damn plank of wood right now. She went ramrod straight like someone strapped her to a pole. "My stepdad used to say that. Except he said that like an onion, the more you peel the layers, the less complex you become and the more you stink."

She grew up hearing that shit? "Sorry, but your stepdad sounds like an ass."

She wasn't facing me, but the muscles at her back and shoulders relaxed again. "You want coffee?" She bent down to open the oven.

"Coffee and croissants sound incredible."

She opened the oven door and another waft of smoke escaped, drifting to the ceiling and sending the smoke alarm off. Jumping to my feet, I grabbed her French book off the table and started fanning the smoke away from the shrieking disk on the ceiling.

She dropped the blackened croissants to the counter, swiping her hand across her forehead. "Maybe just the coffee, then?"

Chapter Nineteen

Shelby

Saturday finally rolled around, and I swear this week moved slower than any other week.

Wear this. Be ready by 6:30. That's all Tate's note had said. No other hints, no matter how hard I tried to pry information out of him. And now it was 6:29 and I was sitting on the couch in a ridiculous red and black ruffled skirt (which, thankfully, I could wear with yoga pants), a tank top that was painted to look like a lace up corset, and my black ballet flats.

There was a knock at the door, and I jumped to open it. "You better have a damn good explanation for this." The first thing I saw was the box in his hand. The second thing I saw was—well, was *Tate*. He wore some sort of weird, old-fashioned pants with suspenders, a white T-shirt, and a newsboy cap. "What the—? What is going on?" At least I felt like less of an idiot now. Now we *both* looked dumb.

"You look amazing." He grinned. "Reagan helped me put the costume together. And you should thank me. She wanted you in a real corset. Something told me you'd be more comfortable in the tank top."

Heat tingled down my body at his declaration. Something he said so easily and probably didn't even think twice about. *Something told me you'd be more comfortable in the tank top.* He knew what made me comfortable. The tank top, a longer skirt. Most guys would have wanted to see my boobs crammed into a corset, but Tate not only *knew* but *respected* what I wanted. "You look pretty good, yourself," I said, smoothing the tank top, even though it didn't have a damn wrinkle in it. "So…you going to tell me what the hell is going on?" I laughed at how ridiculous we looked.

He still didn't answer, just handed me the box in his hand. "You need just a couple more things to complete the look."

I set it on the coffee table, tore the ribbon off the top, and opened it. A feather boa. *Huh.* This just keeps getting weirder. And a feather clip for my hair. At least, I thought it was for my hair.

Before I asked any more questions, he took the feather and moved to clip my bangs back. Fear and anxiety collided in my chest, and I jumped from his touch, pressing a palm to my bangs. "What are you doing?"

"It goes in your hair," he answered cautiously. I knew I was acting like a lunatic. That reaction was extreme, even for me, but I just wasn't ready for him to see my scar. To see the actual damage that permanently marred my face and was a constant reminder of that horrible night.

I swallowed, feeling like something gooey was caught in the back of my throat. "I'll do it," I managed to say, taking the clip from him. I pinned the other side of my hair back and took a quick look in the mirror.

"Ready?" he asked, wrapping the boa around my shoulders.

"For *what*?"

"Your next lesson, mademoiselle."

I locked the door behind me, and as we stepped on the elevator, my eyes trailed down to his feet, which were clad in penny loafers. I tried to hold in my laughter, which only resulted in a weird hiccup-snort hybrid.

His eyes widened, surprised at my laugh. "Did you just snort?"

"Whatever, dude. You're wearing penny loafers. I could pee myself, and you should still be more embarrassed."

"Oh yeah?" He didn't wait for my response, but dug his fingers into my ribs, tickling me. I jumped, screaming and laughing nearly collapsing to the elevator floor. He caught my elbows, ceasing the tickle attack, and helped me to my feet as I caught my breath. "Sure you want to keep testing that theory?"

I shook my head, panting. "Where the hell did you get that outfit, anyway?"

"Reagan found it all in the costume department. She let me borrow it tonight." He adjusted the cap, looking at his reflection in the elevator door. "Though, I think I might keep this hat. Looks damn good on me, wouldn't you say?"

"Oh, definitely," I said, rolling my eyes. "You've got a hat face."

He swept his fingers over the brim in some sort of Bruno Mars-Michael Jackson move. "I know, right?"

"Maybe I didn't mean it as a compliment." I pushed onto my toes, tipping the hat to the side so it sat on an angle on his head.

"Of course it was a compliment. You said it yourself, I've got a hat face. Meaning I look *good* in hats."

"Or your face looks better covered up." I laughed and tugged the brim down over his eyes.

He flicked the edge of the hat, and damn… I had to admit it was a smooth move. He winked, wetting his lips. "The only way my face looks better covered…is if it's covered by your lips."

My heart fluttered, the irregular beat causing my chest to lurch. "Anyone ever tell you how humble you are?"

He grinned, flashing me that dimple almost as if it were deliberate. "Not today." Then, leaning in, he tugged at the feather boa, dragging it across my neck. "I also bet we could make good use of this eventually, too." Warmth spread through my limbs at that, and I tried to calm my somersaulting stomach. Because despite my need to go slow, damn, did my body want to go faster.

Ten minutes later, we were pulling up to the old Charleston train station, which had been converted into a lounge a few years ago. People were milling about, all wearing clothes similar to ours. Hell, most were even more elaborate. In front of the door was a sign that read LE PETITE MOULIN ROUGE.

Tate curled an arm around my waist, guiding me through the front door. "Are we seeing Moulin Rouge tonight?" I asked.

"Close, but not quite. We're *in* the Moulin Rouge tonight."

The lounge had set up tables and decorated the insides of the bar like a small-scale replica of the Moulin Rouge, complete with a stage and dancers, and girls walking around selling cigars. Tate handed tickets to someone standing at the door, and they directed us through the crowd to a table near the front.

"What the…? How did you even know this was happening?" I was shocked that a guy like Tate would go to such lengths to keep the lesson themes alive. It made me excited and nervous, and even though my skin was heated as his hand came in contact with my waist, a chill skittered down my spine.

"My family gets invited to shit like this all the time," he said. We slid into our seats, and Tate shrugged as if this wasn't crazy. Sliding his chair toward mine, he closed what little distance there was between us and rested a hand on my knee. Pleasure blasted through my body, hardening my nipples, and I hugged the feather boa tighter around me, hoping he wouldn't notice my obvious response to his touch.

"It's not just a show, though."

"No?"

He shook his head. "It's also a dance lesson. Before the show starts, they'll teach the women how to cancan."

He draped his arm over my shoulders as my spine bristled. *I'm expected to dance tonight.* I hadn't danced in years. Especially not for an audience. His thumb circled my shoulder, and moisture clung to the back of my neck.

"Unless you don't want to. Then we can watch everyone else learn it and make fun of how crazy they look." He leaned in, his lips brushing against my ear, and I had to suppress another shiver of excitement as he did. I remembered the feel of those lips on mine. I *liked* it.

But more than that, I liked the lengths to which he went to make me comfortable. He was taking it slow, just as he promised. He hadn't kissed me, even though I could see—hell, *feel*—how much he wanted to. I was touched by that. His actions reached down somewhere deep and squeezed something inside of me I thought was long gone. Something I thought I'd never get back. "Although," he whispered, his words leaving warm little puffs of air tickling my ear. "I'm a little bummed I won't get to see you up there flinging your skirt over your head."

He leaned back in his chair, dragging those incredible lips away from my ear, and *God, oh, God,* I wanted nothing more than to grab those suspenders and yank him back into me. "I'll do it," I answered quickly, my body doing the talking, not my brain. Because whatever I'd felt just then, I *really* really wanted to feel it again. I wanted to please him. For the first time in my life, I wanted to show off for a guy I liked.

Tate was a tiny sliver of sunshine in the middle of a hurricane. And maybe it was time to finally follow those instincts. To shelve inhibited Shelby for a night and see what happened. Maybe by finally moving beyond one chapter of my life, I could begin a new one.

My hands curled against the satin skirt, bunching the ruffles against my skin.

"*Bonjour, monsieurs et mademoiselles*." An actress with the show moved to the center of the floor as a spotlight hit her. "Let's bring all the women up here, and we'll begin with the cancan."

"Shelby," Tate said, grabbing my hand and gently pulling me back into my seat as I stood. "You don't have to do this if you don't want to."

I was nervous. More nervous than when I played Clara in The Nutcracker when I was thirteen. Which was *crazy*. It was the cancan. It was meant to be frenetic and clumsy and silly.

Nothing depended on this. Nothing but having fun and letting loose a little.

I took a deep breath and stood, giving Tate my best smile. "I know. I actually think I want to."

I filed into the small crowd of women as our teacher first went over the basic cancan steps. Knee up. Leg up. Bounce, bounce, ruffle your skirt. Repeat. And so on and so forth. When we finally had all the steps, we put it to music with the live band and the rhythm pulsed through my body. It thrummed through my heart, in my veins, and it was as if my mom was right there with me. Everything was better when I danced. When *she* danced. I was never as good as she'd been, but then, few were.

The song ended with a final high kick, and my knee nearly brushed my nose as I launched it in the air. The woman instructing gave me a huge smile and announced into the microphone, "We've got some serious talent in the audience tonight. I better watch out or I may be out of a job." A blush splayed across my face and though I couldn't see it, I could feel it heating all the way up to my hairline. She sent me a wink, and I moved back to where Tate sat, his eyes bugging out, staring.

"Where the hell did you learn to do that?"

The adrenaline of dancing and applause hummed inside me and skimmed over my flesh. "I'm an onion, remember?"

"Shit, you're not an onion. You're a cake. Still lots of layers to discover, but sweet. Delicious." He did this funny growl thing and nipped my shoulder before pulling back to examine my face. "Seriously, where did you learn that? Your leg was, like, parallel to your body."

I didn't want to explain it. I didn't want to get sad again or feel all the things that usually went hand in hand with dance for me. Instead, I glanced at Tate's strong profile, his tanned complexion and sharp cheekbones. I didn't want to talk. I just wanted to be. And to enjoy. And in the spirit of following that same instinct that pushed me onto stage, I lifted a hand to Tate's hair and ran my fingers through it. "I'm going to kiss you," I said.

His eyes widened and darkened all at once. "You do that, and I'm not going to stop you."

"Good." I dragged my thumbs down the sides of his face and pulled his mouth near mine. Parting my lips, I brushed them gently across his, teasing him, taunting him with a promise not yet fulfilled.

He groaned as one hand scooped under my jaw. His fingers trembled against my skin, vibrating with restraint, and he hissed, his lips moving against mine as he spoke. "Shelby, please—"

I didn't let him finish the plea. Pressing my tongue beyond his lips, I moved my mouth hard against his. He crushed me against his body, his hand landing at my hips and squeezing, pulling me into him. I didn't resist. I followed my instincts—followed every gut wrenching, aching pull I had to this guy, and so far, it was serving me well.

I arched farther into the kiss, letting my hand slip under his shirt. My fingers trailed over hard, carved muscle, and his skin was just as hot to touch on the outside as I was on the inside.

Distantly, I heard the sound of an announcer. "The show is starting," I managed to pant, pulling back from his embrace.

"Fuck the fucking show," he growled, claiming my lips with his once more. His hands roamed over my back in long, possessive sweeps until he curved that hand up the back of my neck, stopping suddenly, just short of my hair. *My hair.* I had freaked out when he brushed my hair away. More than once, really. And judging from the way his stomach muscles clenched as he nearly reached my hair, he remembered all too well the reaction I had.

"But these tickets must have cost a fortune."

"Shelby,"—he moved his hands to either side of my face, looking deep into my eyes—"I don't care how much they cost. You want to get out of here?"

I swallowed. This would take us to the next stage. I didn't know if I was ready for it. But I knew I *wanted* to be. "Yeah," I said. "I want to get out of here."

I didn't have to say it twice. Tate had my hand in his, and I don't know how the hell he got us home in such record time, because next thing I knew, we were clambering off the elevator, falling onto the couch, my mouth latched to his.

The couch dipped beneath our weight, groaning.

Or was that Tate?

His lips landed at the base of my throat, dragging up to my ear with a soft nibble that shot raw, biting heat between my legs. A whimper pushed beyond my tightly pressed lips, and

I lifted my pelvis to brush against his, the pressure releasing only a small part of the ache between my thighs.

I slid my hands down his back, yanking the suspenders down over his shoulders, and beneath my touch, his impossibly taut muscles twitched, flexing against my fingers.

Was this moving too fast? What if all these feelings still aren't enough for me to—

I grunted, squeezing my eyes shut against the nagging thoughts, as though darkening the room could also darken my mind.

With a deep breath, I drew my lips to his neck, kissing along the muscles there, roped with tension.

What if he grabs my hair again? What if he sees my scar? My neck was heavy as thoughts itched and threatened to push through.

Bad thoughts.

Doubtful thoughts.

Too many fucking thoughts.

No, not this time. I wasn't going to let fear ruin this amazing night. There was no threat here. And as I pushed those thoughts away, it made room for something new—a feeling that was raw and fresh and made me feel more alive than I had in years.

I opened my mouth, deepening the kiss, sweeping my lips over his. Our movements morphed from frenetic to tender. We were surrounded by the satin and lace and ruffles of my skirt as it bunched around our waists.

Gripping the skirt at the back, he yanked it open with a growl, sending a couple of buttons scattering the floor. I gasped and looked down at the ripped skirt. "Reagan's going to kill you," I whispered.

"I'll write the costume department a check," he said and pulled it over my head, tossing it aside as his hands slid up my hips and sides with an admiring growl.

I speared my greedy tongue back into his mouth, licking over his. Lust, thick and heady, stirred in my chest, quickly followed by a flare of aching need. His eyes fluttered open as he pulled away from our kiss, I moaned, not ready for it to be over. Anticipating my plea, he captured my lower lip between his teeth as my breasts heaved with rapid breaths. "Shelby," Tate said, and he sounded as unraveled as I felt.

I arched my back, and in doing so, despite the layers of clothing still between us, his erection pushed against my clit. I gasped with the sudden burst along all the nerves of my body.

He wet his lips, and his eyes were that impossible shade of blue. "Is this okay?" His grip on my waist was heavy, and when I looked down, I saw his white knuckles. What he really wanted to know was whether or not I was okay.

"Yes." Gripping his hand in mine, I slid his palm up my torso, landing it on my breast. "So is this," I whispered, squeezing for him. His fingers worked my nipple through my shirt, taking over where I had left off.

I moved my hand to his erection, sliding it over his shaft. "And this."

His right arm trembled as he held his weight over me. "Shelby," he said, "this doesn't exactly feel slow."

I grunted. Right now, slow was the last thing on my mind. I wanted fast and sweaty. I gripped him harder, and he groaned, dropping his head to my neck. "Are you sure?" The question was muffled against my shoulder.

"Yes," I croaked. "If it's too much, I'll stop you, I swear—"

He leaned back, tugging his shirt off, and he had those old fashioned pants off in seconds. He pulled a condom from his wallet, setting it beside us on the coffee table, and in another quick movement, my tank top and bra were off, followed quickly by my yoga pants. A breath sucked quietly through his parted lips.

"No panties?" He shook his head as a bemused grin

curved his lips. "You're killing me Shelby."

His lips came crashing down onto mine once more, and I tightened, throbbing for him. Moving down between my legs, he slid his tongue along my length.

Oh God. What if the same thing happens again? What if I start giggling like last time, or worse?

A bubble of doubt expanded in my chest. I needed to do something, fast, to change the pattern. Cupping his face, I pulled him back up to my lips and kissed him. "I need you inside of me," I said. Taking the condom, I ripped it open and slid it on.

"Holy shit," he whispered. "You are so hot." He pushed gently inside of me, pausing halfway. One ache was replaced with an entirely different kind, and I gasped as he waited a moment before moving slowly. His hips thrust in slow, controlled motions, and restraint tightened his features as he examined my face. Sweat pushed out of his pores with each disciplined circling of his hips, and he ran a hand down the side of my ribs. "You okay?" he asked in a gravely voice.

I nodded. Using my heels, I pushed my hips up, meeting him in a deeper thrust. He hit the swollen knot deep inside of me, setting my nerve endings alive, tingling down my legs until my toes curled against the leather couch.

His thumb worked my clit, moving in quick circles, and the tension built inside of me, coiling and uncoiling, over and over again, until I thought I'd explode. It wasn't fair—this was so freaking easy for some women.

I quickened my breaths, matching the faster rhythm in which he slid in and out of me. His hips rotated, flicking at the end of each thrust, claiming me, branding me, as tension and heat spiked in my body. Faster and faster he pumped, eyes on me in an intense stare that would every now and then be broken with a kiss.

"Shelby—I'm so fucking close…I don't know if I can hold

it. Are you—"

He quickened the movements against my clit, and I had to hand it to him…he definitely knew what he was doing. But I was nowhere near an orgasm yet. It felt amazing, and he was so sexy over me, inside me, slick with sweat.

"Shelby—"

Oh God. What do I say? Do I fake it, just to make him feel better? No, that wasn't a solution. Do I just moan and then talk it out after? That would be good. The adult thing to do…talk it out, I mean. Not fake it. *Oh, hell, how long have I just been laying here, staring at him with my mouth open? That's* real *sexy.*

"Shelby," he grunted, crying out my name once more with a final thrust and shivering above me.

"I can't come," I shouted. "I never have." I cringed as soon as the words left my mouth. He twitched, his orgasm pulsing inside of me, and with a shattered breath, his eyes grew wide.

"*W-what?*"

Well, fuck. Any of the other options would have been better than *that*.

Chapter Twenty

Tate

"You what?" No way had I heard that right. Pushing off from the couch, I sat back on my heels and studied Shelby as she covered her face with her hands.

"Oh God. I'm sorry. That was…I'm so stupid."

"Uh…" For the first time in I didn't know how long, I had absolutely nothing to say. "Just with me? Did I do something wro—"

"No." She cut me off. After sitting up, she reached for her shirt. "I swear, it's not you—it's me." Shelby groaned, throwing her head back, and the movement created the most sensuous curve to her neck. "God, that sounds lame, but it's true. I've never been able to—not with myself, not with anyone."

"Not even with *yourself*?" I repeated, quietly. I mean… didn't *everyone* masturbate? I thought that happened early, even for girls.

She shook her head and squeezed my hand. "I'm sorry."

"Whoa, whoa, whoa…" I held up my free hand and shook

the cobwebs from my head. "Let me get this straight. You didn't come. You can't come. And you're apologizing to me for it?" I laughed at the ridiculousness of that, and scooped a hand through my hair.

Her eyes widened.

"Shelby, you don't need to apologize. Not for that. Not ever."

"It *feels* like I should apologize. Because that was really hot. Right up until I ruined it." She hugged the shirt into her body, covering her breasts. Gone was the confident girl who straddled me, licking her way up my neck. In her place was someone who needed a shield, a mask.

I gently took her hands in mine, and with a small tug, I pulled her back into my arms. Her skin was smooth against my fingertips, and I ran my hands up and down her spine. Damn, she felt good in my arms. Soft breasts pressed into my chest, and with each breath she took, they pushed into me harder. "Are you okay?" I asked quietly.

She nodded, not moving from where her cheek nestled into my neck.

"Do you want to talk about why?"

This time, she shook her head no.

"Okay." I curled my arms tighter around her and cradled the back of her head with my palm. Blond hair tangled through my fingers, and I swept the strands from base to tip in soft strokes. Her body only tensed for a moment this time as I brushed my hands through her hair. It was progress. Did she even realize it? That she was letting me touch her hair?

She let me hold her there for a hot second before she pushed away, shoving her arms into the tank top and hopping back into her yoga pants.

"I, um, I should really go," she muttered, head down, avoiding eye contact.

"Shelby, wait—"

She didn't slow down, and instead rushed around my living room, gathering her things. This was her MO, how she handled stress—she fled from it.

"Shelby," I said again, this time loud enough to stop her. Our eyes collided, and a spray of pink flushed across her cheeks. "It's okay if you don't want to talk about this tonight," I managed to say. I got up and moved to her slowly, slipping my palm to her hip. "It's even okay if you don't want to talk about it tomorrow or the next day." Cupping my other hand around her jaw, I dipped my forehead to hers, and our noses brushed.

She swallowed hard. "This whole thing is humiliating," she whispered.

Humiliating. I didn't know how to respond to that. Tell her it was okay? Shit, I didn't know. Maybe it wasn't okay. Maybe *she* wasn't okay. Was it a health thing? Just the thought of that caused my stomach to hollow out. "You *never* have to feel embarrassed around me. Ever. I mean it."

She pushed onto her toes, pressing her mouth gently to mine, her hands lingering at my jaw.

"Please tell me that's not a good-bye kiss," I said.

That earned me a small smile. "It's not a good-bye kiss," she said.

"Good. Cause I want to see you. Like, a lot more."

That got me an even bigger smile. "Still? Even after tonight?"

God, what assholes had this girl been dating? Who the hell would break up with someone over this? But again, I couldn't say that to her. I couldn't downplay what happened and tell her it was no big deal.

It clearly was a big deal to her, even if it certainly wasn't a deal *breaker* for me. Shit. This was hard. I felt like I was swimming through toxic waste with nowhere to go for safety. So instead, I just pulled her into my arms and held her in that hug an extra moment. "Yeah, I still want to see you. Even after tonight." I brushed my lips across her forehead, lingering there a second longer. "Buddy and I will bring you croissants in the morning."

Looking to the floor, she swept her knuckle under her eye, and I could have sworn that a tear stained her cheek.

"I'd like that," she said.

As she got on the elevator, I felt a momentary jolt of unease. Before the elevator doors closed, she came running back out throwing her arms around my neck and kissed me once more good night. Hard. Her lips and tongue working mine in such a needy, intense way that she left me literally panting when she broke the kiss and ran back onto the elevator with a little wave.

"Night, Tate."

"Night, Betty." But the doors had already closed before I said it.

...

Long after Shelby left, I lay in bed, staring at my ceiling. I was used to sleepless nights. Had more than my fair share, actually.

I missed Shelby.

I wanted her here beside me. I wanted to smell the coconut and vanilla in her hair, and watermelon Chap Stick on her lips all night in my dreams.

Questions swarmed in my head, and I hated that she didn't trust me enough to open up. What did most guys say to that kind of information? She must have told other boyfriends, right?

I flipped the sheets off of me, and a wave of cool air brushed over my bare chest. My dick was a fucking steel pipe, and my gym shorts tented as proof of how hot this damn girl made me. I was so turned on that it went beyond frustrating and dived right into the deep end of painful.

I slipped a hand beneath the band of my shorts, fisting my cock. Electricity shot through my veins. Masturbation used to be enough. It used to get me through each sleepless night. But it was as though Shelby flipped a switch in me. What had always sufficed now barely got my engine revved.

An image of Shelby appeared, her golden eyes simmering as she straddled me, lifting up and down against my dick. I groaned, stroking myself, and damn it felt good, fanning the flames and making my skin burn hotter. I jerked, grunting as I came, all the while imagining Shelby crying out in pleasure right along with me. I swallowed, guilt burning through me. Shelby wasn't a virgin—and yet, she hadn't had an orgasm. After I cleaned up, I grabbed my iPad, typing "how to get a girl off" into Google. Oh my God. If the guys ever checked my browser history, they'd annihilate me. Within seconds, thousands—no, tens of thousands of articles filled my screen. I looked at the clock. One thirty.

I should go to sleep. I had practice later. But this seemed wildly more important than anything else in my life.

I clicked on the first article, consuming it entirely within a matter of minutes. Then the next. And the next. They lead me to a handful of books about the G-spot and female orgasms. I one-clicked them and then set my phone alarm for eight a.m. so that I was up in time to bring Shelby croissants. Then, I clicked open the first page to *The G-spot* and settled in to read. If I was going to have sleepless nights, they might as well be productive ones.

Chapter Twenty-One

Shelby

Tate kept his promise the following morning and brought me croissants with jam and butter. He also kept his promise Monday morning with a meat and cheese plate for breakfast (very French of him). In fact, he'd kept it almost every morning since that Saturday night two weeks ago.

Now, I rushed around my apartment, cleaning frantically while simultaneously applying some makeup. I didn't wear it often, but now and then, I'd brush some powder over my nose and lip gloss over my pout. Our week had been extra busy, and we hadn't had a lot of one-on-one time. In the two weeks since I told Tate about my little, um, issue, he had barely laid a hand on me. Yeah, we'd kissed and participated in some over the clothes stuff, but below the belt?

Nothing.

Nada.

I was tired of being treated like a friggin' porcelain doll—and tonight? Tonight, that was going to change.

There was a knock at the door, and I stalled. An armful of dirty laundry was tucked against my body in one arm and my toothbrush stuck out of my foamy mouth. I ran for my bedroom, chucking the laundry in my hamper and spit into the sink, rinsing the toothpaste down. "Coming," I called and fluffed my hair, smoothing the bangs down over my scar.

Swinging the door open, I leaned a shoulder against the molding, lowering my eyelids in what I hoped was a sexy way. "Hey, you," I said, dropping my voice an octave.

Reagan stood there, grinning from ear to ear, and slipped me a knowing wink. "Keep your panties on. It's just me."

I huffed a sigh, letting her in and shutting the door behind her. "What are you doing here?" I asked as she handed me a wine bottle. "And how'd you get by the doorman?"

She rolled her eyes. "Oh, please. Lou loves me. Recognizes me well enough to know I can be just let up." Reagan barged into the kitchen, rummaging through my drawers until she found a bottle opener. "Besides, I'm here to hang out with my best friend, whom I haven't seen in two weeks." She dropped onto my couch, tucking her feet under her.

"Reagan, it's not a good night—"

"Yeah, I know. Because you're seeing your boy toy, right?"

"He's helping me with French—"

"Kissing?" she finished with a smile, and patted the couch beside her. I sighed, falling beside her. "Girl, you know I love you, and no one is happier than me that your hoo-ha is getting some attention. But you can't leave Harrison and I hanging."

"We all just had brunch."

"Yeah—weeks ago, for an hour, before you ran off for another date."

I opened my mouth with a retort before I snapped it shut. She was right. I don't remember the last time Reagan and I hung out just the two of us. It had been longer than three weeks, for sure—since before the night at Petite Moulin

Rouge—whereas we used to see each other almost daily.

"I suck."

"You sure do—otherwise, I doubt a guy like Tate would be with you." She laughed, popping the wine open and pouring us each a glass.

"*Reagan.*"

"Oh, relax. I have to get it all out now before big brother Harrison shows up. He'll freak if I make blow job jokes about you in front of him." She tapped the edge of her glass to mine, holding it up. "To best friends and the guys that can never come between them."

I nodded, taking a sip. "Speaking of—Tate really *is* supposed to help me study tonight. We have a test tomorrow."

Reagan took a glance at her watch. "It's only six. Why don't we all—and by that, I mean you, me, Harrison, *and* Tate—have a few drinks, and then Harrison and I will leave you to it."

I took a deep breath. "I don't know how well that'll go over with the boys, but in theory, it's a good idea."

"You're a loveable girl that both boys feel territorial over. What'd you expect to happen?"

I rolled my eyes. "Harrison doesn't love me *that* way."

She shrugged and sipped her wine. "As if that matters. Besides…Tate gave Harrison tiny éclairs for Christ's sake, Shelby. *Tiny éclairs.*"

"So?" I sent her a questioning look and she rolled her eyes in spite of me with a snort.

"No guy wants another man's leftovers."

I laughed. "I know there's an innuendo in there somewhere, but I'm afraid to ask."

Reagan patted my head, pushing her bottom lip out in a pout. "Oh, sweet Shelby."

Ten minutes of chitchat and catching up flew by. Man, I didn't realize how much I missed our girl time until now.

I wasn't intentionally ignoring them, but it was easy to let friendships slip when you were consumed with lust.

A knock on the door cut us off in the middle of a giggle fit, and Reagan hopped up to answer, finding Tate and Harrison outside, locked in a glaring showdown.

As soon as the door was open, Tate's attention turned to me, then he glanced at Reagan. "I didn't realize this was going to be a party."

"We were surprising Shelby," Reagan said, beaming at all of us with her full wattage smile. She took Harrison's hand, tugging him inside, and he handed me a bouquet of peonies with a kiss on the cheek.

"I know they're your favorite. And I felt like I needed to apologize for my grumpiness the last couple weeks," he said quietly.

"Thanks, Harrison." I filled a vase with water and tucked the flowers inside, pretty sure Reagan had instructed him to bring them to me.

"Shelby and I thought it'd be fun to all share a bottle of wine and get to know each other a little before your study session."

"Sounds good to me," Tate said, sauntering toward me. "So long as we get some studying in for that French test tomorrow." He tapped a finger to the tip of my nose. The air between us crackled as he moved in, pressing his lips to mine in a quick but tender kiss.

"Studying, huh?" Harrison's low voice was quiet, but I jumped at it all the same. "Then you won't mind if I join you?" His brow lifted right along with his smirk. "Since I'm in the same class, too, and all."

Tate's hands on my hips tightened. "If you feel you need the help, absolutely." Then, looking over my shoulder, he sent a grin to Reagan. "Is it French wine, at least? We sorta have a theme going here…"

She shrugged, looking at the label. "Um, *Château Diana*. Sounds French, right?"

He laughed and held up a "wait a minute" finger. "I'll be right back." Backing out the door, he rushed down the hallway and onto the elevator. As soon as the door shut behind him, Reagan was on her feet, smacking Harrison's shoulder, and I was on the other one.

"Ow, *ow*!" he shouted, covering his head. "What the hell?"

"What the hell? *What the hell*?" I repeated. Was he really asking that? He had to know he was being a complete dick. Instead of answering his question, I kept hitting him.

And thank God for Reagan, who jumped in on my behalf. "Harrison Richard Thomson, I swear to God, I promised our best friend a civilized night where we'd share a couple glasses of wine and be on our way. If you do not give us that, I swear by all things holy—"

"Okay, *okay*." He raked a hand through his hair, rubbing his shoulder and looking back and forth between both of us. "Shit."

"What's your problem, anyway?" I folded my arms, narrowing my eyes.

Harrison shook his head. "I just think he seems a little…I dunno. Slimy." He shrugged. "But you seem happy. For the first time in—" He swallowed hard and held my stare.

There was another soft knock and Tate let himself back in, holding up a bottle. "Now *this* is wine. If we're gonna study French, we might as well immerse ourselves, right?"

He grinned at the group, shooting me a wink as Reagan's smile lit up toward me. *I like him*, she mouthed silently.

The remainder of the bottle was drunk without any further drama, and I think I owed that, in part, to Reagan. The glares she kept shooting at Harrison kept him in line, and combined with my hand clasped around Tate's, it seemed to be the recipe for success. At least, no one killed one another.

So I called it a win.

After about an hour, Reagan and Harrison said their goodbyes, and Tate and I hit the books, equipped with a second bottle of wine, cookies, and steak tartare. Rare steak? *Ew.* I poked mine with a fork for a few minutes before ordering my own Chinese takeout. When it arrived twenty minutes later, Tate gave me a chastising look. "Not very French," he *tsked.*

"Oh, please," I said, sliding one of the Chinese food boxes toward him. "Even the French switch it up now and then, right?"

Studying with Tate could barely be defined as that. Yeah, my attention was split, trying to figure out the phrases in French and create an answer that made even the least bit of sense. But mostly it was just us hanging out, speaking in another language. If only my previous French classes had been this awesome, maybe I wouldn't have failed my first test.

"What's that grin for?" he asked, spearing a piece of chicken with a chopstick.

I shrugged, playing off the smile. "Nothing. I just never knew I could like…*French* so much."

"How could you not?" He swallowed the chicken and sipped his wine, gaze dipping to my exposed décolletage. With a heaving breath, he cleared his throat, looking back to his chicken and broccoli. He pinched a bite between his chopsticks, but it slipped through, landing on my floor with a splat. "Son of a bitch," he murmured. "I never did learn how to use these damn things."

"They didn't have sushi in prep school?"

"No, we did—I just never quite got the hang of it." He paused, looking up at me from over his takeout box. "You're mocking me."

"Here." I laughed and got up from the table. "Let me tutor *you* on something for a change." Standing next to his chair, I slid my arms around his and placed the chopsticks properly between his fingers. "There. Now pinch. Try the broccoli—chicken is slippery."

He grasped the broccoli, slowly bringing it to his mouth. Just before it reached his lips, it popped out of the chopsticks, splattering back into the takeout box.

As his head turned, his nose brushed my breast, and I sucked in a breath, startled by just how close his lips were. He made a sort of *hmm* then parted his lips. A devious glint caught the light in his eyes, and that same heat as before spiraled between my legs.

What was it about this guy? From the moment we met, my body had reacted differently around him. Was it just that I finally found someone I was extremely attracted to? Did our pheromones simply match up perfectly? Or was it more than that? Because it felt as though something larger than both of us had brought us together. I mean, he was *so* not my type. And not only because he was spoiled and rich and privileged and…and…

God, so fucking hot. And surprisingly smart. The tips of my breasts tightened and pushed, straining against my bra and T-shirt. Tate growled, pulling me against him, and closed his mouth over my nipple. The fabric scraped against me, and I gasped as he tugged the shirt down, freeing one breast. His hot tongue glided in circles over me, finishing in quick, flicking movements.

I scraped my fingers into his hair, dragging him closer and tighter as he pulled my other breast out, repeating the motions.

I tilted my head back, eyes drifting closed as wetness and warmth rushed through my body. His hands trailed down my sides, landing on my hips, and with a squeeze, he pushed me away. When I looked back down, his biceps were tight, and I was at arm's length, panting, wanting.

He released me, wiping a finger over his lips and tapping

the French book. "Sorry," he said, and his voice sounded hollow, as though I was hearing him through a conch shell. "You need to study. And I need to learn self-control."

Lowering myself, I straddled his lap, facing him, my legs clamped around his hips and pushed into the arms of my kitchen chair. His erection pressed against me in the perfect spot, and I bit back a whimper, tugging my bottom lip between my teeth. "Self-control is overrated," I whispered dragging my lips across his.

He kissed me back, but his hands stayed on my shoulders, like he was ready to end things if we went too far. My face burned—did I make a mistake telling him I couldn't orgasm? Ever since, it seemed that he was handling me with kid gloves. Tonight was the first time my breasts had seen the light of day in his presence since our petite Moulin Rouge night. Usually, guys took the opposite approach; they saw me as a challenge, thinking they had some sort of magic penis that would make me come instantly. While I didn't *love* this about my previous partners, I also didn't love being treated like I was made out of glass. "Tate," I whispered, pulling back.

"I got a new app for us to practice your French with."

I sighed, sliding off his lap and pulling my chair closer beside him as he pulled his iPad out of his backpack and set it in front of me. He turned it on, punching in his code while also reaching for the wine. Those extra few seconds gave me a glance his screen—and at what he'd been reading.

I suddenly forgot all about my French lesson and my sex drive, and blinked, reading the passage from the book that was open. *The Elusive Orgasm.* I clenched the iPad in my hand, tightly, in case he tried to tear it away from me. It was the sort of book written for women in situations like mine. Women who couldn't climax.

"No, don't—" Tate started, reaching for the iPad, but quickly gave up, dropping his face into a hand.

"What's this?" I asked, skimming the page that was open on the screen. He didn't answer at first, but dragged his hand down over his nose, landing at his stubble and scratching his chin.

"I, uh, I don't know. I just wanted to learn more. Know more about what—if anything—I could do to, I don't know… help." He shook his head, grabbing the iPad from me and clicking open a French learning app. "It was stupid, I know. I'm sorry—"

"No," I cut in, grasping his face between my hands. "Not stupid." I shook my head. All through my adult life, guys just did with me what they did with every girl. But here in front of me was a guy willing to read, and learn, and research. Tingles swirled down my chest, dropping into my stomach.

"It's sweet. And wonderful. And…and it makes me feel really special."

Wrapping his hand around the back of my neck, he pulled me gently down to his lips. "Shelby, you *are* special."

I slid my hand up his thigh until he caught my hand, head falling back with a groan.

"*Qu'est-ce que je vais faire avec toi?*" he asked.

"I don't know," I said. "What are you going to do with me, Tate?"

Mischief and arousal sparked in those crystalline eyes of his. "I know what I want to do," he said quietly.

My eyes flicked to the iPad. "Why don't you show me what you've learned in your little private reading sessions?"

He swallowed so hard that I saw the muscles at his throat contract. "Okay," he said, nodding. "If you can translate this sentence in under five seconds." A deep breath dragged through his lips, and the words flew past his tongue, faster than I'd ever heard him speak French to me before. "*Je veux va te faire foutre tellement dur. Je vais t'emmener au septieme ciel avec ma langue et ma queue.*"

My mind flew through the French words I knew. Shit. Shit, shit, shit… It went so quickly, I barely got the words, let alone the order of them. *Avec ma queue…* with my…What the hell was *queue*?

"And…time," Tate whispered, pressing a kiss to my jaw. "Five seconds is up. Time to study."

"That's not fair. You went too fast."

He shrugged. "You think Ceele is going to wait for you to be ready? You think he's going to slow his speech patterns to make it easier?"

Damn him. "Well, next time *you're* turned on and ready to, you know…I'll be sure to bring up Ceele, as well." I gave him a playful tap on the cheek.

A deep laugh rumbled from Tate's chest and he nodded, sliding the French book back over to me. "Fair enough. Now study."

Chapter Twenty-Two

Shelby

I chose the wrong damn night to pick up a shift at Magnolia's. The night dragged on. And on a Saturday—a night that we were almost guaranteed tips, I'd hardly served three tables. And yet, my manager refused to release any of the waitstaff.

I wiped down my two-top that just paid, flicking a glance at the bill. They tipped okay—I'd seen much worse from students on a date, that was for sure. I centered the vase and flower on the table and reset the condiments.

Out of the corner of my eye, I glimpsed a flash of emerald green as the front door swung open. When I looked up, Reagan and Harrison crawled into one of the bar top tables. Her skintight green dress hugged her slim curves, standing out in a sea of beige and black.

Clutching the rag, I headed over. "Hey guys, what are you doing here?" I did a quick wipe down of their table before flopping onto my elbows in front of them.

"Whoa, it's so quiet. Like a funeral is happening here,"

Reagan said.

"Yeah, weird juju tonight," I answered.

Harrison gave me a sympathetic half smile. "Sorry. I can promise that we tip well, though."

I rolled my eyes. "Too bad I won't be the one to get it. The bartender waits on this section."

Reagan leaned over, looking beyond me to where Dave poured a beer. Her eyes drifted up and down as she wet her lips. "Mm, he can serve me for sure."

Harrison shook his head, busying himself with the menu.

"Him?" I cast a glance over my shoulder at Dave. "He's so old, though."

Reagan scrunched her face. "Oh, come on. He can't be older than what? Thirty?"

I shrugged.

"Well, I'd still rather have you as a waitress," Harrison said. "When are you going to get licensed as a bartender so *you* serve us at the bar, instead?"

I looked again toward the bar. This time I saw Dave's dark gaze collide with Reagan's, and he smirked.

When I turned back around, I was met with Reagan's raised brow. "Seriously, what's his story?" she asked.

"I'm not sure. I thought I heard him say he was married, though."

She shook her head. "No ring."

"No intelligent bartender would wear a wedding ring," Harrison chimed in.

"See? Harrison knows what's up." I winked.

As I turned, I slammed into Dave, who was smoothing his crisp white dress shirt. "Hey now," he joked, nudging me with an elbow. "Don't be stealing my tables when it's slow." He flashed Reagan a smile.

"Dave, these are my friends, Harrison and Reagan. Take good care of them." I rested a hand on his shoulder before pushing off to see how long I'd have to wait before getting another tip.

At the hostess stand, I was peering around Alexis to see the seating chart when Ross, my manager came up behind me. "Sorry it's been so slow, Stevens. You wanna be cut?"

Thank *God*. "Sure. Thanks for letting me fill in, though."

Ross smiled and placed a hand on his bulging belly. "We miss you around here. You ever wanna come back, there's always a spot for you."

"Thanks." I smiled. Ross was a good boss. And in the restaurant business, that was sometimes hard to find.

"Actually—you wanna work over Parents' Weekend?"

I grinned. Oh, *hell* yeah. Parents' Weekend was the best.

"Guaranteed to be a good night for tips," Ross continued as if he had to convince me to come in. "And most of our student servers want the weekend off because their own parents—" Ross's face dropped, his cheeks turning a ruddy color. "Crap. I'm sorry, Shelby. I wasn't thinking."

A knot bulged in my throat at the thought of my mom. "It's okay, Ross. I'd love to take a shift. At least one night that weekend."

He sighed and ran a hand over his goatee. "Perfect. I'll put you on the schedule and let you know."

I glanced at Reagan and Harrison, whose drinks just arrived, and untied my apron. "You cool with me having a drink or two with my friends over there?"

He chuckled with a glance at the bar, the heaviness lifting from his sagging features. "Hell, not like we have any other customers hanging around. Knock yourself out."

My phone buzzed, and Tate's message blinked at me.

Want to come over tonight when I'm done with poker?

Sure. I'm at Magnolia's with Harrison and Reagan. I'll

swing by after.

"So, what *are* you two doing here?" I sank into a seat, and even though it wasn't a busy night at all, my feet still throbbed from being on them all day. Dave put a glass of white wine in front of me with a wink. "Thank you," I called after him as he went back to the bar.

"Well," Harrison's smile widened as he pulled out his phone. "We know how hard you've been working—studying, waitressing, tutoring—all that."

"*And*," Reagan cut in, "we wanted to get you something."

I opened my mouth, ready to object, when Reagan held up a hand. "Don't fucking fight us on this, Shelby. Your birthday is coming up, and you need it."

From his back pocket, Harrison pulled an envelope and set it down in front of me. A deep breath expanded in my lungs, and I let it out slowly. "Guys—I don't like charity."

"I know," Harrison began quietly, "but with graduation this year, you're going to be interviewing for jobs soon."

Reagan nudged the envelope closer to me. "And your only 'business' clothes are covered in stains and have a permanent smell of soul food." She glanced around the restaurant. "High end soul food, but still." Her face twisted. "It's not exactly the impression you want to give to the head of the international division of Hilton."

"Hilton?" I snorted, rolling my eyes. "As if I'll even get a job interview there." I opened the envelope to find a Macy's gift card. I swallowed, warmth rising in my throat and prickling behind my eyes. "Thank you, but I can't take this. I have money…I can go buy a new suit."

"It's a birthday gift." Harrison looked to Reagan as though they knew this would be my reaction. "You can't turn down a birthday gift."

I nodded as the tears caught at the back of my throat.

"Thank you," I managed to choke. "My birthday isn't for a month, though."

"Trust me," Reagan said from over her glass of wine. "You'll need a business suit sooner more than later. You'll be surprised how quickly meetings and networking events will pop up."

"You know"—Harrison grinned, leaning back in his chair and taking a gulp of beer—"our test scores will probably be posted on Ceele's forum when we get home." He jerked his head toward the envelope. "We could see if that's just a big fat waste of money."

Crumpling the napkin in my hand, I threw it at his face as he laughed. It bounced off his cheek and landed right in his beer, sending molasses-colored liquid spilling down the sides of the glass. "Why are you even in Ceele's class?" I asked.

"I don't know. I needed an extra elective credit, and it might be fun to travel." Harrison shrugged, picking the saturated napkin from his beer and placing it on the other side of the table. "Get the hell out from under my dad's thumb. No one over there will care that he's a police commissioner in Podunk, South Carolina."

My gut clenched at the mention of his father and my limbs went numb. I needed to be a friend. Harrison had been there for me all through high school, whenever I needed him. And if he needed to talk about his dad, then goddammit, I had to listen. But that didn't mean I had to be sober in doing so.

I turned in my chair, signaling for Dave to get me another wine, then I tipped back, slamming the remaining liquid in my current glass. Reagan wooted from beside me, laughing, but her giggles sounded far away.

"So…" I looked once more to Harrison, blinking my eyes open. "Going to France to get the hell out of here, huh?"

Chapter Twenty-Three

TATE

Saturday night usually meant one thing. Poker night with me and the guys. I sighed, looking at my cards, which really gave me a big, fat nothing of a hand. I couldn't keep my mind on the game. Shelby said she had to work, but was the tutoring center even open on Saturdays? And now she was with her friends at Magnolia's clear on the other side of town? It didn't make any sense. I gulped. Was she lying to me? Even just the thought of that made me grip my cards so tight, I damn near bent the corners. Maybe she was really grabbing a drink with her creepy boss, Ryan.

No. She wasn't Katie. This was Shelby. Sweet, honest, sexy Shelby.

I tossed another chip into the center of the table, not even sure why I wasn't just folding, and glanced up to find Logan studying my face carefully. I cleared my throat and draped my arm over the back of my chair. "Was that Katie I saw you with the other day?" I asked, trying to sound casual.

Logan's jaw twitched, and he nodded. "Yeah. We've been hanging out."

Chase buried his nose deeper into his cards, and Brad eyed me carefully.

"You know to be careful with her, right?"

A grin stretched across Logan's face. "Oh, I'll be careful all right."

I rolled my eyes with a half-snort, half-laugh. "What the hell does that even mean?" I shook my head as Logan upped the bet with another chip. "I'm serious, though. She cares more about your trust fund than you."

"That's A-okay by me." Well, at least I tried. When she poked holes in his condoms and trapped him into a marriage, he couldn't say I didn't warn him.

"Dude." Brad rapped my elbow with his knuckle. "I raised."

Swiping a hand down my face, I threw my cards onto the table. "I'm out." I had nothing. I grunted, pushing back from the table, standing. Bottles clanked against the fridge door as I grabbed another beer. No big deal. The sooner I lost this game, the sooner I could kick these assholes out and see Shelby.

Chase scooped the cards together as Brad stretched back in his chair.

"You see that clip I sent y'all?" Logan asked, southern drawl dripping from his deep voice.

I shook my head, bottle to my lips, mid sip.

"Logan, don't pull that shit up. I'm a porn connoisseur, and that shit doesn't deserve the light of day," Brad grumbled and finished the rest of his beer quickly.

Chase laughed. "It's bad if even Brad won't watch it."

Logan hopped up, grabbing my laptop from the coffee table and opening it so that we could all see it. "Don't be a pussy. This shit is crazy."

Brad shot me a glare, and his chair scraped the floor as he jumped to his feet, storming into the kitchen.

Unease burrowed in my belly. Damn, Brad was a pretty hardened dude. Watched a lot of shit. I knew Chase was joking, but there might be some truth to that statement. If *he* thought this clip was too much, maybe we *shouldn't* be watching it. "Isn't watching porn together gay or something?" I joked in an effort to lighten the mood.

But Logan kept typing an address into the browser and then slid the laptop to Chase and me, presenting it as though we were about to see some fine piece of cinema or something. "And here we go," he said quietly, hitting play.

My heart dropped to my stomach as I processed the clip. A girl was tied to the bed—hands and feet bound, one on each bedpost. She was completely naked, legs spread wide, and blindfolded. Okay, that in itself was kind of hot. Only, the man was rough—really rough. And her screams didn't sound like cries of passion. I gulped, and my chest felt hollow as I continued watching. I slid a glance at Chase, who seemed just as horrified as me. As she screamed *no* another guy came onto the set and shoved his dick into her open mouth.

The laptop clapped as I slammed it shut. "That's enough," I grunted, my voice hoarse.

Brad leaned against the kitchen counter with his back to us, shaking his head.

"Intense, right?" Logan's eyes sparked with desire. Chills ran the length of my spine, and I shook them off. I didn't like this side of Logan. At all. A moment of concern for Katie tightened in my stomach. And *fuck* if I'd ever let this guy anywhere near Shelby.

"Are we going to play fucking poker, or are we going to watch porn together like a bunch of pussies?" Chase said, shuffling the deck. He had already taken his seat back over near the table, his skin, oddly sallow.

"Actually, guys, I think I might call it a night." I cleared my throat, tossing the empty bottles into the recycling.

Chase gestured to my clock. "It's only eleven-thirty."

I shrugged. "It's been a long week."

"We gotta settle up," he said, clearing his throat. "Where you hiding your dough, Michaelson?" Brad pushed off the counter, grabbing his wallet, and a look passed between us. I nodded at him. We'd been friends long enough to understand each other without using words, and he didn't like that video any more than I did.

I nodded toward my backpack as I picked up the remaining empty bottles, cleaning up. "In the front pouch, I think. I owe seventy-five bucks, if you wanna grab it." When I looked up again, Logan had my laptop open again. "I'm serious, Logan. Don't use my computer to look at shit like that."

"I'm not looking at porn, dude," he said. I heard a few more muffled laughs until finally I looked over to find the guys huddled around my laptop, snickering. I crossed over to find them scrolling through my Amazon account where it said *Because you bought The Elusive Orgasm…* followed by a list of other titles on the topic. Their fists were clenched in front of their mouths, covering their laughter.

"Holy shit," Chase said, gasping between laughs. "Tate, you always can come to me if you needed a tutor."

"Have you learned nothing from all the videos I sent you?" Logan finished for him.

"Okay, okay." I snatched the laptop from their hands, closing it and setting it aside on my coffee table. Grabbing my wallet from my backpack, I threw some cash down. "You're all fucking hilarious. Here's your money. Now get the hell out."

One by one, I shoved them out the door and onto the elevator. I couldn't fault them for giving me shit—hell, if I had found those books on any of their laptops, I would have done the same fucking thing. It was just how we operated. But that didn't mean I had to stand there and listen to it in my own home all fucking night.

"Look," Brad said, holding the elevator door open and leaning toward me. His voice was quiet, and his eyes soft in a moment of sincerity. "If you need to talk, or you need a few pointers…I'd be happy to tag in and show her—"

He didn't even finish before the guys were back to howling with laughter. Chase tugged him into the elevator. They're lucky the doors shut before I fucking throttled him and shoved him in there myself.

I sighed, dragging a hand through my hair, and looked around the apartment—considering I just had three drunk guys in here for several hours, the place wasn't quite the disaster it could be.

The elevator dinged once more, and from the kitchen I called out, "Which one of you dumbasses forgot something?"

There was no answer, and I pushed open the door to my foyer to find Shelby, arm outstretched, leaning against the wall in the most sexily disheveled manner I'd fucking ever seen.

And she was pretty damn tipsy.

Chapter Twenty-Four

Shelby

The elevator jolted to a stop, sending my stomach into my throat. The floor was like Jell-O beneath me. As the doors slid open, I slowly made my way into the lobby. It only took Tate a second to hear me enter and come out to the elevators. I rushed at him, throwing my arms around his neck and pressing my lips into the crook of his shoulder. He smelled fresh and clean—sexy, like always.

"Shelby." He exhaled my name as though it was one with his breath. "Are you okay?" He grabbed my hand, tugging me inside, and the room was foggy like mist on a swamp. I inhaled deeply. Cigar smoke?

I knew my hair was a mess, and I probably smelled like a restaurant, but I didn't care. I had Tate in my arms. He grinned down at me, eyebrows raised. "Had a few too many, huh?"

Sighing, I pulled him against me tighter, my breasts aching to be touched, my body tingling for attention. "Not too many." I shook my head. "Just enough."

From his hold on my waist, he lifted me from the floor, and I was floating across his kitchen to the couch. "Well, I'm just glad you're here. Even if you regret your drinks in the morning." His dimples deepened, and I leaned forward, pressing my lips to one in a lingering kiss. God, I wanted him. More than I ever wanted anyone in my life. Every time I saw him, my heart leaped into my throat.

"Shelby," he began, pulling my hand up. "You can set your phone down, you know."

Oh, shit. That's right—I came here for a reason. I shook my head, dragging a hand through my ponytail. "Our grades are posted from our French test," I said, keeping the waver in my voice as smooth as possible.

Tate's face dropped. "They are?" He looked to my phone, then back to me, eyes wide. "Look, no matter what it is, you've worked so hard. Ceele has to see how you've been try—"

My face split into a grin as I held up my phone. "I got a ninety-one," I blurted out.

The breath gushed out of Tate in an exaggerated sigh, and he crushed me into a hug. "Ninety-one—that's great!" Tate hopped to his feet, me still in his arms, and twirled about the room. Buddy followed at our heels, barking and jumping. "Babe, that's amazing. You deserve it."

"I think I might throw up if you keep spinning me," I squeaked. Tate immediately stopped, placing me gently back on my feet. He cupped my jaw, pulling me in for a kiss. Once my knees stopped quivering, I slid my hands down his arms, certain—or at least, fairly confident—that I wouldn't fall if I just held onto him.

"Thank you," I said. "I couldn't have done it without your help."

He rolled his eyes. "Oh, please. You're the smartest girl I know. You would have learned the language and aced that test with or without me."

Scooping his arms behind my neck and lower back, Tate dipped me, his nose brushing against the hollow of my neck. "But it wouldn't have been nearly as fun as it's been with me." He winked.

"You got that right, Archie," I said through a smile.

"I have a surprise for you," he said. "I wasn't planning on giving it to you tonight. I was going to wait until after midterms. But, well, you're here. And you deserve something to celebrate."

A present? Other than Harrison, I didn't think any guy had ever surprised me with a gift for no reason.

He took my hand and pulled me into his bedroom, grabbing a wrapped box from his closet and setting it on the bed. "This is only the first part of the gift. I have to get the rest of it ready." He spun around to face me, grinning and excited, like he'd been waiting to give it to me. I didn't even know what it was, but his thoughtfulness made him that much more sexy. My body heated as I stared at him, my nipples peaking beneath my shirt. Tate growled, dragging me to his lips for a fevered kiss. "Goddamn, just when I think you can't get any sexier."

He left the room, closing the door behind him. With a timid hand, I reached for the box, pulling at the satin red bow. Folded perfectly inside the box was a fluffy pink robe. It was neither overly sexy, nor totally casual, and it had just the tiniest touch of beads and lace decorating the seams. I thought back to my old cotton robe that he'd seen me in a few weeks ago. The pink color had long since faded, and it had frayed along the edging. Shimmying out of my skirt, I yanked my shirt overhead and paused, looking down at my basic cotton panties and sports bra. A groan echoed in my spinning head and I braced myself on the dresser. Could I have chosen less sexy underwear for tonight?

Jeez, think before leaving your apartment, Shelby. Even if you're just going to work.

I mentally face-palmed myself before wiggling out of my underwear and tucking my clothes in the corner of his bedroom.

The robe was so soft across my sensitive skin, like I was wrapped in a cloud. Twirling in front of Tate's full-length mirror, I tied the belt loosely around my hips, the strip of skin between my breasts glistening with a sheen of sweat. The robe was short, the hem only hitting about mid-thigh, leaving a lot of my legs showing. With a quick tug of my ponytail, my hair tumbled down my shoulders in messy waves, and I scrunched it with a hand, licking my lips.

My body was on fire—ready, swollen, and more than wanting this. Wanting Tate. I wandered around his room—he only had a couple of photographs in frames. One of him and a group of guys in some sort of beer pong championship. I assumed the other picture was him and his parents, sitting on a beach somewhere breathtakingly beautiful. His mom was perfect—the quintessential debutante mother. I swallowed hard. My mother had been that woman once. She had spent her days on PTA boards, planning charity events, and attending functions in gowns that cost more than my monthly rent. That had been her life. I gulped. That had been *my* life.

The door clicked and swung open on the other side of the room, and I jumped, startled. Jesus, how drunk was I?

I spun to find Tate standing in the doorway, shirtless, in only his mesh basketball shorts. They hung low on his narrow hips, and the white contrasted with his bronzed skin. He was lean and solid. All that basketball practice was paying off, and his pecs and biceps bulged with the proof. I followed the line of his torso with my eyes, gliding down his solid stomach to the defined muscles that created an arrow from his hips down to his—well, you know. Talk about bulging.

My throat was dry, and a flush of heat swept my body.

"Holy shit," he whispered as he looked me up and down, his eyes lingering on my bare legs. I resisted the desire to hug the robe closed entirely. Instead, in a moment of bravery, I pinched the edging, running my fingers slowly up and down the billowed opening. My knuckles grazed the swell of my breast, and my nipples tightened.

"This is beautiful. Thank you so much."

"I know you have one already, but I thought maybe—"

"I love it," I reiterated.

He cleared his throat, breaking the trance, and rushed to his nightstand where there was another wrapped present.

I put my hands to my hips. "You don't have to buy me things, Tate."

He closed his eyes, breathing silently for a moment while a peaceful smile tilted his lips.

"I love that you said that," he whispered, the smile widening. "But *this* gift, especially, you're really going to want." Lacing our fingers, he guided me out of the bedroom, and I followed without further argument. He threw a grin at me from over his shoulder. "You got an A on your test. You deserve a reward."

I rolled my eyes. My head was foggy, but not *that* foggy. "An A minus. And you only just found that out now."

He stopped in front of the bathroom door. "I knew you would." There was tenderness in his voice, and it cracked as he studied me. He turned away, forcing himself to break eye contact, and he fiddled with the doorknob.

I narrowed my eyes, giving him a sidelong glance. "What's going on, Tate?"

"Well," he started. "You wanted to know what I had learned in my…um…reading. And you're tipsy, but not drunk. It might be a good time to try something new."

My pulse jumped at the mention of the orgasm books. What could they possibly have said about my own body that I didn't know already? Well, probably a lot, actually, considering I had no idea what I was doing half the time. What I didn't know about orgasms could fill a library.

"One of the key things it said was that the likelihood of a man bringing your first orgasm is really low." His lips twitched into a half smile as he continued. "As much as I would love to be the exception to this, the realistic approach is that you need to know how to please yourself before anyone else." With his turn of the knob, the bathroom door swung open to a low-lit bubble bath, and a couple of candles in the corner.

I curled my arm around Tate's waist, tugging him into my body. As he hit a button on his phone, soft music played through the speakers. "This is for us?" I blinked up at him as those steel eyes of his flashed an almost silvery blue.

"This is for *you*. And this—this is for you, too. I don't know if you have one or not, but, well…it should at least help. And if it doesn't happen tonight, that's okay. I just want you to relax and enjoy yourself."

I opened the second gift to find a small, waterproof Pocket Rocket. My face burned, and I was too mortified to look up at him yet. His chuckle from above made me snap my attention forward, and he raised an eyebrow.

"I didn't want it to embarrass you…it's just…I don't know. Every girl should have one, right?"

Reagan had said the exact same thing to me once. But every time I went to buy one, I chickened out.

I dragged a deep breath through my nose and sighed it out. "You're right—it's really thoughtful. Thank you." I turned the toy over in my hands. I had no idea how to use one of them, but holy shit, I wasn't about to admit that to Tate. It had to be pretty self-explanatory, right?

"Here, let me." He took the box from my hands and opened it, holding the small device out to me. "I already put batteries in and washed it," he whispered.

Instead of taking it from him, I stepped back, slipping the robe from my shoulders. It fell, pooling by my feet. I moved to the tub, bending slowly to drag my hand across the bubbles. A sharp breath behind me was followed by a shuffle of footsteps, and when I looked over my shoulder, Tate was staring at me, leaning against the sink.

"I think you should stay—and help."

His eyes flickered, the orange glow of the candlelight contrasting with the cool blue in his eyes. "I'll meet you half way," he whispered. "I'll stay and *watch*—if you're comfortable with that."

Holy hell. *Was* I comfortable with that? I wasn't sure I was comfortable with *any* of it, to be honest. My insides felt two sizes too large for my skin, and the room temperature must have spiked twenty degrees. But despite my nerves, I found myself nodding.

I dipped a toe into the bath water, and after a moment, lowered in the tub. Tate sat on the toilet, watching intently. Bubbles encompassed me, popping along my heated skin like a thousand tiny kisses over my body. The temperature of the water combined with Tate's searing gaze had me melting like a piece of candy left in the midday sun.

Was I really doing this? In front of him?

Hell, I was the one who'd asked him to stay.

It was new. And I wanted it. I wanted him here, experiencing this with me. My hand fluttered down between my breasts, slick with water and soap. As my fingers skimmed across my nipples, the ache between my thighs tightened. My fingernails dragged slowly down my stomach, and I caught my lip between my teeth, snapping my eyes open. He was staring as though there was nowhere else he wanted to be. As the edges of my fingers brushed between my legs, adrenaline spiked, my muscles instinctually bucking against my touch.

"Tate," I panted, and his lips tipped into a barely there

smile.

"Yeah, babe?"

"I–I can't…"

His eyes softened, but he cut me off. "Does it feel good?"

I nodded, my breath shattering through my clenched teeth.

His smile widened. "Then, yes, you can." The low, throaty growl of his voice was darker than usual. "Turn your new toy on." Was it a command? A request?

Did I care?

My heart was running a marathon in my chest, slamming into my ribs with each frenetic beat. What was I doing? Beneath the surface of the water, I flipped the vibrator on, and it hummed against my body as I slowly moved it down. Gently at first, I pressed it against my clit, and I jumped at the fiery contact. Holy shit—no finger in history could achieve that sensation. With another deep breath, I brushed it against myself once more. This time my grunt came from the back of my throat.

Tate's cheeks reddened as he breathed heavily. I had no idea what the fuck I was doing. Not that that mattered, because everything was working just fine. The vibrator turned the small flame within me into a raging inferno, and Tate watching me simply added the accelerant.

With the vibrator barely touching me, I stroked myself, and the ache, the tingle, flared down to my toes, which curled against the porcelain tub. A moan escaped as I pushed the vibrator deeper. Wow. Okay, yep—that felt good. Water splashed around me as I rocked my hips in circles, the water growing clearer as the bubbles melted away. The tension mounted inside of me, spreading to my chest, and a swell of panic caught in my throat. What was I doing? This wasn't me. I didn't masturbate with a hot guy watching me from the toilet. I wasn't satin and silk. I was cotton. Boring, plain cotton. My moan turned into a gasp as pressure clamped onto my throat. Oh God. No. I squeezed my eyes shut, pushing my toes into the bathtub. Not here. Not with Tate—I could not have another panic attack in front of him. I opened my eyes, searching for him, and this time concern marred his brows. His gaze washed over me like a calming wave, and I breathed in his demeanor. "I need you," I whispered. Damn, that was hard as hell to admit, and yet, it slipped out easier than I expected. I blamed the alcohol. With my admission, his lips parted. He was on his feet in seconds, crouching beside the tub, his hand brushing gently across my cheek.

"I'm here," he rasped. His touch was a comfort I hadn't experienced from a man before. I grasped the edge of the tub with my free hand, knuckles almost as white as the bubbles dissolving around me. The panic melted, disappearing into a sea of abandon and passion.

"Touch me," I whimpered, pushing the vibrator firmer against myself. It sent another jolt straight through me.

His lips quirked and that dimple appeared. "I don't think you need my hand right now," he chuckled. "You're doing perfectly on your own."

"But I want your hands on me," I whispered. When I opened my eyes, I saw Tate shaking his head.

"Nope," he whispered, leaning back. "I'm here—but you have to do this yourself, Shelby."

"I hate you," I managed to say through a trembling smile, and shot him a quick glance from the corner of my eyes.

His grin was the only response I got. I closed my eyes and imagined Tate's hand between my legs—imagined his lips on my neck, traveling up to my mouth and ravaging me. A whip lashed through my body as the tension shattered, diffusing my thought-ridden mind into an array of random images and— feelings. Oh God, the feelings. I spasmed around the vibrator, and my swollen, hot flesh cooled as the tremors rocked through me. They spiraled down to my fingertips and toes, my spine straightening as the tingles quieted.

I panted. The water had turned tepid somewhere between my getting in and my first ever orgasm.

My first *ever* orgasm.

Holy. Shit.

It actually happened.

I opened my eyes. Tate sat with one leg up, elbow resting across it. "Welcome back." His grin widened, if that was even possible.

I sighed, lowering my face and head into the water to rinse away the sweat that had gathered along my hairline. Tate's eyes flashed as I stood in the tub, dripping water like Niagara Falls.

Grabbing the largest, fluffiest towel from a hook on the door, he wrapped it around me. His hands clasped my shoulders, pulling me in for a kiss. "That might have been the sexiest fucking thing I've ever witnessed." His breath was warm against my mouth, and as his grin pressed into my lips, all I responded with was a soft sigh.

Instead of words, I slid my hand up his thigh, landing with a grip on his erection. It was steel in my fist, and I worked it in up and down strokes. Within a couple of seconds, he gently held my wrist, lowering my hand. "Shelby," he whispered. "Tonight's about you. Only you."

And with that, he lowered to his knees. He darted a tongue out gently, licking my length and sucking my clit into his mouth. I cried out, grasping his hair. Oh my God…no, I couldn't. Not this soon after. How could someone go from zero orgasms to two in a ro—*Oh*. His tongue delved inside, thrusting deep before he moved back to my clit, flickering his tongue in a motion so quick it put the vibrator to shame. Heat slammed into my veins, traveling fast like a river, and I tensed with the flash of delicious warmth. A shiver skated across my skin with his deep, raspy chuckle from between my legs. His hands held my hips in a way that made me feel safe. His tongue worked deeper, more urgently against me, and his hand slid from my thigh to my ass where he cupped the tender skin there. I nearly toppled over as lightning struck twice, sending another bolt directly into my heart and, well—elsewhere.

He smiled up at me proudly and pushed to his feet. He smoothed my wet hair back, and I closed my eyes against his tender hold. Then, he stilled, hands frozen in my hair. Silently, he leaned in closer to examine me. Not my eyes, but…oh God. No. My stomach dropped to the floor, and I slapped a hand to my temple, where my wet hair had revealed the angry scar that traveled the edge of my hairline.

Fear and panic erupted inside of me, drowning any bit of happiness and passion I had felt earlier. I squeezed my eyes shut, willing the scene before me to disappear. This was not how this was supposed to play out.

"What happened?" he whispered. And there on his face, I saw it—the same thing I saw on everyone who discovered my scar. Sadness. Pity.

Yanking out of his hold, I smoothed my wet hair into place over the scar, clasping the towel around my dripping body.

My lip trembled as I stumbled back a step, heel colliding with the cold tub. "I need to go," I croaked.

His shoulders stiffened, and he stepped in my way as I attempted to push past him. "Christ, Shelby...*talk* to me."

"Please, just let me go." My voice broke right along with my heart as I moved past Tate and into the bedroom where I'd left my clothes piled.

He followed behind me, even though he said nothing. When I spun around, half dressed, he barred the doorway, arms outstretched, blocking my way.

"You can't keep me here," I yelled, my voice shrieking in a way I hadn't meant it to.

He moved forward with both hands up. "Stop running, Shelby. Talk to me. Maybe I can help."

I snorted at that, shoving my arms into my shirt. "I'm beyond help. You should know that by now."

Chapter Twenty-Five

TATE

"Well, that's just bullshit," I grunted as Shelby pushed past me, grabbing her bag from my coffee table.

"You wouldn't understand." Her voice cracked as she rummaged around her bag then scoured the room. "Where's my phone," she said, more to herself than me.

"What? What wouldn't I understand?" I dipped to meet her gaze, but she was doing everything in her power to ignore me. "Shelby." I gripped her shoulders, squeezing harder than I meant to. Beneath my grasp, she yelped and fell to the couch, curling her knees to her chin.

"Fuck." I rubbed a hand over my eyes and lowered myself, sitting beside her but at a distance. "I–I'm sorry. I—Jesus, I'm sorry. I don't know what else to say. I need you to talk to me."

"I don't know that I can," she snapped.

I lifted my hands, dropping them to my thighs in defeat. "All I've had are these little glimpses of understanding that I've gotten between the times that you *don't* fucking talk to me. I like you. I really do, but if we're going to keep seeing each other, I need you to let me in."

"That's not true," she whispered, shaking her head, and a silent tear slid down her face.

I swallowed. "It *is* true. I don't know how to help. Or hell, how to even talk to you about certain topics if you won't open up even a little."

Her face turned whiter than the wet towel clenched in her hands.

Shit. Please don't cry more. "Would it help if I shared something first?" I asked.

She didn't say yes, but she didn't say no, either.

I took a deep breath. "My family sucks," I said, and she rolled her eyes, shoving to her feet once more. "No, hear me out." I held up a hand, but didn't dare to touch her as she sank back down next to me, alert, her spine stiff, ready to leave at any moment. But at least I had her sitting again. Emotion twisted in me—I had never admitted this out loud. It was weird, foreign. And even though I spoke a couple of languages fluently, the words got lost somewhere between my brain and my tongue.

"My dad has never said I love you. My mom only ever hugged me—hell, *touched* me—when there were cameras around. And sometimes…" I dragged another deep breath in through my nose. Did I sound utterly ridiculous? Too *oh, poor little rich boy*? But it was true. And I knew that it had fucked me up. "Sometimes I think I was only born because it was the right political move at the time for them."

"That's terrible." Shelby shook her head.

I used the movement to scoot closer and put my hand on her knee. To her credit, she barely flinched. "My life was a whirlwind of events and shit I didn't give a crap about. And freshman year here, I met a girl who I thought loved me back. We had a year of dating exclusively. I took her to every event and party. I bought her dinners and gowns and hired limos…" My voice cracked, and I rolled my eyes to the ceiling. "And I was young and naive enough to think that she was in it for me.

"When our first year was over, I proposed, only my parents wouldn't give me access to my trust fund for a ring. She was annoyed, but it wasn't until I presented her with a pre-nup that she flipped out. She made a lot of good arguments about how insulting a pre-nup is, and so I used every bit of money saved from my allowance to buy her a small ring until my trust was released. Only when I went over to her place, I found her in bed with some random dude. I'd never even seen him before. She didn't want to marry me. I was interchangeable, as long as she got a certain lifestyle. She wanted to be the governor's daughter-in-law, and that was it."

Shelby snorted, rolling her eyes at that. "As if *that* life is something to desire."

My eyes widened at that. "*Exactly*. See? That's why I need you to not run. I need you, Shelby. And, I mean, maybe I'm wrong…but I think you need me, too."

A sad smile tilted one side of her mouth. "Since when did you become so co-dependent?"

Relief flooded through me. A joke—thank God for that. "Just because you can't see my scars doesn't mean they don't exist."

Shelby stood slowly, tossing the pillow back on the couch, and hoisted her purse onto her shoulder, moving toward the elevator. I let her go this time. Emotion swelled in my chest, and I thought I might throw up.

There was a sniffle from the doorway, and when I peeked an eye open, Shelby leaned against the door. "You coming?" she said with a jerk of her head.

I jumped to my feet, grabbing the nearest T-shirt and shoving my head through it. "Where?" I asked, stuffing my keys and wallet into my pocket. But it didn't matter. I didn't care where we were going. Because I'd follow her just about anywhere.

Shelby swallowed, working her jaw, deep in thought. "We're going to the only place I've ever felt comfortable talking."

...

Shelby's car was in the shop again, and I didn't trust her intoxication levels yet, so I drove. And with a series of twists and turns, we finally ended up pulling into the empty parking lot of a wealthy neighborhood playground. I turned the ignition, cutting the engine off. "Shelby—"

"Shhhh." With puckered lips, she lifted a finger, silencing me. After another moment, she unclicked her seat belt and opened the passenger door. "Come on," she finally said.

I followed her to the middle of a playground. We were surrounded by jungle gyms, metal climbing bars, and a series of mirrors. Shelby circled the play area, sliding her hands along the bars as though they were long lost friends. "My mom used to take me here." Her voice cracked.

I looked around the playground. It was in the middle of an extremely wealthy section of town. We were surrounded by mini-mansions, similar to the sort in the neighborhood I grew up in if you doubled the lot sizes. "You grew up here?" I asked quietly.

She nodded, her stare vacant. "Kind of." Shelby paused in front of one of the mirrors, grasping the metal bar in front of her. As she swung her leg back and forth in graceful movements, I followed the line of her muscular leg and pointed toe. "My mom was a professional ballerina before she had me. She was good, too—at least according to the reviews she had cut out of the newspaper and saved. She traveled the world with a Ukrainian company. And somewhere along the way, my presence surprised her. She never danced again after having me. It took most of her energy, as a single mom of an infant, and of course, I "ruined" her body by ballet's unrealistic standards. Even when she stuck her finger down her throat to get her figure back—they still rejected her."

Anger flared inside me at that. It wasn't fair and yet, it was the same story for a lot of women in sports as well. Unease churned in my stomach. I didn't know where this was going. Shelby seemed like she was in her own world. She wasn't talking to me; she was talking at me.

I said nothing, but sat in the middle of a roundabout, waiting for her to continue.

"So, she married my stepdad. Ex-stepdad, I should say. He was fine, I guess, for a while. I always wanted to be a ballerina, though…just like my mom. But he refused to pay for lessons. He just about refused anything I wanted. His son was the most important, and I was secondary." Shelby shrugged and stretched her leg overhead in a ballet move that seemed to defy physics. Wow. I'd seen her high kick during the cancan lessons, but this was a whole different sort of grace. I chewed my bottom lip, digging my heel into the mulch, and continued listening. "So, my mom would bring me here and give me lessons herself."

Shelby's voice drifted off, and I waited a few minutes, but she offered me nothing else. I moved in behind her, hugging from behind. "How did she die?"

Shelby gulped, and I could hear the sob building in her throat. But she was stronger than that, and with one more swallow, it disappeared. "Cancer. About three months ago." She blinked, and her eyelashes flicked the tear from her eyes, but her face showed no other signs of tears. "She was my best friend."

I stood there, holding her, questions flooding my mind, but I didn't want to push her beyond what she was comfortable sharing. "What else?" I whispered, dropping my chin to her shoulder and watching her lips move in the reflection.

Her eyes clenched shut, pain twisting in those beautiful features. I hated seeing her this way. Hated seeing her writhe with painful memories. "The scar—" she started, voice breaking. "I was at a party my freshman year of high school. And…and someone put something in my drink. I felt weird and so…disconnected. And I knew something was wrong. Really, really wrong. That's kind of the thing with roofies— you can't think rationally. All I knew was that I had to get away from the party and whoever drugged my drink. It was late. Like, really late. Probably four in the morning. And as I was walking, a police car pulled up. I don't remember much. Just sensory things—sweat dripping onto the back of my neck as he—he pushed himself into my mouth."

Anger like I had never known before sliced through my body, and my face heated with the admission. "He was a cop?" I didn't mean to raise my voice, and Shelby flinched at the volume. Despite how I joked around that first night I met Shelby, I actually really respected cops. I knew a lot through my dad's position and most were really great, trying to make the world a better place. But every now and then, abuse of power like this happened. And I had to bite down on my tongue to stop any further outbursts, so hard that the coppery tang of blood filled my mouth.

Shelby didn't answer me. "He had me by the hair, and was so forceful that he ripped a fistful out."

I pulled her tighter into my hold, rubbing my hands up and down her arms. She shivered despite the warm night and turned to face me. Only she didn't look at me. Instead, she focused on the ground. "What else?" I whispered, my voice trembling.

"I was fucked up, but still cognizant enough to know I didn't want what was happening. I said no. I said it over and over again, and when he didn't stop, I bit down on him."

I clamped my eyes shut, not wanting to know more, but needing to.

Her voice forced my eyes back open, and in the moonlight, I caught my reflection in her irises' amber depths. "He was livid—grabbed my hair, slammed me against the window. My face connected with some equipment he had there, slicing across my forehead." She gulped as tears fell silently down her cheeks, staining her skin with slick streaks.

I nodded, cupping her jaw. "Please tell me that guy is rotting away in jail."

"He died in the line of duty a couple months later. As I'd run from his car, he'd threatened me and my family if I ever said anything.

"I was so embarrassed, broken and mortified, I didn't tell anyone until after he was gone, but by then"—her voice cracked as she pulled from my grasp—"there was no proof. No evidence by then. I didn't even get stitches for my cut that night. I just went home, washed it, and cut my bangs to cover it. That's why the scar is so bad. I told everyone that I slipped and hit my head."

She was visibly trembling, and she hugged her arms across her torso. I so badly wanted to hold her and ease away any residual pain. But as I stepped forward, she leaned away from me. I knew I had to wait.

"My stepdad was more concerned about his job and appearances than about my well-being." Her tone completely shifted from scared and traumatized to angry. She nearly spat the words. "He told my mom and I that 'even if it was true' there was no one left to prosecute." Her eyes sparked like a flame ready to ignite an uncontrollable fire. "But my mom believed me. Without question. And so did the cop we reported it to after she separated from my stepdad. Most of the officers we dealt with after were really great. I just wish it had been one of them who'd found me walking that night."

"Fuck," I hissed, "I'm so sorry." My chest was an empty pit, and each pounding of my heart echoed in my head like a fist beating a drum. I knew shit like this happened. I'd heard stories, seen reports of rape on the news and around campus. But never anyone I knew. At least, not anyone who had *told* me.

She peeled away from my grasp, crossing to the other end of the playground. "I don't want your pity. I don't want your sympathy. It's the exact reason I didn't want you or anyone to know."

"It's not pity, Shelby. It's…it's…" What was it exactly? I didn't know if I had words for it. My response faded into the night, and silence sat thick between us. "Dance for me," I finally whispered.

Shelby twirled, whipping around to face me once more, her features completely unreadable. "What?"

I swallowed. "Let me see you dance."

A ragged laugh broke through her sigh. "The cancan? I don't even remember it."

"No. Ballet, like your mom taught you."

An exhausted chuckle rang like music in my ears. Thank God for that laugh of hers. She sighed in a "why not" way, and I leaned against the monkey bars as she took her place in the center of the playground.

There was no music—no beat other than the rhythm of my heart thrumming in my chest. Her body moved seamlessly from one position to the next, like running water twisting and turning around bends and rocks. Beginning with her heels together, one leg scooped around in a muscular point before lifting back behind her head, her torso tilting parallel to the ground. Part of me wanted to run with arms out to catch her if she fell, while the other part of me was glued where I was, enchanted by this side of a woman I'd spent so much time with lately.

What else didn't I know about her? I quickly looked away, pinching the bridge of my nose as if this could clip the rush of emotion.

Shelby ended with a spin, landing with one arm curved above her head. As she brought her hands down, she shrugged, and the insecurities that had momentarily disappeared rushed back.

The lines of her muscles flexed, and I could see years of hard work and training in the roped tension that held her legs and arms in place. But it wasn't her physicality that had me speechless. The real strength was deeper than the various masses of cells beneath her skin and couldn't be seen in a physical way. That power, that fortitude was in her, a part of her.

"That was the most beautiful thing I've ever seen," I said, moving toward her. I slid my arms around her waist, and she fell into me as I absorbed her weight. I brushed her still damp hair away from her face and brought my lips to her temple where the edge of the scar dipped behind her hairline. She shivered, but let me. "I'm so sorry that happened to you. If that guy was still alive, I'd kill him. And the fact that your stepdad…" I trailed off, shaking my head. No, that wasn't what she needed to hear. She didn't need to hear more about how cruel the world had been to her. I cleared my throat and tried again. "You're the most amazingly strong person I've ever met. You think I pity you?" I shook my head. "How could I pity someone so amazing? I'm in awe of you, Shelby."

A ragged breath pulsed through her parted lips, and she pressed her mouth to mine, dragging her tongue along my bottom lip. "Take me home," she whispered. "Your home."

I curled my arm around her shoulders as we walked back to the car. Her stomach growled. Had she eaten yet tonight? Did she need something to soak up that alcohol? "Let's make a pit stop first."

"For what?"

"Provisions," I said, gently poking a finger to her ribs. She squirmed, ticklish. "We need crullers for the morning."

She rolled her eyes, threading her fingers in mine. "Where the hell are you going to find crullers this late?"

I arched an eyebrow, opening the passenger door for her.

"Oh, right," she snorted. "I forgot that you have magical ways of finding delicious baked goods." She smiled, and though it wasn't a huge grin, it was something. It was playful. Sarcastic. The Shelby I'd come to know so well.

I leaned down into the car's doorframe as she buckled her seat belt. "Guess where we're not finding these crullers?" I brushed my mouth gently across hers and whispered, remembering those terrible burned croissants she made. "In your oven."

. . .

An hour later, we had already dug into the stash of crullers. Shelby sat on my kitchen counter, legs swinging off the edge, and I stood between her knees.

"I had no idea the gas stations had fresh baked goods," she said, shaking her head in disbelief. "I mean, other than crappy plastic-wrapped ones."

"I can't believe you doubted me," I said, reaching for the second cruller. She slapped my hand just before my fingers brushed the glazed deliciousness.

"And *I* can't believe you were about to steal the last doughnut," she said.

"*Cruller*," I corrected and then offered her my biggest pout and puppy dog eyes. Even Buddy, sitting at our heels, whimpered along with me. "Come on. We can get more tomorrow."

"We promised each other we'd only have one each and share that one in the morning," she scolded playfully, finger pointing in my face. Crystalized sugar from the glaze coated that index finger, and I opened my mouth, sucking the sweetness from the tip.

She gasped, but didn't pull away. "Mm," I moaned as she slowly withdrew her finger from my lips. "Sweet."

With a coy smirk, she dipped her finger into the cruller, scraping the glaze off before spreading it across her bottom lip. "Not as sweet as this," she said. Grabbing the collar of my shirt, she pulled me into her, pressing those sticky, sweet lips to mine. Tiny granules of sugar were the only thing that separated us, and the sweet flavor combined with her watermelon Chap Stick was intoxicating. With no coaxing at all, she opened her mouth against mine, stroking her tongue into me. I curved my hands around her waist, and her legs locked around my hips.

"I want you," she whispered. I stepped back to move to the bedroom, but she pulled me back using her heels wrapped around my back as leverage. "No, here. *Now*."

Oh my God, that was hot. Her skirt draped loosely around her hips and thighs. As I brushed a knuckle down the length of her sex, the soft cotton of her panty scraped my skin. I pushed it to the side and was met with her wet heat. Groaning, I pushed a finger gently inside of her and was rewarded with her sexy moan. "Like that?" I whispered, pulsing my finger in and out of her, circling my thumb over her clit.

She didn't answer with words but bit her lip, nodding and grinding into my hand even more. I continued my movements, alternating between tortuously slow, and fast movements until she gripped my neck, twisting her fingers into my hair. She could take all the time she needed for all I cared—this was my definition of perfection. Pleasing her, it was all I wanted to do. I didn't even care if I came.

Okay, maybe "didn't care" was too strong, but it certainly

wasn't a priority.

"Oh God, Tate..." Her eyes flew open, looking wildly around.

"What? What's the matter?" I asked, pulling my hands back instinctively.

"No—it's, it's me...panic..." Her words were choppy and breathless.

Scooping my hand behind her neck, I carefully tilted her head so that her eyes met mine. "Shelby, breathe. We can stop. Anytime. But breathe. And look at me."

Her chest heaved in and out, and her palms pushed into my shoulders, the pressure increasing. Slowly, she returned to normal. "Do you want me to stop?"

She swallowed and finally shook her head. "No," she managed in a small voice. "I'm okay."

She didn't look okay. Sweat dotted her forehead, and I swiped my thumb across her brow, kissing the area just above her eyebrow.

"I'm okay," she reiterated. Her eyes fluttered closed, and using her heels, she pulled me closer, crushing our bodies together. Cautiously, I moved my finger, brushing lightly between her legs once more. She moaned as I increased pressure, circling harder, faster, watching her face carefully for any signs of tension or hesitation. Was she going to freak out again? Maybe I should just stop entirely. It'd been a long night.

"I want you"—she panted— "inside of me." I'd heard her say that before, only to have her panic and run.

"Not yet." I nibbled her ear, and her shiver trembled against my body, her sex tightening around my finger. "I want to feel you come again, Shelby." I quickened the pace of my finger and increased pressure to her clit with my thumb. After a few moments, she cried out, hips bucking against the heel of my hand. Muscles exploded around my finger, convulsing as she moaned, nipping my shoulder. Pulling back, her eyes met mine, flicking back and forth over my face. She opened her mouth to speak, only no words came out. And that was okay—we didn't need words right now. Instead, she sloped her lips over mine in a sweet kiss that just barely brushed my lips.

Her hand drifted down, slipping below the waistband of my basketball shorts, and she sprung my erection free. I grasped her around the waist with one arm, not wanting to let go, and with the other pulled a condom out of my wallet. Shelby's hand was around me, stroking in a firm grip, and I was momentarily blinded with pleasure. Ripping the foil with my teeth, I moved my shaking hand, unrolling the condom over myself. Shelby took over, finishing for me and guiding me inside of her. I melded my mouth to hers, fusing our lips together in a kiss that could melt metal. This girl made me feel more alive, more amazing than anyone I had ever met before—and she was mine. Here, in my arms. She thrust her hips onto mine, and her body gripped me tighter than I ever imagined possible. I trembled, gaining control of my senses, forcing myself to slow down. I didn't want to hurt her. It had to be enjoyable for Shelby, first and foremost.

She clamped her legs tighter, urging me to move more. I pulled out slowly, dragging myself out of her almost entirely and stopped with just my head at her slick entrance. Rolling my hips in circles, I drove back into her, controlled but firm. From below, she moaned, squirming against me, and I shifted my hands to her ass, lifting her and driving myself deeper inside. Her eyes opened to a slit, revealing a sliver of almond, and her head fell back against the bar behind her. Through lips swollen from kissing, small rushes of air escaped to the sound of my name. She kept moaning it, over and over until I thought I was going to explode.

I kneaded her breast through her shirt, brushing my

thumb over her sensitive nipple, and she scraped her nails down my back with another cry.

My climax heated at the base of my pelvis, building with intensity. Through a jagged breath, I managed to speak. "Shelby—I–I can't hold on much longer," I winced with the words, thrusting into her.

She hugged me closer, her teeth scraping my shoulder. "Don't wait. Come…"

It was all I needed to hear. I thrust once more inside of her, as deep as possible, and let go. My orgasm rushed from my pelvis in a shudder up my torso, and I think I screamed out her name. She leveraged my body, riding me until every shiver had run its course.

I pushed myself off the counter, brushing her hair out of her eyes. Pressing my lips to her forehead, I caressed my thumb down her neck. "You okay?"

She nodded, and a heavy breath sighed from her chest. "I'm so okay. Better than."

I nodded. "I know the feeling." I slowly withdrew, taking the condom off, tying a knot at the end and tossing it in the garbage. "Let's go to bed. You'll stay the night, right?" I swallowed hard, and it went down like a lump. It would kill me to not wake up beside her tomorrow.

She raised an eyebrow and lifted a small smile. "As long as we can have a repeat of that."

I laughed. "Some of us need sleep."

She snorted and burrowed closer into my neck. "Fine. Then I expect some first thing in the morning."

I rolled my eyes, tugging her skirt back in place. "You're so demanding."

"So…" There was hesitancy in her voice. "Guess it's bedtime?" She slid off the counter. Was it in my head? The slight shift in her demeanor?

"Yeah. You sure you're okay?"

She nodded. "I think so. I haven't talked so much about that time in my life in…in years. Hell, I don't know that I've ever talked about it that much."

"You can tell me anything, babe." She smiled at that, but it didn't quite reach her eyes. "I'm serious," I assured her. "You could confess that you *murdered* someone, and I wouldn't care."

That earned me a larger smile—it even got a giggle out of her. "Really? So if I called you over tomorrow with a chopped up corpse in my freezer…?"

"I'd grab a shovel and pull out a map. There has to be a dozen places around here we could bury a body."

"Okay, okay," she laughed. "This took a weird turn."

"No more secrets, okay?" I said more seriously. She paused, her smile turning tight before she nodded. It was tentative, uncertain. Or was I just reading too much into it?

"No more secrets," she finally said.

Chapter Twenty-Six

TATE

"It's this big talent show at school, and my dad told us...he *promised* me that he'd be there for it. I'm singing a solo and everything."

"That's great. I bet he'll love it." I nodded, half listening as Sophia rambled on about her recital and dad while I looked over the test she got back today at school. I'd been volunteering at the center for almost two months now, and Shelby hadn't fudged my hours since that first day when we initially set up the agreement. There was no way I could abuse her power like that and risk everything she'd worked so hard for here at the center. Besides, I kind of liked Sophia. She was a pretty cool kid.

"I bet he'll bring me flowers. Roses, probably." She talked about her dad constantly, but I had never met him—and I noticed that if she brought him up in front of her mom, the woman tightened up visibly. I pushed the thought of Sophia's dad from my mind, focusing again on the few questions

Sophia missed on the test.

"Good job, kiddo." I patted Sophia gently on the back and pushed my chair onto two legs. "What did I tell you? If you did your homework and paid attention, you would ace long division." I slid her B-plus test back across the table to Sophia and she beamed at me.

"Thanks." There was a gaping hole in her toothy smile where she had lost one. I had seen it each step of the way, from when it barely wiggled, to her basically being able to wiggle it with a whistle, to now—the time when the tooth fairy comes. She had rushed in, pointing at the gap, beaming. Apparently, kids were extremely proud of losing their teeth. I never really knew—when I lost my first tooth, my parents weren't home. But the nanny had told me to put it under my pillow and the tooth fairy would come. But I guess she either failed to inform my parents that I had lost that tooth, or they just simply forgot. Knowing them, it was the latter. So, I woke up the next morning to find a dried, bloody tooth under my pillow, and no gift like all the other kids in my class.

Shelby caught my eye from across the room, sending a smile my way. It had been about two weeks since our night at the playground. But between my basketball schedule and her study/tutoring/work schedule, we rarely saw each other. We were lucky to have Sundays together. Even though Shelby was the busiest person I had ever dated, it was worth every minute of waiting. Today was a great example of how she ran around like a crazy person. She was bouncing between three students who didn't have any tutors, and Ryan had asked her to stay late to get their quarterly tax preparation paperwork out of the way. Acid burned in my stomach at the thought of them working late together, but I pushed the envy down. It was stupid. Shelby was the sincerest, most honest girl I knew…hell, if I couldn't trust her, then I had no hope for the rest of humanity.

I looked back to Sophia. "What's your favorite milkshake flavor?"

She rolled her eyes to the ceiling in thought. "Um, strawberry?"

I laughed. "Is that a question or an answer?"

She smothered her giggle with a hand, and her eyes shot wider. "No. Wait, not strawberry…mint chocolate chip."

I grinned at that. For some reason, Sophia reminded me a lot of Shelby. I had come to know Sophia's mom a little bit, simply with her picking her daughter up on weeknights. Their bond, even with Sophia still so young, reminded me of the stories Shelby would tell of her mom. I wish I had met Shelby a few months earlier—I really would have liked a chance to meet her mother and shake the hand of the woman who raised such an amazing daughter.

"Well," I said, pushing the thoughts away. "How about if tomorrow at tutoring, I bring you a mint chocolate chip milkshake?"

Sophia lit up at that, nodding. "Okay. But wait—you're not here on Thursdays."

Crap, that's right. How could I forget that? "I'll swing by on my way to basketball. Or I'll have Shelby get it for you. I'll have to ask your mom if it's okay, though."

"She'll be fine with it."

I laughed, the sound bubbling up and out of me like water out of a spigot. "I've still got to ask." I ruffled her hair, and she scrunched her nose, smoothing her static strands back down with her palms. "Now, what do you say we get started on your grammar homework."

Sophia sighed, pulling out a big book from her bag. "Oh, okay."

My phone buzzed in my pocket, and I glanced at the screen with a sigh. My mom. She had been calling all week and I had been dodging her pretty successfully. Until now.

"You get started and I'll be back in a minute to check on your progress."

I stepped out to the lobby, sliding the call button on my phone to the right. "Hey, Mom."

"Well, there you are. Have you been avoiding us?"

I rolled my eyes, flopping into a chair. God, I'd rather be anywhere…having any conversation but this one. "No, of course not. Remember that little community service I've had to do? Yeah, it keeps me pretty busy."

"Well," she huffed, ignoring my pointed comment. "I've been trying to reach you. Your father and I are going to be coming into Charleston on Friday for Parents' Weekend."

"What?" My grip on the armrest tightened. "Why? I thought you guys were going skiing this weekend?"

She let loose an exhausted sigh, and I resisted the urge to snort at that. What she had to be exhausted over was beyond me. "Your father's people said that with elections coming up, some family outings would do us good. Never mind the fact that we did this whole parent weekend thing your freshman year."

My throat closed up. Yep, one visit four years ago, and suddenly they're freaking parents of the year. That wasn't entirely true, though—they'd usually come down during basketball season for a game or two…just never without their entourage. My skin wrinkled under my hands as I rubbed my eyes. "Okay, fine. You're coming Friday. What's expected of me?"

"Well, we're going to get in late Friday night—we'll just go right to the hotel. Then, we'll pick you up Saturday morning for the Parents' Weekend brunch, go see the matinee of the little musical your school is putting on, and then we figured dinner. You pick the restaurant."

I swallowed, my heart jumping. "Can I bring someone to dinner?"

"Of course. Is it Brad? Oh, we just love Brad."

"No, Mom." I cleared my throat. "It's a girl. I–I've met someone, and I think you're really going to like her." Well…as much as they could like anyone, that is. Shelby was smart and going places. And based on the neighborhood she grew up in, she came from "good breeding" as my mom would call it. Not the kind of girl they'd worry over signing a pre-nup or getting pregnant just to trap me.

"Oh?" My mom's voice sounded genuinely shocked. "Really?" There was the hint of a smile in her voice with that question, and I had to laugh.

"Yes, really. She's great, Mom. She's beautiful and sweet and funny and—"

"Does she have money?"

My smile dropped and my heart squeezed for Shelby. She was too good for this family of mine. If I really loved her, I wouldn't even bring her into this mess. But I'm a selfish bastard. I sighed, falling back against the chair. "Yeah. I mean, I think so. She lives in the building below me. *You* know how hard it is to get an apartment in there." There was a *hmmm* from the other end of the line. "Mom? Please don't embarrass me."

"Oh, sweetie. Don't be ridiculous. We can't wait to meet her. What's her name?"

I opened my mouth to answer and quickly snapped it shut. Oh, hell no. I was not giving them her name. They'd have an investigator looking into every aspect of her life the second they knew. "Well, I'm not sure if she's available Saturday…it's kind of last minute. I'll check and let you know."

"It's only last minute because you wouldn't answer your phone," she sneered pointedly.

Through the glass doors, I saw Sophia waving me over. I sent her a nod. "I have to go, Mom. Duty calls." And before she said good-bye, I hung up.

Pushing back through the doors, I nearly tripped over my own feet. In one of the private rooms, Shelby was standing, bent over some paperwork. Behind her—that son of a bitch, Ryan leered at her ass, his hand branding her lower back. I knew nothing was going on—they were colleagues and friends—but that jealousy raged like an inferno in my gut. I was blinded by it, rational or not. With a deep breath, I held a finger up to Sophia and charged the door.

My hand struck the tempered glass as I shoved it open, and a startled Shelby and Ryan both jumped, spinning to find me there, red in the face.

"Hey, Tate," Ryan said casually, standing upright. "Everything okay out there?"

It even annoyed me how friendly he was to me. Like I wouldn't notice the way he was leering at my girlfriend. I pressed my lips together, biting the inside of my cheek to stop myself from saying something stupid. "Things are…fine," I managed through a coarse rasp. "I just need to ask Shelby a question."

The two exchanged a look, and Shelby nodded. Without another word, Ryan turned, leaving the room and shutting the door behind him. Shelby's gaze swept over me, concern marring her eyebrows. "What's going on?" She ran her palm down my shoulder to my hand, and I gritted my teeth.

"What were you two doing in here?" I tried to keep the accusations down, but there was an edge of anger that I just couldn't shake.

She tilted her head, pulling back, but I held on to her hand, pulling her into me. "What do you mean? I was prepping the receipts for tonight, but I had some questions about the categories."

I dropped my voice. "He was staring at your ass. Did you not see him? Or did you just not care to stop him?"

She wrenched her hand from mine. "He was not. Tate,

he's my boss. He and I have to work together and you need to deal with that. He's also my friend. Don't be an asshole." She whispered the curse, looking beyond me to make sure there were no children outside the door.

I rolled my eyes, diving a hand through my hair. "You can't possibly tell me that the way he looks at you is innocent?"

She sighed, her eyes squeezing shut. "Maybe. Maybe not. But he's my boss. So, unless you expect me to quit, you need to find a way to deal with it. He's never been inappropriate with me."

I threw up my hands. "Fine. I'm just saying that I think you need to watch out for him. If I wasn't in the picture, he'd probably be working an angle to get into your pants right this second."

Shelby glanced out the window, folding her arms. "Then how is it that he and I have worked together for years and he hasn't tried a thing?"

I shrugged. "Look, I don't know. He's a moron first of all. I wouldn't have gone a week working beside you without acting on it."

She raised an eyebrow, but the slightest smile peeked through her angry facade. "I think we all know that. Trust me, Tate. You have nothing to worry about. Even if you're right about Ryan having feelings for me...*I* would never cheat on you."

God, I was such a moron. This was about Katie. Shelby was my first real relationship since I was cheated on, and it was fucking with my head. "I know," I whispered. "I know that. I can't help it that I get jealous. Especially because you've been spending so much time here at work—"

Shelby sighed, wrapping her arms around my neck. And God, her body...those tight curves, and the way her strong legs would clamp around my hips and ride me to orgasm.

"I'm busy." She wet her lips, looking up at me through

long, black lashes. "A lot, I know. With my jobs and school and friends—"

Jobs. Plural?

"But I'll make time for you whenever I can…you know that," she continued.

I groaned, placing my hands on her shoulders and pushing her back. "Control yourself." I grinned. But it was too late… I'd need a few minutes before I went back out there. "I just talked to my mom. She and my dad are coming for Parents' Weekend, and they want to meet you."

The natural flush Shelby almost always sported drained quickly. "Oh?" was all she offered.

I shrugged. "Yeah…I mean, I know parent dinners are boring, and my parents suck balls, but it's a free meal, right? And I get to pick the place."

Her shoulders were rigid around her ears. "Where are we going?"

"I was thinking that new place, Ice, where all the food is served cold."

Shelby's chest deflated with a small sigh. "Oh. Um, yeah… okay. I mean, parents aren't really my thing, but if you want us to meet, then sure. When are you thinking?"

"Saturday night is their only available evening. And be prepared—they'll probably have their media entourage following them."

This time I knew I wasn't imagining it. Her whole body went rigid. "I can't Saturday."

Anger fumed inside of me. Fucking Ryan. "Work?" I said through tight lips.

She nodded, twisting a piece of paper between nervous fingers.

"Fucking asshole," I muttered, looking in the direction Ryan had run off…the coward. If you want my fucking lady, come fight me for her and show some cojones.

"Ryan has nothing to do with it," she said, nostrils flaring like a bull seeing red. "You know what? I don't have to explain or justify myself to you. I'm done with this conversation. When you decide to grow up, let me know. I was going to suggest that I switch my work to Friday, but now? Fuck it. If your parents want to do brunch on Saturday or Sunday, let me know. Otherwise, I'll see you later."

She stormed off, slamming the door behind her.

Well, shit. That could have gone better.

Chapter Twenty-Seven

Shelby

The glass door was cold beneath my palm as I shoved it open and stalked into the other room. How dare he? He didn't get to helicopter over me like some sort of overprotective Neanderthal. I wasn't even working here at the center that Saturday, but now I was too pissed to explain that. Nor should I *have* to.

"Shelby," Tate's quiet voice said behind me. I didn't even hear him walk up.

His face sagged. "I'm sorry. I think talking to my parents set me on edge. And I don't love—" He paused with a quick glance around the room. "I don't love that you and Ryan work so closely together, but I handled it all wrong. You have a right to work when and where and with whoever you want."

"Whomever," I said quietly, almost on a reflex.

He smiled softly, reaching a tentative hand to my waist and tugging me closer. "Smart-ass," he whispered, dipping his lips over my cheek. A shiver danced down my spine, and if we weren't in a public place, I might have pushed those lips to a whole other area of my body. Because, damn, this boy knew what he was doing most of the time. Scratch that—all of the time.

"Tate, on Saturday night, I'm not going to be working here—"

"It doesn't matter where you're going to be. Or who you're going to be with. In fact, don't tell me. I don't care. I don't even want to know." Tate cleared his throat and put a more respectable distance between us. "Instead of Saturday night—my parents and I have a brunch thing that morning with the school, but I'm sure you can come, too. Would that work better?"

I nodded. "Brunch on Saturday would be…" What? Not great. Because Jesus I did not want to meet these people. These so-called "parents" of his that spent more time on their tans then they did with their son were not the sort of people I wanted to waste one of my few free mornings with. It was the same sort of bullshit I had always seen with the wealthiest kids, and I hated that Tate had that sort of childhood. The sort where parents pay other people to do the parenting for them so they could simply disappear—whether that was in the physical sense or simply the emotional. Or both.

But I wasn't doing this for *them*. I was doing it for Tate. He had been so sweet these past several weeks. Understanding and patient. I needed to extend that same courtesy with his emotional baggage. So, despite my many, many reservations, I cleared my throat, finishing my sentence. "Brunch on Saturday would be…great. We'll have fun," I managed to add without an eye roll.

Yeah, fun. If I made it through the morning without flinging pancakes at his parents.

• • •

The rest of the week dragged on. And as the weekend approached, that feeling of dread dropped lower and lower into my stomach. What the hell was I thinking going to brunch with them? These people embodied everything that I vowed to never be a part of again.

But, here I was…putting on a too-expensive dress and staining my lips with the perfect shade of rose colored lip gloss. I stood in front of my full-length mirror and gave a little twirl, holding out my hands. The girl staring back at me was a fragmented vision of both who I used to be and who I was to become. I wasn't going to be poor the rest of my life, that was for sure. But I didn't want to become the Michaelsons.

"Well?"

"You look great," Reagan squealed, hopping up from my futon and running over. She smoothed the Kate Spade wrap dress down my hips. "Jesus, it fits you better than it does me."

I rolled my eyes. "I highly doubt that."

She stepped back, examining me. "No, really, it does. *Look* at yourself. My boobs nearly bust out of it, but you make it look classy. Sophisticated."

I sighed, looking again to the mirror. "What do I do with my hair?"

"Sit," Reagan commanded, pointing to the floor, and I did as she said. She twisted my hair into a low bun, pulling out several wisps to frame my bangs and jaw. "There…demure, but sexy."

"Tate likes it when I wear my hair down."

She rolled her eyes, flipping her own fire-engine red hair over a shoulder. "Every guy feels that way. Until they see something new. Trust me. This sophisticated look? He'll love it."

Reagan rummaged through her duffle bag and pulled out a pair or low-heeled Jimmy Choos. "Here…these match the dress perfectly."

I took the shoe, turning it over in my hands. "I can't wear

these. They cost you more than this damn apartment." Okay, not really…but almost.

"You *can* wear them, and you *will* wear them. Besides, they cost my dad, not me. What's the point in having a best friend if we can't raid each other's closets?"

I arched a brow, crossing my arms. "Oh? You want to raid my closet, do you? What exactly would you like to borrow? Perhaps this vintage T-shirt featuring our favorite Care Bear? Or would you rather borrow these Gap jeans which I bought, *gasp*, off the rack."

"All right, all right. You don't need to be a bitch about it. Just put on the damn shoes." Reagan laughed. "Besides, once you're a high powered business woman and I'm a starving actress, I plan to raid your closet weekly for auditions." She grinned and lifted a pillow from my bed. "If you weren't already done up to the nines and about to meet your boyfriend's governor father, I swear I'd pummel you with this pillow."

"You could *try*." I smiled at her in the mirror while slipping my pearl earrings in. "But we both know I'm the reigning pillow fight champion."

She burst out in a fit of giggles, clenching the pillow as though she were really debating going all girl-slumber-party on my ass, when a knock at the door quieted us. "Oh my God, they're here," she whispered.

I grabbed my purse, rushing for the door. "You'll let yourself out?"

She nodded, shutting herself in my bedroom and hiding while I answered the door. A very dapper Tate stood on the other side, and a grin stretched across his cheeks as his gaze swept my body from the tips of Reagan's Jimmy Choos to the top of my French-twisted head. His smile was just the breath of fresh air that I needed, and he tugged me close, brushing his lips along mine.

"Wow. You look—wow," he said.

I smoothed the sides of my bun, and as I stepped forward, my heel caught on the carpet, and I stumbled into his shoulder. Jesus. Some things didn't change.

Tate chuckled and brushed his hand across my hip. "They just got here. They're waiting up in my apartment." He pushed the button for the elevator, flashing me a smile and squeezing my hip with his free hand.

"Tate, c'mon. Stop." But despite my protest, I smiled.

"Stop what?" he asked, his voice a raspy shell of what it usually was.

"Stop looking at me like *I'm* what's for breakfast."

"Mmm," he sighed, tugging me against his body once more. The elevator kicked into gear as he smoothed his lips along my neck and collarbone. "I wish."

Gripping my hips, he pulled me into his already bulging erection, and I giggled into his shoulder. "Are you ever not in the mood, Tate?"

"Not around you."

The elevator bounced to a stop, and we quickly parted, jumping to opposite sides. I smoothed my dress, and Tate adjusted his erection before taking my hand.

As we stepped into Tate's foyer, the door to the kitchen was wide open. The first thing I saw was a splash of hot pink. No...*fuchsia*. His mother was tall. Really tall. Standing at his kitchen counter, she must have been five eleven, at least. And in her pink dress, paired with a black cashmere cardigan and matching heels that made her at least two inches taller, she was supermodel beautiful.

I found myself unable to tear my eyes away until I was met with an older version of Tate. Again...tall. His dad smiled warmly, a few lines creasing his otherwise unaged face, and he took my hand in both of his, pulling me in for a kiss on each cheek.

"Ah, this must be Shelby. It's lovely to meet you," his

father said.

Tate rolled his eyes as his mom approached me next, her face void of any emotion. Was it because another woman was finally competing for her little boy's attention? Or was it simply a case of too much Botox? Considering what Tate had told me about his childhood, I assumed it to be the latter. She pulled me in for one of those weird air-hugs—the kind where someone clearly doesn't really want to touch you so they keep as much space between your bodies as possible. Yeah, that was the hug I got from Mrs. Michaelson.

If you're not comfortable being pressed boob to boob with a person, then a handshake will suffice. I ducked my head to cover my smirk as my mom's sage wisdom rang in my ears. I studied Tate's mom carefully. In some ways, she was a lot like mine—at least, back when my mom was married to wealth. There was a time she owned gorgeous dresses and had her hair done weekly.

"Come on over, Shelby," Tate's dad said, pulling out a seat at the counter. "We just opened some champagne and are having mimosas before we leave."

Tate's mom poured four glasses of champagne, adding a splash of orange juice to two of them. "Do you like Bellinis or mimosas? We've got either peach or orange. I, personally, like a good Bellini."

"Peach would be wonderful, thank you, Mrs. Michaelson."

She tittered, handing me my glass and tapped the edge. "Oh, sweetheart. Please, call me Tabby."

I nodded and took a sip of the sweet bubbly.

"So, Shelby," Tate's dad went on, "please don't take this the wrong way, but Tate's told us nothing about you. Not even your last name."

I slid Tate a look, raising my eyebrow, and he shrugged with an eye roll. While some girls would have been pissed, I preferred it that way. The way people like the Michaelson's operated, they'd have an assistant researching everything about me as soon as I gave them my name. They'd know where and when I was born, every address where I'd ever lived, as well as my shoe size. But, thank God, Tate wasn't like that.

"Um, well...I live right downstairs. Tate and I met the day I moved in. I'm an international business major, and when French was really hard for me, Tate offered to tutor me."

"So nice of Tatum, wasn't it?" Tabby looked out the window, her Bellini nearly empty and her eyes glistening with boredom. When his parents looked away, I mouthed *Tatum?* to him, suppressing a laugh. Tate lowered his brows into a cartoonish scowl. I was definitely going to call him by his full name later. Mercilessly. In front of other people.

"What else? What do your parents do?" Mr. Michaelson asked.

I cleared my throat. God, I hated this question. I wasn't ashamed of my mom...not at all. But people like this? They would eat me alive and throw my carcass to their dogs for dessert. "Well, my mom was a ballerina before she had me..."

Tabby lit up at that, clapping. "Oh, how lovely. With who? Alvin Ailey? ABC?"

I swallowed. "Back in her prime, she danced in Europe with Donestk. But she remarried after, when I was a kid, and never managed to get back to dancing after that—"

Tabby nodded, eyes wide. "Oh yes. It's not an easy job being married to guys like these."

A knot tightened low in my belly. I hadn't said anything about *who* my mom was married to. Mrs. Michaelson either just assumed I was like them...or she knew my family history already. Neither scenario would surprise me. "Nope, not an easy job at all," I said cautiously. If they'd been looking into me, then they probably already knew about my mom's divorce. "In fact, she went back to waitr—"

"And what about you?" Tabby asked pointedly, cutting

me off.

"Excuse me?" I set the champagne glass gently down on the marble counter, running my finger along the base.

"What about yourself? Tate mentioned you volunteer at the tutoring center?"

There was something in the way she stared at me that set my teeth on edge and my radar to pinging all over the place. "Well, I actually work there. I hold the position of assistant director—"

"Do you want to be a teacher?"

I exchanged looks with Tate who rolled his eyes and stepped in. "Mom, she told you already, she's majoring in international business."

"Oh, right, right. I guess I'm just trying to figure out why you spend so much time working in a place that's unrelated to your major." She held my gaze with her intense blue stare—those same blue eyes that Tate had, like a clear sky on a summer day. Only on her, it looked icy, not warm and inviting like Tate.

"I like to give back to the community where I grew up," I said slowly, licking my lips and pushing away what was left in my champagne glass. I had very little desire to let my guard down around these people. "I think it's important."

She laughed, the tinny noise like a cheese grater on my nerves. Even her chuckle was condescending. "Then why take their money? Why not just volunteer?"

"The money is nominal," I answered, my words growing more clipped as my fuse shortened. "My paychecks are barely anything, and I work well beyond the hours I get paid for."

"Then why cash their checks at all?" She wore a berry shade of gloss and worked her thin lips across each other, smoothing the lipstick.

What could I say to that? My financial standing was none of their business, and it had no impact on my relationship with Tate. Before I could answer, Mr. Michaelson cut in with another question. "Tate says you keep pretty busy. Are they demanding over at the tutoring center?"

With another deep breath, I turned my attention to the much friendlier Mr. Michaelson. But I didn't let that smooth smile and buttery voice gain my trust. The cutest kitten could deliver the deepest scratch.

"I do keep very busy. So does Tate." I sent him a grin before continuing with what felt like a job interview. "I think it's a good thing that we both have our own lives."

"So, the tutoring center is your only job?"

Again, my breath stalled. Tons of students waited tables to pay their way through school. There was no shame in hard work to get where you needed to be.

Tate's hand on my back was the reassurance I needed. When I looked up, he was glaring at his father. I opened my mouth to answer, but Tate spoke first. "Dad, back off. She works at the tutoring center because she loves it, and that's the sort of generous person she is. She took me to Shoreburg Park where she grew up—I think I'd know if she had another job." He blew out a sigh and widened his eyes at me in a sort of silent apology. Wait? Did *Tate* think I was rich? I flipped back through our history…oh God. Oh, shit. I mean, I guess I never really came right out and said that my bank account was thin, but I didn't think I alluded to being rich other than a few jokes when we first met. But I was being sarcastic. And had Magnolia's never come up? I've only done a shift or two since the semester started, but even still—it must have come up at least once, right?

"Actually, Tate…I sometimes wai—"

Mr. Michaelson's phone went off in some sort of alarm. "Oops. We should really get going. Don't want to be late for the brunch."

Oh God…Tate's parents shuffled us out of the penthouse,

and I rode the elevator in a total daze. Just how bad did this look?

"Hey," Tate whispered, giving a gentle tug to a wisp of hair that curled around my jaw. "Everything okay?"

I swallowed, nodding. "Yeah." I darted a quick glance at Tate's parents. They were several steps ahead, getting into their SUV. "I just—I think I need to talk to you about something."

Tate stopped walking, holding my hand and halting my movement as well. "What's wrong?"

"Nothing—I'm fine. We're fine. I just think I maybe need to clarify some things. I have another—"

"Tate. Shelby. Come on, we'll be late," his mom called from the passenger window. We moved slowly toward the car.

"Let's talk tonight," he said, rubbing a hand down my arm. "After my parents and I do dinner."

"I'd rather not wait—"

"Babe, whatever it is, it'll be fine. As long as what you're about to tell me isn't that you're an axe murderer..."

A smile curved my lips. "I thought you said you'd help bury the body?"

He froze before laughing. "You're right, I did. See? There you go. Whatever it is, it'll be fine. And I'll be sure to have my shovel ready for when we talk after dinner."

Despite the nerves bouncing in my belly, I laughed. "Okay," I said as he tugged me in, sliding an arm around my waist and pressing a warm kiss to my temple. "But we *have* to talk about this tonight. You're still going to Ice for dinner?" I asked.

"Oh, yeah. Shrimp cocktail, oysters, and ceviche. I wish you were coming. It's gonna be cool."

I nodded, tossing him a grin. "Well, with a name like *Ice*, how can it not?"

Tate groaned and gave me a quick peck on the nose. "You are such a dork. It's a good thing you're cute."

Chapter Twenty-Eight

TATE

Brunch didn't go nearly as terribly as it could have. We were only stopped twice to pose for pictures. And Shelby was amazing...of course. She dodged each of the parents' nosy ass questions with grace while not letting their snooty order of soft poached eggs with hollandaise—seriously, Mom? It's called eggs benedict. Just order fucking eggs benedict—throw off her poise. And though Shelby was quiet through most of the brunch, I knew my parents. Things could have gone a hell of a lot worse.

The rest of the day went smoothly, though it was boring without Shelby to make the time go faster. I mean, Reagan was cool and all, but musicals just aren't my thing. And then, of course, there were more photo ops after that. Dad's "people" wanted images of us around campus. By the time dinner rolled around, I was grumbling almost as loud as my stomach.

My dad pulled into a parking lot in front of a historic pink house. "What are we doing here?" I groaned. "Ice is eight blocks the other way."

"We're not eating at Ice," my dad snapped. Here it comes. This was the man I knew—the man the cameras never saw. Stubborn. Pig-headed. And with no regard for what others want.

"What the hell? Mom said I could choose the restaurant."

"I take my *bourbon* on the rocks, not my goddamn dinner," he sneered through tight lips. I sighed, unbuckling my seat belt as he tossed his keys to the valet. There was no use arguing with him at this point. Not when he got into a mood like this. And hell, I was damn hungry, and we were already here.

A young girl stood at the hostess podium, scrolling through names. "Yes, Mr. Michaelson. Right this way." We followed her through the old southern manor, which had been converted into a restaurant. Jesus, the walls were all painted pink like the outside. Every table had a bouquet of magnolias. Very original. The tables were some sort of dark wood with matching chairs—the sort of furniture you'd find in your grandmother's house.

The girl stopped in front of a table next to the bay window. "The best seat in the house, Governor," she said.

"And the special request I had when I called?"

"Already taken care of." She smiled first at him, then my mom, and finally she settled on me. She was a student—I recognized her from around campus. After a second's glance, she strode back to her station at the front of the house.

"God, I need a martini," my mom said, squinting at the menu. No matter how much she denied it, the woman needed reading glasses. For her, age did not bring wisdom, apparently—only more vanity. "That show was dreadful. God, I hate community theater."

"It's not community theater—it's college theater," I

snapped, feeling suddenly defensive for Reagan's sake. I thought she was great—I mean, I don't really have much to compare it to, but still. Damn, there was no way I could ever remember all those lines like she did.

"That's even worse," my dad cut in. "That just means those poor kids expect to make a living out of it."

I sort of half groaned, half sighed at that. There was no winning with them. Their snobbery knew no bounds. "Well, then why go see it at all?"

"Oh, honey." Mom made a noise that gargled in the back of her throat. "We were *invited*. They expect us to do all these things during our visit."

"Silly me," I said, mostly to myself. "Here I thought you wanted to come hang out with me."

My mom rolled her eyes, and I was amazed she managed to show that much emotion through all her Botox. "You're so sensitive today. Of course we're here to see you."

"Really?" I slapped the menu onto the table, waiting for either of them to make eye contact. But I'd be waiting the whole damn night. Their eyes stayed glued on the menus. "Dad, how many meetings do you have lined up for tomorrow?"

"Two, why?" he answered robotically, with no clue that he'd just made my point.

A middle-aged dude with chestnut hair and a goatee came over, grinning wide. "Good evening, Governor Michaelson, Mrs. Michaelson."

My dad stood, taking his hand. "Good evening. Thank you for being able to accommodate us on such short notice."

The man waved my father's gratitude away and bent to offer my mom his hand as well. "No problem at all. Would you mind a photograph? We love documenting all public figures who eat at our establishment."

"Of course." My dad's chuckle bellowed through the

restaurant, and my mother offered him as warm of a smile as she could. Both turned to glare at me. "Come on, Tate. Stand up so we can all have a picture." I inwardly groaned. It was bad enough having to grow up doing this, going out with friends and seeing my picture up behind the bar or in the entryway to a restaurant. Now it was following me to fucking college, too.

The flash popped, and I honestly didn't know whether or not I smiled. Nor did I care. I would order my steak, eat quietly, and get the fuck home and away from them.

I fell back into my chair and placed my napkin back on my lap, then I heard a familiar voice above me.

"Good evening and welcome to Magnolia's. My name's—" Her voice squeaked when we both looked up at the same moment, catching each other's eyes.

"*Shelby?*"

Chapter Twenty-Nine

TATE

Her face went stark white, stiffer than the starched table cloth. My body tingled, heating at the sight of her here. As our waitress. Why was she waiting tables? What the fuck was going on? "Wha-what are you doing here?" I stuttered.

Her blush turned to a full-on crimson. "I work here," she said quietly. "I mean...sort of. I used to, and I'm just filling in for extra cash over Parents' Weekend."

I turned to my father. No emotion registered on his face, or on my mom's. "You knew about this," I said quietly.

"Shelby." My dad smiled, but his eyes were dead. "Could you give us a minute?"

"Of course," she whispered, backing away.

"You knew she worked here," I said again.

"Well, of course we knew." My mom rolled her eyes, sipping her water. "You can't drop a bomb like having a girlfriend on us and expect us not to do a little digging."

"But...I didn't tell you her name or anything—"

"Son, please. Give us some credit."

I snorted. "Right. Silly me. I forgot for a moment that you have eyes fucking everywhere, don't you?"

"Watch your language." He was quiet but venomous, and I didn't give a shit about my language right now.

"A few calls and you knew *exactly* who I was spending my time with."

"Son." My dad leaned in, lowering his voice. "We love you. Can we focus on the more important issue here? This girl told you she came from wealth, right? She claimed to live in a wealthy part of town on the North End?" My dad shook his head. "There has never been a Shelby Stevens living in North Charleston. After your first sham of an engagement, I'm surprised *you* didn't do some digging yourself. When are you going to learn?"

My body went numb, and I couldn't feel my fingers. It was as though all my blood was replaced with cold gel that congealed and slowed my heart. "No," I whispered. "That's not possible."

"There is, however, a record of a Shelby Stevens who lived with her mother, Dee Stevens, in the trailer park down near that tutoring center where you're volunteering, up until a few years ago, when she moved into the dorms. It looks like her mother died on July tenth." Mom clicked her tongue handing me some sort of printout that, I guess, had the proof of all this. But I didn't even look—I couldn't look. Anger and sadness clogged my throat like a gunked up drainpipe. How the fuck was this happening to me a second time? How could I possibly be so bad at judging people? The tightness in my chest was suddenly overwhelming, and my breath was puttering through my lips like a bad carburetor.

"Tatum." My mom placed her hand over mine. Her fingers were frigid, and her acrylic nails scraped along the back of my hand. "There are a lot of young girls out there who would take advantage of you for one thing and one thing only. They see dollar signs in your eyes—"

"Not Shelby," I choked.

"That's what you said about that other girl," Dad muttered under his breath, his nose buried deep in the menu again.

Mom shot him a look before turning her attention back to me. "Then why didn't she tell you? Why didn't she tell you of this job? Of her real home? The fact that her mother was *also* a waitress at some dreadful little diner—"

Oh God. Was her mom ever a ballerina? Or was it all a lie? I pushed out of my chair, nearly knocking it back. "I have to go. I have to get out of here."

I ran out of the restaurant, and the night air was humid and sticky. It pushed down on me, oppressive like my fucking life. Inside, my parents were still at their table by the window. A new waitress showed them a bottle of wine. Did they even care that my heart was fucking shattered? Did they give a shit that their only son just ran out of the restaurant? I swallowed, and it tasted like bitterness and anger. Would they toast to a job well done with that seventy-five dollar Chianti? Toast to the successful breakup of their little boy and the woman he loved.

"Tate." I looked up to find Shelby running down the stairs toward me. "Tate, I was trying to tell you—it's what I needed to talk to you about. I swear, I wasn't hiding it from you. I was about to mention it the other night, too, and you cut me off. And it just—I didn't think it really mattered that much—"

"What about North Charleston? That playground? Did that never come up, either?"

Confusion crumpled her beautiful face, and I didn't know whether I wanted to run from her or grab her and kiss her. "What? What are you talking abou—"

"Why would you lie about that? You think I really care that you grew up in a trailer park? You think that would affect how I saw you?"

"No. Tate, *no*. Those are terrible memories for me. I hate talking about it with anyone. It took me years to even tell Reagan—"

"You lied. You lied to me, Shelby. What the fuck? Even after I told you about Katie and how—" My voice rose, and even though I was yelling and I knew I shouldn't be, I couldn't help it. I cut myself off.

She shook her head, tears springing from her eyes. "I didn't. I didn't lie to you. It was just a misunderstanding, Tate."

"I can't do this right now." I backed away, moving in the direction of the apartment complex. "I need some time to think."

"What are you going to do? Walk home? It's like twenty blocks."

That was exactly what I was going to do. It was just what I needed.

"Tate. Stop. *Please*. Talk to me. I lov—" Her sob choked the words, stopping them before she finished. I squeezed my eyes shut, feeling moisture slide down my cheeks. No. I can't be in love with a liar. Not again.

I would not end up with another Katie.

And I would not end up like my parents.

Chapter Thirty

Shelby

There was a pounding on my door that echoed in my head. I crawled out of bed with a glance at the clock. Ten thirty on a Friday night. Who the hell was that?

I opened the door just in time before Reagan nearly broke the damn thing down. She still had full stage makeup on, fake eyelashes and all, but she was in a teeny skirt and low cut tank top.

She looked me up and down, and her aggressive demeanor shifted immediately. "Oh, Shelby. Have you been in bed all day?"

I sniffed, rubbing my swollen eyes, and shook my head. "No…I went to class."

"Please tell me you put on pants."

I rolled my eyes. "Of course." Sweatpants counted, right?

"What about the tutoring center?"

I swallowed and let my silence answer the question for me. I'd called in on every day that Tate would normally be there. Ryan seemed to be okay with that, and to be honest, the days I *did* show up, I didn't exactly look healthy.

Reagan sighed, dropping her duffel bag on my futon. I had already given her the whole story, and we had played it out together time and time again over pints of Haagen Dazs. We pretty much came to the conclusion that while, yeah, I should have told him about living in a trailer park, Tate was completely overreacting. But in light of his history with that ex, I guessed it was understandable. All except for the fact that he wouldn't let me explain. And after almost a week of trying, I'd pretty much given up.

That didn't make it hurt any less, though.

The intercom phone to my doorman rang, and Reagan ran to answer it. "Hi. Yep, I'll be down in two seconds to grab it."

I furled my eyebrows at her. "Who's that?"

She swallowed, not quite looking at me, but grabbed her wallet. "Pizza."

"I don't want to eat," I said, flopping onto my futon.

Reagan rolled her eyes. "You are eating. And after there's something in your stomach, you, me, and Harrison are going out and getting you trashed."

"I'll compromise. I'll take the pizza, but I am not going out."

"Yeah, we'll see," she muttered, throwing my door open.

I grabbed my keys, following her downstairs. "I'm serious, Reagan. I don't want to go anywhere."

"Girl, you have *got* to get out of this apartment. It's getting an old lady smell, and you're not even in your mid-twenties yet. I'm a little worried that if I open your closet, I'll find you hoarding cats or something."

The elevator pinged, and when the doors open, Tate was inside, dressed in black pants and an electric blue button-down shirt—the same shirt he was wearing the first day we met. Panic swelled in my chest, and even though I wanted to run and hide, my feet were cemented to the ground.

And fuck me hard. There was a girl clinging to his arm. Not just any girl, either. Veronica. Well, *Chrissy*, actually. But whatever. Nothing could have prepared me for how much that fucking hurt. She leaned in close to Tate, tucking her clutch under her arm. His eyes locked with mine for only a second before he looked away. My heart damn near skipped a beat within that moment.

Her throaty chuckle skimmed beneath my skin and irritated worse than a breakout of freaking poison ivy.

Reagan rolled her eyes, lips pursed. "We'll wait for the next one," she snapped.

My whole body was suddenly flushed with heat, and I looked down at myself. My T-shirt had stains all over it. My sweatpants had holes everywhere. My hair was all ratty tangles piled on top of my head. Yeah, I was a friggin' mess. And not even a hot one.

The elevator doors slid closed, and Reagan's hand fell on my arm, rubbing in reassuring strokes. "Shelby," she whispered, and I clamped my eyes shut.

"You get the pizza. I'll go shower," I whispered. Because, damn, she was right. If Tate was moving on already, maybe I should, too.

I didn't wait for her response. I just turned and walked back to my room in a daze.

...

An hour and a half later, Harrison, Reagan, and I walked into the dark club. We flashed our IDs, and I immediately sidled up to the bar.

"What are you drinking tonight?" Reagan shouted over the music.

"Alcohol," I grumbled.

Harrison sighed and Reagan snickered. "Done and done," she said, leaning over the bar to get the bartender's attention. Within a few minutes, I had a row of shots lined in front of me, and one by one, I slammed all three.

"Holy shit," Reagan said. "Some of those were for us, y'know."

I slapped a twenty onto the bar and signaled the bartender for another round. "Look," I murmured. "I've got yoga pants on under these jeans. I am one bad moment away from hopping in a cab and falling back into a pit of chocolate and Netflix. You want to test me on this?"

Reagan rolled her eyes. "You do not have yoga pants—"

I lifted an eyebrow and popped the button of my jeans, revealing the cotton leggings beneath the waistband. Reagan went silent, passing a look to Harrison. "I stand corrected. And here I thought *I* was the overdramatic one."

"You wanted me out. There better be a damn drink in my hands at all times."

Reagan nodded and gestured again at our cute bartender. "And a whiskey sour, please."

"And three waters," Harrison added, only to be met with Reagan's scowl. "Glare all you want. If we're gonna be slamming drinks, at least hydrate between."

"You don't like whiskey," I said to Reagan.

"Bitch, it's for you. You want alcohol? You've got it." She tossed my twenty back at me, and handed her card to the bartender as he filled a tumbler with Jim Beam.

I examined him for a moment. He was cute. Dark hair. Tall. I didn't realize I was staring at him until his grin widened. Crap.

Reagan took my hand, pulling me onto the dance floor. Harrison joined, staying a bit behind Reagan as she swayed against me, but my heart just wasn't in it. I don't know what happened to my sense of rhythm, but nerves and insecurity had taken over my body, and I just stood there beside Reagan, swaying like a lame duck to the music.

Reagan took my free hand, shaking me to the music. "Girl, loosen up. It feels like I'm dancing with a two-by-four."

"That's giving me too much credit right now."

Before long, I was only slurping icy water at the bottom of my glass and was to the point that the nasty taste of alcohol was almost ignorable.

The walls seemed to be spinning. Reagan still held my hand, but had shifted her attention to some guy grinding near her. Even Harrison seemed to have found someone to dance on. And here I was, just me and Jim Beam having our own love affair.

Harrison's voice was closer now, leaning down to catch my eye even though his hand was still curved around another girl's waist. "You okay, Shelbs?"

I nodded, but the floor seemed to lurch beneath my feet. Maybe three shots at once was a bad idea.

"Oh, she's fine." Reagan pushed Harrison to the side, ignoring her dance partner and sidling up beside me once more. "Go get her another drink."

The two exchanged a look that in my inebriated state, I couldn't quite decipher. He eventually sighed and went off to the bar.

"Well, well, well," Reagan whispered in my ear. "I think we hooked us a catch." Clasping my hand, she twirled me, and directly behind me was a guy, several inches taller than me with a cute "boy next door" sort of face. He smiled, sliding a hand around my waist, and pulled me in.

He moved to the beat perfectly, dragging me along with his sway. Damn, he knew how to move those hips, and I was glad that he was in the lead because I didn't quite trust my own balance.

A cold, wet tumbler appeared in my hand, and I looked

up to find Reagan smiling, dancing with Harrison. "We're right here," she mouthed to me.

A chill crawled over my body. I wasn't sure about this. It had taken me weeks, months even, to trust Tate enough to open up, and look where that landed me. Drunk, alone, and in double-layered pants. I wasn't sure I was ready to start all over again. I tugged my halter-top higher over my cleavage. I felt lost in my own skin, like I wouldn't have recognized myself in a mirror.

"You a student?" he asked, his lips brushing my ear as he spoke.

I gulped and nodded, shoving the straw into my mouth and sipping to give myself something to do. "You?"

He nodded. "Grad student. Architecture. I'm Matt."

"Shelby," I rasped.

"Shelby. That's cute."

A big, dumb grin spread along my face, and my skin prickled. The song ended, and I backed up, nearly knocking into Harrison behind me. "Thanks for the dance," I said.

He tilted his head, one side of his mouth tipping higher. "Who said it had to just be the one?"

My lungs stretched with a deep breath, and as the lights swirled around me—around the dance floor—I looked beyond Matt's shoulder, connecting to two azure eyes fixed right on me.

Tate. Fuck me. Tate was *here*? My initial reaction was momentary excitement at the thought of seeing him. And then reality cut through my alcohol infused fog, and I remembered there was no longer an *us*. Chrissy was still hanging on to him, but his eyes stayed locked on me. His hardened scowl was like a punch to the throat, and I backed away from Matt, shaking my head.

"Maybe later," I said to him, doing my best to offer a smile, though I was pretty sure it was wobbly like my stomach.

I handed my drink to Reagan and whispered in her ear. "I need the bathroom."

She gave me an uncertain look. "Need me to come?"

I shook my head. "No, I'm fine," I lied. I needed a moment. A place to breathe, to *be*, without Tate. He was fucking everywhere. He was in my thoughts, my apartment, my classes, the tutoring center… There was no escape.

As I pushed past my friends, bobbing and weaving through the raucously dancing crowd, I glanced back to see Tate stiffen, his eyes following me through the club. On a deep breath, I looked away, and when I finally broke away from the dance floor, I looked once more and found his spot against the wall empty.

Part of me was sad to see he had left. Was seeing me here too hard on him? Was the thought of me dancing with another guy too much?

The room spun, and people bumped into me as I rushed for the bathroom door. Though I was pretty sure the floor wasn't uneven, it felt like I was walking on cobblestone streets and I just couldn't get my footing. I just needed to splash a little water on my face, and then I'd be fine.

"What are you doing, Shelby?" Tate was suddenly right in front of me, and he caught my arm.

I lost my balance as the room seemed to pitch to the right. Even through his dark glare, he was still so beautiful.

In a moment of false clarity, I yanked my elbow from his grasp. "Dancing. Drinking. You don't recognize a good time?"

"No," he growled. "I recognize reckless behavior."

My laugh cracked in my throat. "Oh? So, when you do it, you're letting loose. When I do it, I'm reckless? Welcome to the world of hypocrites, Tate. Then again, you were fucking born into that world, weren't you?"

Turning, I stumbled, doing my best to make it through the bathroom door, but Tate was in front of me in seconds, bracing my arms and stopping me. "Shelby, you need to go home. Sleep this off."

"Fuck you, Tate." I tried to shove him away, but it came across more as a fumble, and my hands clumsily landed on his chest. God, his chest. I must have been drunk because I found myself tracing his muscles with my fingertips. Even though I was fuming mad, I was mesmerized by him, unable to tear my hands away from his body.

"Shelby, stop."

His pecs heaved with each breath, and he wet his lips. He still wanted me. Even with Chrissy waiting for him on the dance floor—he wanted *me*. I stepped toward him, and he backed up, putting the same space between us.

Liquid courage roared through my veins and a smile tipped my lips as I took another step. "Shelby, think," he said quietly. "You're going to regret this in the morning."

I raised a brow. "Probably. But my mom said there's no shame in regretting action. Regret not acting."

I pushed onto my toes and pressed my lips to Tate's. The muscles beneath my palms tightened, and even though he gasped, within seconds, he plunged his tongue into my mouth. I moaned, and I didn't know if the room was spinning as a result of his kiss, the whiskey, or both.

After another moment, Tate's hands pressed into my shoulders, and he pushed me back. Gently at first, but he finally held me at arm's length.

"Oh God," I whispered, brushing my fingers to my wet lips. Heat burned in my cheeks and down to the pit of my stomach as a moment of dizziness passed in my foggy head.

Tate didn't respond immediately, but his eyes traveled over my face. He looked—sad. Or something. He thrust a hand into his hair, the ends standing up between his fingers. "Shelby…we should talk, but not here—"

I squirmed and stepped back from him. "I *know* we

should talk. That's what I said last week. It's what I've *been* saying all week." Liquor sloshed in my stomach, and a rapid wave of sickness rushed over me. Oh God. I can't get sick in front of him. It would just prove how right he was. This? Tonight? It wasn't me.

"I'll come over tonight after—"

"No," I said quickly, and for the first time in a week, I got it.

"It's over," I whispered.

I said it more for myself than for Tate. And once the words left my mouth, I knew it was true. We were over. "I never lied to you. But you wouldn't let me explain that. I don't think the truth matters anymore. I get it. You were burned before. But I can't be with someone who doesn't believe in me. We're done." Pain twisted and coiled in my chest, and my heart stuttered as I said the words. *We're done*. It was true. I sensed the finality in those words and my heart dropped, empty and hollow.

And there was no way Tate's parents would let their only son end up with someone like me. They orchestrated our breakup. Maybe it was best that way. Better that it happened before we had too much time and emotion invested.

"Shelby." His voice cracked.

"I said no." I held up a hand, and though the tears threatened to rise, it was a different sort of cry than I'd had all week. It was good-bye. Tears of defeat. Before, I'd held on to hope that he would forgive me and we'd move on. But now? Alcohol apparently offered me clarity I hadn't been able to achieve before. I swallowed as a tear trickled down my cheek.

"It's okay. I get it."

"You don't get anything," he growled. He reached out for me once more, but I dodged his hands, slipping into the bathroom, where I texted Reagan to come find me.

Tate and I were officially over.

Chapter Thirty-One

Tate

I watched through the crowd as Reagan ushered Shelby out of the bathroom, and it was only moments later that they left, hopefully to go home and not to another club. Based on how drunk Shelby was, I doubted they could even *make* it to another bar. And it wasn't just wishful thinking on my part.

What did she mean by the fact she'd never lied to me? She *had*. That had to have been the alcohol talking.

I drove Chrissy and Brad back to their apartments, but not before having to pry Chrissy off my body. That wasn't supposed to be what tonight was about. But of course, the second she got wind that Shelby and I were over, she was climbing all up on me. I pulled into my spot at the apartment and looked up to Shelby's window—I knew it was hers by the orchid sitting on the ledge. It looked like the light was still on, and I rushed inside, impatiently pressing the elevator button.

I was still pissed, but we had to talk.

When I got to her door, there was a quiet shuffling coming

from inside. I knocked, and all movement stilled. When the door finally creaked open, Harrison peeked out. His eyes narrowed, as did mine, my fists involuntarily closing. Absolute fury bubbled in my stomach as I took in his untucked shirt and disheveled hair. Shelby was wasted. I had to except that if we were really over, she was going to move on. But the thought of someone taking advantage of her when she was drunk was too much.

"What do you want?" Harrison whispered.

"What the fuck are you doi—"

Harrison put a finger to his lips. "Shhhh." He grabbed a set of keys and came out into the hallway, shutting the door behind him. "Shelby's asleep. Finally."

"What the fuck are you doing here?" I whispered.

Harrison raised an eyebrow, seeming unfazed by my confrontation. "Me? I'll always be here," he said with a tilt of his chin. He drove his hands into his pockets and rocked back on his heels casually. "And unlike you, I never left."

"Fuck you," I spat and grabbed the collar of his shirt. The bastard smirked at me.

"Go ahead," he whispered, sticking his jaw toward me. "Go for it. Fucking punch me. See how far it gets you, hitting the police commissioner's son, asshole. You'll be doing community service for the next year." I shoved him, and he fell back into the wall, still smiling in that smug ass way. "And for that matter, see how far it gets you with Shelby."

"Shelby and I are done."

"Oh?" He snorted. "Then why are you here?"

I sighed. That was a damn good question. *Why was I here?* Because she seemed so sad and undone. "I want to make sure she's okay."

"She's fine," he answered quickly. "You can go home now."

"And…" I paused. "I wanted to make sure we were okay

to coexist as needed. French class, the tutoring center…"

Harrison shook his head and looked toward the ceiling lights. "You're un-fucking-believable, you know that? You dump an amazing girl over the stupidest fucking reason I ever heard. Then you parade around your latest date, and when she *finally* gets herself out of bed to do something fun, you approach her and fuck with her mind, showing up at her door in the middle of the night." Harrison ran a hand through his hair, scratching the back of his neck. "Well, whatever happened between you two at the club, believe me when I say she seems to get it. There was an eerie calm to her as we left, and she seems to understand that you two are over. It was kind of scary."

I snorted. "Well, that happened fast considering she kissed me at the club."

"A kiss good-bye," he said, talking over me, then lowered his voice back to a whisper. "She told me so herself."

There was no way that was a good-bye kiss. "And I bet you just couldn't wait to swoop in here and be her shoulder to cry on."

"I don't have to swoop anywhere. I *am* her shoulder to cry on. Always have been. And always will be." Harrison sighed. "But since you have no idea what you're talking about, I'm going to guess Shelby never told you how we know each other?"

I shook my head. "There's a lot Shelby never told me." Despite the fact that I'd shared just about everything about myself.

"Yeah, she's been through hell and back. She doesn't like talking about it for obvious reasons." Harrison pinched the bridge of his nose. "Shelby's not just *like* a sister to me. She *is* my sister. My stepsister."

Chapter Thirty-Two

Tate

Shock resonated through my body. "What? No. She always said you were more than friends. Family. She never talked about you as her stepbrother, or about her stepdad."

Harrison snorted. "Yeah. She and my dad aren't exactly *close*. The Thomson family isn't really something she wants to claim or acknowledge much, other than me. And even that's probably fucking hard for her. Telling people I'm her stepbrother raises questions about her mom and my dad. Is that shit you'd want to have to explain to nosey fucking people?"

I swallowed hard, feeling my face get hot. Harrison didn't stop his rant, or hell, even pause it.

"So all that fucking 'chemistry' you claim to see between us is totally in your head, man. I love her, yeah. But as a sister. Her mom married my dad when we were in grade school. Dee Stevens was the closest thing to a mother I ever had. And the fact that that woman put up with my father…" His voice dropped off, and he shook his head. "I'm kind of convinced she stayed married to him as long as she did simply for my sake."

"You're Shelby's stepbrother," I repeated, dumbfounded. That meant his dad—Harrison's dad—was her asshole stepfather. The one she told me about, who hadn't believed she was raped.

He nodded. "Yep. My dad didn't want Dee working. He wanted her home to take care of Shelby and me. She had the talent to go back to dancing at that point, but she chose to be a full-time mom instead. Meanwhile, my dad must have had a dozen affairs.

"The first one seemed to devastate her, but we were really close. I'm pretty certain she didn't want to leave me alone with my father. But after that night—that awful night in high school, something in Shelby changed. She withdrew and stopped dancing. Her grades dropped. It wasn't until Officer Devlin's death that she finally told us what happened to her. She told me first, and I convinced her to tell my dad. I knew he wasn't a great husband, but I never thought he'd be so cold as not to believe her. That was Dee's last straw. She didn't care that the pre-nup left her with nothing. No skills, no job, no savings. She didn't care that she had to work her ass off as a waitress. She left, and the only reason she ever looked back was for me. Dee continued raising me as if I were her own son, even after the divorce."

"But...my dad said that no Shelby Stevens ever lived in the North End—"

Harrison rolled his eyes. "No. But she wasn't Shelby Stevens. Both she and Dee took the Thomson name—up until the divorce. It was a shit ton of work, but Dee wasn't about to let Shelby stay a Thomson after that."

I hissed a curse and buried my face in my hands. My parents *had* to have known that. They had to have found a marriage license or something. With all the resources at their fingertips? There wasn't a doubt in my mind that they purposefully omitted that fact. "What have I done?" I whispered, running both hands through my hair. My insides felt numb.

"Tate—trust me when I tell you that Shelby doesn't want your money. She never wants to have to rely on anyone for anything. It's her number one goal in life to earn her own living. Be honest...did she actually lie to you? Or was it possibly just a misunderstanding?"

I gulped. I didn't even know anymore. Everything was sort of foggy. What exactly *did* Shelby tell me? "I–I don't know."

"Well, *I* do. Because *I* know Shelby. And the answer is no. She didn't. Believe me...if something was omitted, it was because she thought you knew or she assumed it wasn't a big deal. And the fact that it *was* a big deal speaks more to your character than hers."

Dread struck me hard, and though I hadn't had much to drink, it was still sobering. "I need to talk to her." I moved to push past Harrison into her apartment, and he stopped me with only one hand.

"Hell no, Tate. She's completely drunk, and finally asleep. And if you think I trust you in there alone with my passed out sister, you've got a rude awakening coming."

I looked back and forth between Harrison and her front door, finally nodding. "Okay," I held up two hands in surrender. "Will you tell her I came by? And that I want to talk."

He nodded, eyes softening. "I'll tell her. Though, I'm sure it won't do much. When Shelby's done, she's done. She moves on."

"But you'll tell her?" I added more urgently.

He paused and finally nodded. "In the morning. I promise I'll tell her."

Chapter Thirty-Three

Tate

"They gave me a *second* solo. My dad promised he would be there. He promised he'd make it, and even though my mom said not to get my hopes up, he wouldn't promise and then *not* come, right?" Sophia bounced in her seat, the yellow number two pencil causing squiggle lines in the margins of her paper.

Oh my God. Was she still talking about this concert? "Ummm, right." I was only half listening as I stared at Shelby from across the room. She split her time with two older students, and as she bent over the shoulder of one, my eyes wandered to her ass. It was as though she cocked that hip just for me.

"You'll come, right?"

"Huh?"

"To my recital. Will you be able to make it?"

I cleared my throat, pulling my attention back to Sophia. "I'll try. When is it?"

"I just told you. Tomorrow night. Seven p.m."

"Of course I'll come." My eyes drifted again to Shelby, and an idea formed, a moment of excitement flaring with the thought. "You should invite Shelby, too. I bet she'd love to see you perform."

"Yeah." Sophia jumped to her feet, running over to Shelby, who smoothed her bangs over her scar in that same way she always did. How did I not notice that habit sooner? Sophia's excited voice rang through the small room, and Shelby's wide smile was like the first warm day after winter. God, she was stunning.

"Oh, man," Shelby said, crouching down to Sophia's level. "I would love to, but I already have plans for tomorrow night."

Sophia's smile dipped into a pout, but she nodded. The girl was used to disappointment, but it squeezed my heart all the same. And apparently, it had the same effect on Shelby. Her eyebrows tilted down, and she pulled Sophia in for a hug. "Hold on a sec, okay?"

Shelby pushed to her feet, walking over to Ryan. She lifted onto her toes, whispering in his ear. Every muscle in my body clenched as his hand landed at the base of her neck, his thumb stroking down between her shoulder blades. He smiled at her and nodded before Shelby rushed back over to Sophia.

"Ryan and I will both be there," she said, grinning, and Sophia nearly tackled her in a hug.

My throat bottomed out into my guts. I wasn't really sure what happened the rest of the day. The thought of Ryan and Shelby going anywhere together made my stomach churn, and I wasn't positive, but I thought I might puke.

When Sophia's mom arrived to take her home, I grabbed my time sheet, dropping it in front of Shelby.

She glanced up quickly before checking the time on her phone.

"Three and a half hours," she said quietly. "I thought you

had basketball on Thursdays?" She scribbled onto the sheet, placing her signature at the bottom.

"Yeah. I did. But Sophia has a test tomorrow. They'll be fine at practice without me for a day."

Her sharp breath registered in my ears, and she opened her mouth, looking up at me. But no words came out. She sat there, frozen, brown eyes locked with mine.

"Shelby—" I whispered, but she cut me off quickly, handing me the hours sheet.

"You can file this. You know where it goes, right?"

Ryan walked up, and my hands flexed at my sides. God, how I wanted to deck that guy right in his pretty-boy face. He wore khakis, for Christ's sake. *Khakis*. What was Shelby doing with a khaki-wearing goody two-shoes?

"Ready to go?" he asked, and she looked up at him with a warm smile, the same smile that used to be reserved for me. Damn, did that hurt.

"Yeah," she said quietly.

"I'll walk out with y'all," I said without thinking.

The two exchanged looks, but I didn't let either of them say no. Instead, I grabbed my shit and hauled ass to catch them before they left. As we walked into the parking lot, I searched for Shelby's car…only it was nowhere. *Oh God. Please don't tell me she's going to his place.*

"Oh, shoot." Ryan snapped, turning back for the front door. "I forgot my phone." He rushed back inside, leaving Shelby and me awkwardly rocking onto our heels in the parking lot.

"Where's your car?" I blurted out.

Shelby sighed, eyes tilting to the cresting moon. The bluish hue cast a spotlight on her face. "It broke down. Again," she said quietly.

"Why didn't you tell me? I could have given you a ride—"

"I didn't need a ride. Ryan's helping me out."

"Shelby…we live in the same building. No matter how close or on the way Ryan is, I can guarantee it's even less of a hassle for me. Besides, we could use the time to talk—"

"We have nothing to talk about," she cut in, but still didn't look at me. I wasn't sure if that was a good sign or not.

"Please." I debated taking her hand. But even as her scowl softened, I knew that was probably a bad idea.

"You were right to end things," she said quietly, finally turning her head to me. Her mouth turned down at the corners in the tiniest little frown that I wanted to kiss back into a smile. "We're too different. We'd never work."

I gulped, shaking my head. My heart shattered. Harrison had warned me. But I wasn't convinced. She wanted to believe that, yes—but she didn't entirely. Not yet. And I had to prove to her that she was wrong. "*Je parie que je peux te faire changer d'avis.*"

"No, you can't change my mind," she answered.

My eyes widened, and I stared at her, my face splitting into a grin. "You didn't even miss a beat, Shelby."

Her own smile twitched, and I swore there was a tear in her eye. "I had a great tutor."

I sighed. "So, when do you pick up your car?"

That hint of a smile vanished, and she fiddled with her messenger bag. "I'm not. There's a buyer interested in it, and I need the money to buy something more reliable." She shrugged as if this were some sort of nothing piece of news.

"You can't sell that car, Shelb. Come on…"

"Come on, what? I have no choice. I can't afford to keep fixing it up." Her voice broke, and she shook her head. "It's not up for debate. It's not a practical car for me."

The door behind us swung open, and Ryan came bumbling out. He was like a cartoon, some sort of gangly character that belonged on *Schoolhouse Rock*, not on Shelby's arm. "Ready to go?" He grinned like an idiot, holding out an elbow for her to take. Which she did, slowly killing pieces of my soul each time they touched.

She nodded. "Yeah."

"Want to get a milkshake first?" he asked, seemingly forgetting that I was beside them at all.

"Sure," Shelby whispered. "Why not?"

I don't know how long I stood there watching them through the window of the diner. Watching them drinking milkshakes. Eating fries. Talking and laughing. It ripped me apart.

But at least she was smiling.

Chapter Thirty-Four

Shelby

Sophia's concert was your typical grade-school recital—and she was adorable. Her eyes scanned the audience, and during her solo, she waved. At first I thought it was at me, but when I turned around, two rows back from me was Tate, a big bouquet of flowers in his lap.

Damn him. Damn him for orchestrating my being here. And damn him for being sweet and perfect to this little girl who needed a strong, male figure in her life more than anything.

My throat closed, and I promised myself I would not cry. I snuck a sideways glance at Ryan. Sweet Ryan. When he asked me on this date, I'd been so taken aback that I'd said yes. I should have liked him. He was handsome, respectful, and sweet. We both came from hard-working parents. He knew my past. And he didn't care. I've never felt like he was judging me.

He reached for my hand, and I pulled away, reaching

instead to check my phone.

There was no heat, no spark. And after being with Tate where every moment together was like being in the center of a molten hot volcano? No way I was going back to lukewarm relationships.

I wanted to like Ryan, but I just didn't.

And it was stupid of me to lead him on.

I glanced back over my shoulder at Tate again, scratching my neck and pretending as though I was casually looking around the auditorium. His steely eyes were right on me, and that lush mouth of his curled into a smile. Dimples appeared on either side of his lips. I jumped, spinning forward in my seat. Damn. Totally caught.

"You all right?" Ryan whispered, leaning in. The group chorus finished their final song, and I winced, hearing Tate's distinct whistle as he jumped to his feet, cheering for Sophia.

"I'm fine." I forced a smile, clapping, and stood as well.

...

The rest of our night was…well, boring. Terribly boring.

Life had never been boring with Tate.

I missed him so much it hurt. And stupid Reagan…she was the one who convinced me to go out with Ryan. Follow our friendship where it led us.

The best way to get over someone is to get under someone else.

The silver lining was that Ryan *couldn't* think this was going well.

Oh God. What if he thought this was going well?

I stole a glance at him as he drove me back to the apartments. Music hummed on the radio—bad top 40s music that Tate and I would have mocked mercilessly—and Ryan sang along, tapping his fingers in rhythm on the steering wheel.

Pulling into an empty space in front of the building, he put the car in park and climbed out along with me. I froze, standing beside his Kia. "Oh. Um, you don't have to walk me in…"

"Of course I do." He offered me a small smile, locking the doors before taking my hand. Sweaty. Ick.

"Okay…" I followed him to the front door, stopping just before punching in my code. He could not come in…not even inside the building lobby. There had to be no pretense whatsoever that I was letting him up to my apartment. "Well. Thanks," I said, doing my best to sound casual. Apart from punching him on the shoulder, I don't know what I could have done. But according to Reagan, this was how most people date.

Except, the way Ryan was looking at me…shit. He *did* think this was a good date. There were beads of sweat along his hairline, and he licked his lips, his smile twitching nervously. Leaning in, his hand fell to my waist, and I jumped backward and slammed against the brick building, groaning as my head bounced into the concrete wall.

I laughed in spite of myself, rubbing the back of my head, offering an apologetic look up to Ryan. "Ouch," I chuckled.

"That looked like it hurt." He laughed, too, but his eyebrows crinkled in the center. He curled his other hand around the back of my head. "You okay?"

"Yeah." I nodded with a shrug. "Just…clumsy." Yeah. Clumsy and trying to get away from you, I added silently. "Well, thanks again for dinner…"

Before I could finish my sentence, Ryan leaned down, pressing his lips gently to mine. I didn't exactly resist, but I didn't entirely give in, either. He opened his mouth, working my lips by sliding them along mine. *Shit…what do I do with my hands?* They were hanging at my sides like I was having my first kiss in middle school again. I lifted them, first landing on his shoulders, but then thought better of that and slid them to his elbows.

Elbows? God, Shelby…you are an idiot.

I moved them back up, settling around his neck, and just as I was satisfied, the kiss was over and he was pulling back.

Well, shit. Even if it had been an exciting kiss, how would I have known it? "Uh, thanks," I said. *Thanks? I really am an idiot.*

Ryan chuckled at that, and sighed, falling against the wall next to me and scratching under his eyebrow. "I really hoped for a bit more of a reaction than that." He looked over, smiling, and I sighed.

"I'm sorry—" I started, and he cut me off with a wave of his hand.

"Don't worry about it." With a squeeze to my upper arm, he winked, leaning in and brushing his clean-shaven jaw against my cheek with a quick peck. "Friends?"

I nodded as he walked back to his car.

I spun to punch the code into my building and nearly walked right into Tate, standing there staring at us.

Chapter Thirty-Five

Shelby

Crap. How long had he been there watching? Not that it mattered. He raised an eyebrow, and I shoved past him, opening the door. I kind of wanted to slam it on his fingers, but resisted the urge, mostly because it would have been a felony. Okay, maybe not a felony, but at least a misdemeanor.

"What are you doing here?"

He shrugged. "What? Am I not allowed to come home to my own apartment?"

I hissed an annoyed sigh. "Were you following us?"

He snorted at that, hitting the call button for the elevator. "Don't flatter yourself."

I hesitated. Maybe I should wait for the next elevator. Tate rolled his eyes, stepping in and kicking a foot in front of the doors. "Don't be ridiculous. Get on the elevator, Shelby."

I narrowed my eyes to slits, glaring at him.

"What?" He raised an eyebrow. "Are you afraid I'll bite? Or are you afraid I'll give you a lamer kiss than the one you just got?"

Anger seethed in my chest. "You're such an ass." I rushed inside with the accusation and Tate pulled his foot from the door, letting it close.

His smirk lifted even more, and I puffed a breath causing my bangs to blow past my forehead. "Congratulations," I sneered. "You got me alone in an elevator. What are you going to do with these thirty seconds?"

Tate snorted. "I wouldn't waste it with a passionless kiss, that's for sure. Tell me something—" He spun, leaning into me, heat radiating off his body. He wore a fitted T-shirt and jeans, and goddamn, did he make that look good. "Does he like it when you grab his *elbows*?" Tate snorted, shaking his head.

For all of a second I thought it was going to be a serious question. "Having trouble with your own sex life, Tate? Is it so dry that you have to watch mine to get your kicks?"

"My sex life," he growled, all humor gone, "is nonexistent since we broke up."

It was my turn to snort, and I rolled my eyes. "Yeah, *okay*."

"It's true," he said quietly, moving so that he was no longer looking at me. "I don't waste my time with crappy kisses."

"Our kiss was not crappy…" But I couldn't even finish the sentence, because it was a total shit kiss. And I didn't even think it was Ryan's fault. There was nothing wrong with his lips or hands or anything. It was all me. I was the dunce.

"No? You're telling me that was a good kiss? That one I just saw out there?"

"*Yes*," I lied.

"Then what would you call this one?" Tate scooped his hands into my hair and tugged me against his body. I fell into his kiss as his lips wrapped around mine and his tongue delved inside my mouth. Oh God, was that good. Excitement exploded in my belly and swirled into my throat. I don't know what came over me, but my hands dove into his hair, yanking the strands between my fingers. His back slammed into the mirrored wall behind him, and my pelvis pressed against his, circling his hips. His hand tucked into my back pocket, and he squeezed my ass.

Both of his hands scraped up my back until he was cupping my face with tender fingers. He pushed me away, ending the kiss, and I was left with stars blinding my eyes as the elevator dinged, opening on my floor.

"*That*," he said, "is a good fucking kiss, Shelby. No matter what happens between us, don't forget the difference."

I stood there, panting, unsure of what to do next. Did I get off the elevator? Go home? Ignore that amazing kiss that sent spirals of molten heat curling to my toes? My hesitation answered for me, and as the elevator doors shut, I jumped for the button to open them again. Tate's chuckle rumbled through my body. "Shit," I whispered.

His chest pressed against my back, and as badly as I wanted to turn and be enveloped in his arms, I couldn't bring myself to do that. Not again. He was right to end things with us. I had to keep telling myself that. He was right that we were a terrible match. Only…if I truly believed that, why couldn't I step away?

His lips were moist on my ear, and his hot breath trickled down my neck. "Shelby," he whispered. "I'm so sorry. I fucked everything up. My parents got into my head. They played me, using my past with Katie—"

"Just shut up," I said, turning to face him. I pulled the elevator stop button because there was no way in hell I was having this conversation in either of our apartments. "When we first met, I thought you were a spoiled brat. And, well, you kind of were. But then you started coming to the tutoring center more and more, and you were so good with Sophia and with me…" My voice cracked as I faded out, shaking my head. "I just… I thought you were going to be different. And I *didn't* lie to you—"

"I know," he said. "I'm an idiot. My parents have had a lifetime of learning how to manipulate me. They won the round, but they've only won the game if we let them. If we walk away from each other when we don't want to."

"Who says I don't want to?" I asked, folding my arms.

His smile was lightning fast and just as striking. "Because you could have left this conversation at any time and you haven't."

"Is that a challenge? Because I'm just about done here—"

"No, wait. I have a surprise for you upstairs."

I rolled my eyes at that. "The last thing I want is for you to throw your money around to get me back."

"I know. It's not like that. Please, come up. Just for a second."

I don't know why I agreed. Curiosity, maybe. Or simply because I missed him.

Because *damn* did I miss him.

I leaned over and hit the button, starting the elevator moving once more. Silently, we made our way into his apartment, and Buddy came trotting over, hopping around, tail wagging, when he saw me. I knelt to pet him and allowed myself to nuzzle the long fur at his neck before I stood back up and faced Tate. "Okay," I said, "what's this surprise?"

"Let me start with the fact that I had no idea you'd be coming up tonight, so I'm a little unprepared. *But…*" He rushed around the kitchen, pulling out a milkshake machine like the one they have at diners—classic spindles that frothed the shake while blending. "I bought this earlier this week. It's supposed to be the best." He also grabbed mint chocolate chip ice cream from his freezer, milk from the fridge, and a sealed envelope from a drawer. He handed the letter to me and got to work on the milkshake.

"Tate, this is really weird. What are you—?"

"Just read."

I opened the sealed letter, which had Cathy's name scribbled along the edge.

My dearest Shelby, I'll make this short. This boy's a keeper. I don't know what happened to split you up, and I will say to always trust your instincts wherever they may lead you. That being said, he has come into the diner the last four days learning how to make you your perfect milkshake. It's really not that hard to make a milkshake, but I think he just wanted it perfect for you. Think hard before throwing this fish back. I love you, sweet girl. -Cathy

Tears sprung into my eyes, wet and fresh and salty, and damn, they burned. "You learned how to make me a milkshake?"

He paused, sliding over a glass of the mint chip shake. "I tried to learn. You tell me. How'd I do?"

I lifted the glass to my lips, ignoring the single tear that slid down the side of my nose. "It's good," I said, hiccupping. "Really good."

He grinned proudly. "But not as good as Cathy's right?"

"No one's ever will be."

His smile dropped into something more serene. "Maybe if you gave me a few more tries."

We stood there staring at each other, suspended in time. Suspended between what my heart wanted and what my head kept trying to talk me out of. God, I was exhausted. Tate screwed up. That was obvious. But if I was being honest with myself, I screwed up a lot in the first month we knew each other. I ran out on him and never wanted to talk things out. But he never gave up. He never stopped trying to make me happy. Even here, now.

He clutched the edge of the marble counter, clearing his throat. "Well, really, this machine is for you to take." He was rambling, filling the silence. I knew the technique because I'd damn near perfected it. "So that after graduation you can still have milkshakes whenever you want. I'm sure Cathy will show you how to use it, too. There's a really specific ratio and measuring tool she uses, and this weird cup tipping technique she practically patented—"

I didn't let him finish the thought. Dropping the letter, I rushed him, crashing into his lips with another kiss. This one was even more chaotic than before in the elevator, slipping into dangerous territory.

His hands curved around my ass, and before I knew it, my feet were off the floor and we were falling into his bed. My pants were off, and I kicked them away, tearing my shirt over my head as well. The soft bedspread pressed against my back, and I spread my legs as Tate leaned into the crook, fitting perfectly. His lips came to mine magnetically once more.

He paused, sitting back and examining me. Tingles shivered across my body and goose bumps prickled along my skin. He shook his head, looking away, and I sat up on my elbows. "What?" I swallowed, not exactly sure I wanted to know why he'd paused.

He tugged at his hair and lowered on top of me. Skin sizzled on skin, and his erection pressed against me just perfectly. But he ignored that—for the moment, at least—and gently brushed back my hair.

"I just didn't know if I'd ever get to see you this way again. I didn't know if I'd ever have you in my arms again, let alone my bed." He brushed his lips across each of my eyes, then my cheeks, and then paused as my bangs flipped up past my scar. "I love you, Shelby."

A terrified breath dragged through my lips. Yes, he knew about my scar now. But covering myself had become such a habit, I didn't quite know how to react to someone examining it—examining *me* so closely.

A whimper escaped my parted lips as he gently kissed the length of my scar, finishing at the tip of my hairline.

"Tate." His name was hoarse coming from me—more than usual—and I cleared my throat. "I lo—"

He pressed his mouth to mine, stopping the admission, and I gasped.

"What the hell?" I asked, half joking and half serious.

"Don't say it yet." His eyes flickered, and a jolt of sadness lapped at my heels. "Just—I want you to be absolutely certain when you say it. Not just because I've said it, or because you're in my bed, or—"

"That's not why I'm saying it," I added quietly.

He closed his eyes, nodding. "Okay. Just…take your time, okay?"

I nodded and debated saying those three words despite his misgivings. I did love him, though that was terrifying.

"See?" he said quietly. "That. That's what I want to avoid. That fear in your eyes when you say it." He brushed the pad of his thumb over my cheekbone, a smile flickering at the corners of his mouth. "Because you *will* say it," he added playfully, "I want you to do so without hesitation. I can wait."

I nodded, at a loss for words.

"Now." Tate wiggled his eyebrows then trailed his lips down my breasts and stomach, nibbling on the string of my panties. "We have some lost time to make up for."

• • •

I stretched in Tate's bed, and his Egyptian cotton sheets tangled around my shins. My God, that was amazing. Somewhere after the third time, we must have fallen asleep. A slice of warm sunlight slid between his curtains, and I glanced at the clock. Seven a.m.

I moaned, rolling on my side, and pressed my lips against Tate's unshaven jaw. The stubble scraped the tender skin at my chin, and I nibbled down his neck.

"Woman," he joked, his voice raspy with a case of the mornings. "You're gonna wipe me out."

I straddled his muscular thigh, and my dampness pressed into his bare skin. He, too, groaned, taking me in a kiss.

"It's Saturday," he grumbled. "Don't you ever sleep?"

I sighed, turning away from him onto my back. "I have a paper to write." I pushed off my elbows, sitting up. "I should get going."

"Nuh-uh," he grunted, wrapping an arm around my bare waist and tugging me back into bed. He rolled on top of me.

My hips bucked off the bed, and I yelped a pleasured cry, laughing immediately after. "Tate."

"Write your paper here," he said. "After." He dragged his lips down to my nipples, and his tongue circled me there before he scraped his teeth across my sensitive skin. His fingers stroked my clit in slow, but rhythmic movements and—oh God—I was close. Again. Who knew that I could go from never to multiples within a few weeks. My body jolted as he increased pressure, and he drove a finger inside of me, thrusting in and out as his thumb worked magical circles.

My toes dug into the bedding as my muscles stiffened, exploding around his hand. A gasped cry came from deep in my belly, and when I was done, Tate fell back, licking his fingers.

"There," he murmured. "Go write your paper. My laptop is on the coffee table. Password is bestbuddy, all one word." He peeked one eye open, arching a brow. "But don't you dare go anywhere. I expect you back in this bed within a couple of hours."

I rolled on top of him, straddling his morning wood. "And

just what will you be doing while I'm doing homework?"

"Dreaming," he sighed, eyes fluttering closed. "Of you." He smirked, and I squeezed his cheeks with one hand.

"Yeah, right." I laughed, hopping off of him, and slipped on a T-shirt and boxers before grabbing a robe that hung on a chair next to the bed. I wanted to smell him as I worked on my paper.

I walked out into his living room, grabbed Buddy's leash, and took him for a quick pee before getting started. When I opened the laptop, I typed in Tate's password.

Tate's email account automatically pulled up. I quickly minimized the screen as half a dozen porn pop-up ads popped open. Holy shit, Tate. I know guys like porn, but seriously? Damn. That was a lot of porn.

I clicked out of each of them, and when I opened Safari, his browser history popped up. I swallowed, looking over my shoulder. He had done so much for me—getting me to open up, talk about myself…orgasm. Maybe there was a fantasy I could fulfill for him. Something he'd always wanted to explore but never had.

I pulled open the history, and the first was a threesome. Anxiety clenched in my stomach and I looked at Buddy. "No way in hell," I said to the dog. He whined and rolled onto his back, offering me his belly. I clicked on the next couple of links…most of which featured blow jobs.

No surprise there. Boys loved their head. But I do that with no problem.

I gulped. Shit, I hope it was no problem. Was he watching the porn because I wasn't good enough at it? I shook the thought away. No, not a chance. I was just being insecure.

I checked the time—I'd watch one more and then work on the paper. I clicked the next link down.

Nothing could have prepared me for what popped onto the screen. A blonde woman—she looked young. Like, maybe a teenager. And she was blindfolded, bound hand and foot to a bed. All air halted in my chest. No. God, no. This wasn't Tate's porn. He couldn't be watching this. The woman screamed no, and I flinched, muting the volume. She writhed and shook her head as two different men forced themselves on her. My stomach lurched.

How could he? Tears rose, pricking the back of my eyes, and I looked away, pausing the video. I couldn't watch another second. If this was his fantasy—if this was the shit that he got off to when I wasn't around, I couldn't be with this man. Why else would this video be in his history? He'd watched it at least one time.

And that was one time too many.

I stroked Buddy's head, my tears falling into his fur, and kissed him on the nose. Leaving the screen open on the rape porn, I dressed quietly and slipped out of his apartment.

Chapter Thirty-Six

TATE

I woke up to find Buddy's snout pressed against my face, snorting. Groaning, I rolled over, scratching his head. "Okay, boy. I know…you're hungry."

I grunted, forcing myself out of bed, and padded my way into the kitchen, rubbing a hand over my face. "Shelby?" I called and no one answered. Maybe she ran downstairs for some notes or something. Grabbing Buddy's bowl, I poured him some kibble and dropped it in front of his nose. He inhaled it, sliding the metal bowl around the kitchen. The marble tile was chilly against my feet, and I rushed over to the couch where my open laptop was resting on the coffee table. I brushed a finger against the trackpad, kicking the screensaver into life.

My breath stalled as I saw the paused video that fucking Logan sent on the screen. "Oh, fuck. No, no, no…" I just barely remembered to put a shirt and shoes on before running out my door and banging on Shelby's.

"Come on," I said while knocking. "Answer, dammit."

I grabbed my phone and dialed her number with no luck. No shock there. I dialed Harrison—gritting my teeth as I pushed send.

He answered on the third ring, sounding gravelly with sleep. "Hello?"

"Harrison…it's Tate. Any chance Shelby is with you?"

"What? What's wrong? Is she okay…?"

I gulped, not able to answer that question honestly. "I–I think so. She's just pissed at me. Again."

Harrison sighed, and I heard a bed creak and the quiet murmur of a woman's whisper. Harrison had a girlfriend? "What the hell did you do now?"

"Nothing, I swear." I fell back against her door, sliding down to a crouch. "It's a… misunderstanding. Another one."

Harrison groaned again. "Look, man. I don't know. She's not here. And she hasn't gotten a new car yet. Not that it would stop her from just walking somewhere. But, if she's walking, I'd guess it would be somewhere safe."

Her safe place—like a wealthy neighborhood playground. "Thanks, Harrison," I said.

"Don't make me regret it, asshole. Be good to her."

I swallowed. "I'm trying. I never want to hurt her again."

"I'm not sure why, but I trust you." I couldn't be certain, but I thought I heard a smile in Harrison's voice.

I hung up and ran for my car, pulling up Google maps for the North End. It wasn't a far drive by any means, but I didn't want to waste time wandering around looking for the place.

Within a few minutes, I pulled into the parking lot and jumped out of my car. It was Saturday morning, and the playground was a proverbial nightclub for toddlers, hopping with kids and nannies and parents. I snorted, shaking my head like a horse, and jogged over to the monkey bar area. Probably more nannies than mommies, knowing the sort of families that lived in this neighborhood. The sight of these kids being closer to the familial employees stirred up anger and emotions that I much preferred to keep pressed down deep in my gut.

I scanned the crowded park for Shelby. Shit…I looked out of place here. A random young woman at a playground never raised any red flags. A random young man? I might was well be wearing a giant "Predator" sign on my shirt.

It was far away, but at the top of the hill a woman sat in the grass. I squinted, shading my eyes from the morning sun. That could be her, though it was hard to tell. Fuck it, there was only one way to find out.

I jogged to the top of the hill, staying at the girl's back. And as I got closer, it was definitely Shelby. She still wore the same clothes as last night, only now, she hugged the cardigan tighter around her.

As I walked up, I made sure to stir up some noise so as not to scare her. But she didn't react. Not a flinch; not once did she turn to see who was approaching. Maybe she already knew. Maybe she didn't care. I plopped down in the grass beside her. The dampness permeated my mesh shorts and was chilly against my bare calves. She was probably cold, I thought, noting the goose bumps that covered her legs.

"Shelby," I whispered, finally gathering the courage to steal a look at her. Dried tears stained her cheeks, and her eyes were a bright, bloodshot red.

Still no response.

I leaned back on my hands, watching the kids below us playing. They were happy. Carefree. "It wasn't my video, Shelbs. You've got to believe me." When she still didn't answer, my own tears climbed into my throat. Shit, I can't cry in front of her. "You've got to trust me."

Finally, she sniffled, wiping her nose with the sleeve of her cardigan. "I don't think I'm capable of trust, Tate."

I closed my eyes as a breeze rushed across my skin and over my face. At least she was talking to me. "Are you capable of listening?" I asked quietly.

She nodded, but even that took a moment of thought first. I pulled out my phone, finding my email exchange with Logan the day after he showed us that video. "Read this," I said. She gently took my phone, and after a minute, a smile twitched at the corners of her lips.

"Fuck you, Logan. Don't show me shit like that ever again. That was disgusting, and I don't want any part of it," she read aloud.

"And what's the date that I sent that?"

She swallowed, her throat working tightly. "September twenty-fourth."

I nodded. "He showed that stupid video to all of us during poker night a few weeks ago. I sent him the email the next day, and he hasn't been invited back to a game since."

"What did he say? How could he possibly justify this?"

A sharp pang caught my heart. It was a damn good question. I scooted closer, wrapping my arm around Shelby and tugging her to me. Her cheek fell to my shoulder, and a breath trembled through her soft pout. "He had a lame excuse about it not being real or whatever. The bottom line is, I don't want to be friends with someone like that."

She nodded. "Okay. Good."

"Shelby," I said, my fingers circling her hip. The silky fabric twisted around my fingers, wrinkling. "I need you to stop running from me every time something happens. It terrifies me when you run away and refuse to talk to me." I held my breath, awaiting her answer.

"Running's my only solution," she said. "It's the only way I know how to cope."

"Then we have to find a better mechanism, don't we?"

She exhaled, pushing off my chest, and pulled her knees

in, hugging them. "Look, sometimes I need space. I need to be alone."

"Okay. And sometimes I need to talk things out. So…can we find a compromise?"

She nodded. "I'll try." And then, her head snapped toward me. "You run, too. You ran when you thought I was after your trust fund."

I nodded. "I apologized for that. It was stupid." After another moment of silence, I added, "How about, when you need space, you just check in and tell me where you are. I'll promise not to come searching for you—to give you your space—as long as I know you're safe, and that we'll talk about whatever it is soon."

She looked up at me, her caramel-colored eyes wet. "I can try that," she whispered, licking her plump lips. "As long as you know I'll probably slip up. I'm used to dealing with my issues alone."

"I know. We'll get there, though. By graduation, you'll trust me more than Harrison, I bet."

She snorted, rolling her eyes. "Harrison's a brother to me. I don't know I'll ever trust a lover as much as a brother."

I laughed, standing and pulling Shelby to her feet as well. Running my fingertips over her jaw, I brushed my lips to hers. "What about a husband?"

She froze, her arms stiffening around my waist. "What?" she asked, breathless.

I crouched onto one knee. Taking her hand, I looked into her eyes, my pulse jumping. "Shelby Stevens, will you do me the honor of…joining me in Paris over winter break?"

She breathed a heavy, relieved sigh, and a smile broke through as she slapped me across the shoulder. "You ass."

I winked, grinning. "Is that a yes?"

She nodded. "Only if I get an A in French this semester."

I hopped to my feet, scooping her into a hug. "Well, that's

clearly a yes, then."

She groaned. "Will your parents be there?"

I shrugged. "Maybe. Maybe not. Honestly? I don't give a shit. We're adults, and I don't need their consent to go to another country with my girlfriend."

She smiled. "They're going to hate me."

I rolled my eyes at that. "They hate everyone. Don't worry." I threaded my fingers into hers. "I'll just convince my dad how much a girl like you will help in the polls, and he'll be fine." She shot me a look of pure daggers, nearly as deadly, too. "What about we go get some breakfast, and then you can finish that paper?"

She nodded, grinning. "Jolie? Croissants?"

I snorted as we started walking back to the car. "What else would we possibly get? And don't worry. That little question you thought I'd ask while on one knee? I'm not asking…*yet*."

She laughed, scuffing her flip-flops in the grass. "I would hope not. I haven't even said I love you…yet."

"Yeah," I added quietly, tucking my other hand into my pocket. "But we both know you do."

She smirked, giving me a sidelong glance.

"But when you do say it," I continued, unable to help the grin stretching my face, "watch out. A diamond will be on that finger in no time," I said, tapping her ring finger.

"A diamond?" She scrunched her nose, shaking her head.

"Um…a sapphire?"

Her smile stretched wider. "There you go." Then with a sigh, she added, "So, I better wait to tell you those three words until I'm ready to be a wife, huh?"

I halted my steps, and she jerked back as I held on to her hand. "Damn…that really backfired."

Her laugh was like poetry, and my entire body warmed with the sound. It felt like ages since I heard that laugh.

"C'mon Archie. Let's go home."

Epilogue

Shelby

Nine Months Later

I pulled up to the tutoring center in my Prius. Tate had convinced me it was worth the extra money because it was so reliable and I'd save that money in gas within a year. The bottom line? He knew cars more than I did, so I trusted him.

My cap and robe hung draped across the backseat. One more day. One more day as a college student, and then I would have a week's break before beginning my job with Hilton. Since my job would involve a ton of travel, Tate and I planned to be based out of Chicago, where he would go to grad school. Well, med school, to be exact.

It was bittersweet. I couldn't wait to begin our life together. And yet, our beginning also meant saying an even bigger good-bye to my mom, in a sense. Good-bye to the tutoring center, and Cathy, and the best French fries and mint chip milkshake I'd ever had. Even though Tate was working on perfecting his milkshakes, they still weren't as good as the diner's. Probably never would be.

I swiped a tear from my eye. But today was about Sophia and her elementary school graduation party at the tutoring center. Confusion slammed into me as I scanned the huge crowd waiting outside.

I carefully climbed out of my car and saw Tate standing at the front of the crowd with a wiggly Sophia holding his hand. A giant red ribbon stretched across the front door and a large white sheet blocked the facade.

Next to Tate was Ryan, flanked by Harrison, Reagan, and numerous students I had tutored through the years. "Tate…" I laughed nervously. "What's going on?"

He met me halfway, taking my hand and pulling me toward the crowd. Sophia and her mom stepped up first, handing me a rose. Sophia's mom smiled warmly, nodding for her daughter to talk.

"I didn't know your mom well. But she always smiled and pretended to grab my nose when she came to visit you. I don't know what it's like not to have a mommy. I hope I don't ever have to know," Sophia finished, so excited she hopped around in place.

She stepped back, and Ryan moved forward, handing me a rose. "When I first got the job here, I almost didn't take it. I didn't know what I was doing with my life." He swallowed, looking at a bench near the front door. "I sat on that bench for an hour, and your mom came over from the diner with a chocolate milkshake for me. She told me to follow my gut, and that the center would be lucky to have me. She's the reason I'm here. She's the reason I'm fulfilled every day in my job. And she's the reason I am addicted to those dang chocolate milkshakes." He grinned, leaned forward, and dropped a chaste kiss to my cheek before moving to the back of the group.

Hot tears burned my eyes as Cathy stepped forward. That's when I lost my shit. I don't even know that I heard what all she said because I collapsed into her arms. She spoke quietly into my ear and whispered that she loved me, and how she still felt my mom's love each day. Pulling back, she squeezed my shoulders, pressing the rose into my palm.

One by one, people from my mom's life—from *my* life—stepped forward, expressing their love for the most important woman I ever knew. After dozens of stories, Reagan handed her phone off to Harrison, and he continued videoing as she dove forward, hugging me. Sobs quivered in my chest, and I looked into the bright sun to stop the tears. If I didn't calm down, I'd become dehydrated in seconds.

"Your mom called me," Reagan said, her own tears falling onto the hot pavement between our feet. "I never told you…but she called me when she was first diagnosed." Reagan didn't even look up into my eyes; she kept her head cast down, bobbing with each word. "She…she told me that I was brought into your life for a reason—to be the next Dee Stevens. She told me not to let you get away with bullshit. She asked me to watch out for you and to make sure you knew when to dance with joy and when to curl up and wallow." Another breath caught in her throat, jagged and broken. "She said that you're too serious for your own good, and that she and I were one and the same. And that she thought I was an early reincarnation of herself."

My stomach twisted at that sentiment. It was a thought that I had always had. Reagan and my mom mirrored each other as though Reagan was another daughter. I wrapped my arms around her neck and cried into her shoulder.

Harrison stepped forward, handing me his rose with a sad smile. My arms were filled with the fragrant flowers. I shook my head. "Please, Harrison. You don't need to say anything—I know. I already know. And she knows…"

His face tightened, and he pressed a kiss to my forehead. "When my dad divorced your mom, I kept apologizing on his behalf, even though it wasn't my fault. It wasn't anything I did, but I still felt responsible for my dad's actions. As I did with you as well. But she never let me get away with that. She just told me that family takes care of each other, and how lucky we all were to have each other. Divorce couldn't separate us. And I don't think death can, either." He pulled me into a hug, then whispering, added, "And I think she would have really liked Tate." He winked and as he pulled away from our hold, he and Tate exchanged a moment of peace before Tate moved in front of me.

"I wish I had known Dee Stevens," he said, taking my hand and pulling me forward. As we moved closer to the front door, the crowd of friends parted. "But in a way, I feel like I sort of do. Through all these people in your life, I've grown to know a woman I'll never meet. And in talking to everyone, I realized, she *and you* are leaving behind a huge legacy here in Charleston. And without you in the city anymore, the gap will be felt by the community. I couldn't figure out what to give you for your graduation gift. It needed to be amazing. Because you're amazing, Shelby. And from what I gather, you get this quality directly from your mom."

Instead of handing me a rose, Tate handed me a pair of scissors and pulled the sheet off of the facade of the tutoring center. Where there used to be a broken-down light-up sign, there was now beautiful new lettering. "Shelby, I give you the Dee Stevens Memorial Tutoring Center." He smiled, and I looked down at the scissors in my hand. "Do the honors, babe."

Everything was shaking. My legs, my hands, even my belly quivered as I cut the giant red ribbon and entered the completely redone tutoring center. "You did this?" I whispered, looking around. The place had been updated. New computers adorned the work centers, and there were actual offices for the employees versus the crowded, dingy cubicles they had to work in before.

"Oh my God, Tate." I crashed into him, a crying mess and swiped my wet cheek across his shoulder. "Thank you."

"That's not all," he said, taking my hand and pulling me around the side of the building. Parked there was my mother's MG Midget. My knees buckled as shock and joy and sadness slammed into me all at once. Tate caught one elbow and Harrison was right there to catch the other before I hit the pavement.

"How—how did you…?"

"I matched your original buyer's offer months ago. I knew you'd regret selling it as soon as you had a job and enough money to afford the maintenance."

"But—what about my Prius?"

"I'll take it," he said with a shrug.

I rolled my eyes, slapping his shoulder. "You *have* a car. A car that you love. You're really going to downsize from an Audi to a Prius?"

He smiled. "I sold my Audi, Shelby. My parents wouldn't let me access my trust fund to donate the money for this." He gestured to the new center. "So, I sold it to pay for the new center." He worked his jaw, moisture clinging to his bright, blue eyes. "My Audi was just a car. Your MG is family. You said so yourself."

The roses all fell from my arms as I lifted onto my toes and pressed my lips to Tate's in a lingering kiss, clasping his face with both hands. "I love you, Tate Michaelson," I said through my tears. "I love you so much."

He grinned against my mouth. "You might have to wait for that sapphire, Shelbs. I sorta just emptied my bank account."

"I don't need a stupid sapphire. My answer's yes. Forever and always…yes."

Acknowledgments

Writing a book is a little like falling out of a tree. It's scary, a whirlwind, can be painful, and also a little fun if you close your eyes, hold out your hands, and trust the branches to catch you. And thankfully, there's been a lot of branches to cushion my fall.

First and foremost, thanks to Jill Marsal, my incredible agent and Candace Havens, my wonderful editor, and everyone at Entangled for their hard work, support, and enthusiasm for this book. It truly takes a village!

To my friends and fellow authors, forgive me if I forget someone! Melissa Rheinlander, my cheerleader, friend, and number one fan. What would I do without you? My critique partners, Krista Amigone, Derek Bishop, Alyssa Cole, and Julia Kelly, your input is invaluable and your talents never ceases to amaze me. Julie Kenner, Hope Tarr, Daisy Prescott, Anissa Garcia, Damon Suede, Martin Biro, Sofia Tate, Lise Horton…and so many more that I'm certain I'm forgetting—thank you. Truly, thank you.

So many thanks go out to my street team and beta readers

and to Women Helping Women, Bellevue Hospital, and Beth Israel's Rape Crisis & Sexual Assault Counseling Programs for their assistance in this book.

There's no amount of words that can convey my gratitude to my mom and dad for always encouraging me to read and instilling in me a love of all books at such a young age. To my family, Bridget, Bo, Adam, Adelynn and Harrison, thank you for dealing with my erratic schedule and crazy deadlines (that somehow always seem to occur over holidays and visits!). I love you guys! Eliza and Maddie, though not related by blood, you two are family. I love you and thank you for your unconditional love and support.

Sean, thank you for being the best hero a girl could ask for and for always acting as a sounding board for ideas and plots. I love you.

And you, dear readers. Thank you for taking time out of your busy lives to spend a few hours with Shelby and Tate.

About the Author

Katana Collins bounced between a lot of different careers, including actor, photographer, television producer and finally after ten years of various jobs, she finally found her niche writing romance novels. With over ten books in a variety of romance genres, (paranormal, new adult, contemporary, and suspense to name a few), she's been keeping very busy these last few years.

She lives in Portland, Maine with her husband and brood of rescue animals. Most days, she can be found hunched over her laptop in a cafe, guzzling gallons of coffee, and wearing fabulous (albeit sometimes impractical) shoes.

Follow her on Instagram and Twitter @katanacollins
www.katanacollins.com

Discover more New Adult titles from Entangled Embrace...

SUMMER GIRL
a novel by A. S. Green

A songwriter is nothing without his muse. Sucks that mine turns out to be Katherine D'Arcy—hot as hell, but the very definition of country-club living and everything I came to this quiet little island to escape. I thought I'd find inspiration here, but I've been unable to write crap. That is until the uptight summer girl arrived to tend the lighthouse and the music began to flow. If only there wasn't that one inconvenient truth I've been keeping from her...

NO FALLING ALLOWED
a novel by Melissa West

Twenty-four hours. That's how long it took my life to flip upside down. Wake up in bed alone after the best night of my life? Check. Get fired? Check. Wealthy parents cut me off when I refuse to follow their path for my life? Check. Now I'm in Cricket Creek, SC—a place where no New Yorker belongs—disowned and broke, with a new job that I can't mess up. Oh yeah, and staring at my one-night stand, who happens to be the complete opposite of my type. Southern. Cocky. Bartender. Who knew Mr. Wrong could feel so right...

Seven Ways to Lose Your Heart
a novel by Tiffany Truitt

In the span of seven days, Annabel Lee will lose her heart. Kennedy Harrison, as reckless with life as Annabel is obsessed with order, never could commit to anything. But he's got a history with Annabel, and for once Kennedy doesn't want to run. Determined to spend time with her before she leaves for college, Kennedy dares her to join him on a road trip to a music festival. And neither of them could ever say no to a dare. What follows is a dizzying week of music, shady hotels, comical dares, and a passion neither one knew existed. But when it ends, Annabel and Kennedy will realize the biggest dare of all might just be falling for each other.

If Only
a novel by A.J. Pine

It's been two years since twenty-year-old Jordan had a boyfriend. Now she's off to spend her junior year in Aberdeen, Scotland, the perfect place to stop waiting for Mr. Right and just enjoy Mr. Right Now. Noah's perfect. After being trapped together outside the train's loo, he kisses her like she's never been kissed before. But Aberdeen is supposed to be about fun rather than waiting for life to happen, and Noah makes Jordan reconsider what love is and how far she's willing to go for the right guy.

Made in the USA
Middletown, DE
24 March 2017